Gothwen

Book One

Darkarrow's Destiny

Matt Carter
Cover Design by Elise Fu

For Nan

Every interest we shared compressed into a world of my
own creation. My only regret is you never had the
chance to read it.

INTRODUCTION

The Continent of Oreldas

The island realm of Oreldas is one of many artificially formed landmasses which dot the flat surface of the bowl-like half of the devastated planet Urunkh. Though how the planet itself came to be devastated is a tale for another time, for this story focuses on Oreldas, and those who inhabit upon it. Those who share it, love it, care for it, and those who would see it burn. Oreldas was once home to countless untamed beasts of all shapes and sizes, mountains which pierced the heavens and disappeared among the clouds, rolling, wild grasslands where cattle grazed and wolves hunted among patches as tall as the average human, and green, towering forests that seemed to harbour a mind of their own, the roots of the trees expanding and snaking across the entire southern region, limited only by what became to be known as The River Dane, separating the wild, green South from the mountainous North.

To the West of Oreldas lies the realm of humans; the bustling, overcrowded, death factory of Soldon, ruled by the Fereldor dynasty. Specifically, by the tyrant king, Argolis Fereldor. A continent that, much like Oreldas, once held a wild, untamed landscape and a diverse ecosystem, but now was little more than a polluted hub of death and decay, where living conditions and work environments were so incredibly toxic, the average life expectancy was half of what it was before the development of industry, most specifically the burning of coal to fuel the fires which heated the vats that boiled and frothed across the entire region, their uses varying from the booming production of alchemical mixtures to the melting of steel for weapons and tools.

A large group of humans, including two of King Argolis' own children; Prince Niltay and his younger sibling, Princess Balmira, were distraught at the state of the world they lived in, and gathered in Soldon's capital city, protesting and gathering the funds and supplies necessary for an expedition to the East, to a land previously visited by explorers but never settled on. The protestors, accused of treason for their blasphemous words against the leadership of Soldon, were banished from the entire continent, and so had little choice but to sail for Oreldas. This may have been their desire, though without funds or supplies, the expedition would prove to be disastrous.

After a week of sailing across unforgiving seas, which swallowed almost half of the original fleet, what remained of the ships eventually arrived on the North-West coast of Oreldas. Fortunately, both of the royal siblings had survived, and so the decision of who was to lead the new civilisation of humans was decided without hesitation. Prince Niltay would become the new king, as was decided by the humans, who had grown accustomed to being led by a strong, male figure, his sister ruling as the Proxy Queen in his absence, particularly during times of raiding and colonial expansion. This decision, however, was ill met by followers of Balmira, who believed her training as one of Soldon's finest military leaders would prove more useful than Niltay's training as his father's accountant. A rift opened between the siblings, separated further by this new expanse of land they found themselves in, with Balmira carving her way East through the various wild and treacherous, some even otherworldly, dangers while her brother remained where the ships landed, constructing his palace and a city to complement this new port.

Balmira continued as far East as possible, until she too came upon a coastline. She ordered the services of a cartographer, who scouted the areas she had not taken, noting down the coastlines of the entire continent as far North as was possible, and as far South as The River Dane. By the time this task had been completed, both Balmira and Niltay had finished construction on basic, wood-based towns for their settlers. Niltay had named his city Marrivel, after his daughter, born during the construction of the city itself, whereas Balmira, honouring her tyrant father, settled with Argolis. This decision, particularly to those who protested Argolis' tyrannical rule, was one which brought great discontent to Balmira's settlers, some of which began to call the city Balmira City instead. The new queen, despite the disgust she felt at seeing the state of her father's realm, never stopped honouring his role as a military leader, hoping that one day, he would once again be proud of her.

Splitting the charted land exactly in the middle, the two Provinces of Niltay and Balmira were formed. The first civilised regions of Oreldas.

To the South of the island, far to the South, was the Isle of Emeralds, Nirndrelluin, The birthplace of the modern-day Elves. Nirndrelluin, unlike Oreldas, was a land covered almost entirely in forests towering as tall as mountains, apart from the coast of golden sands encircling the entire landmass. There were no cliffs, no visible mountains, no green plains. Every aspect of the island was covered in green trees. Among these trees were the Elves, a race of people who had become accustomed to the greenery and adapted to work with it. Unlike the Humans, the Elves were finely attuned to the Magic of the planet, particularly controlling the growth and spread of plants through their mastery of Chlorokinesis. An inherited ability predominantly passed from generation to generation among the elven people, this meant they could bend, shape, and mold the trees into whatever form and size they wished, hollowing out some of them to use as buildings, and manipulating parts of them to accustom to their needs. Every bridge, tower, house, and castle were shaped from the trees themselves, creating extravagant, unbelievable creations of architecture topped by branches of flourishing, deep green leaves which danced in the breeze. Above the houses, where the sunlight poked through the leaves, the trees themselves would seem to offer gardens to the gods, walkways leading upwards to the most beautiful, half-spherical oaken containers a hundred metres in diameter, each one used to grow a different, crucial vegetable for the people below, for the thickness of the canopy prevented most of the vitally needed natural light from reaching the soil at ground level. This also provided an explanation as to why many of the city-dwelling Elves were pale in complexion, cowering or wincing at the sight of direct sunlight during the island's warmer months. The Elves were ruled by an elected queen, one who would come and go when the majority of the people decided. The last queen of Nirndrelluin was Queen Coryphia Rosimer, a peaceful queen who focused on advancing magical studies as opposed to endless, unnecessary war, boosting military strength, or destroying her people's much-loved forests for industry.

The beauty of Nirndrelluin was short-lived, however. The Elves' natural affinity to magic made them a priority target to countless forces of darkness. Deep within the planet's crust, there lies a realm of evil, buried and forgotten. The Blackland, a cave three thousand miles around, with various haunting cave systems and damp caverns around one central sphere of darkness and decay. The exact location of this realm was unknown, it had been lost long ago, save for one entry point at the centre of the planet's flat surface, where once the core of the world itself bubbled and boiled, now little more than a simmering, dormant volcano. Though of course, this access point was sealed by the magical forces of good in the world, and there were little travellers who ever dared to venture that far to the Core Isles. The inhabitants of this doomed realm had instead mastered the art of ritualistic portal travel to various locations they would order their surface minions to attack, for the Demons who dwelled within seldom fought their own battles, utilising the hive-minded nature of their lesser to organise groups to strike the surface. One of these locations was Nirndrelluin. The Demons flooded the land, one touch from their cursed hands setting the trees ablaze. A handful of Elven ships, floating vulnerably around the island, were all that remained. This was the beginning of the Elven expedition.

The small remaining fleet managed to regroup along the northern coast, watching as their entire island burning before them. They sailed North, never again looking back at the destruction they narrowly escaped.

After two weeks of sailing, famished and fatigued, what remained of the Elven people arrived at the South-Western coast of Oreldas. The strongest Elves that remained used their abilities to shape the trees and plants to create what would become a thriving capital city, named after the fallen Queen, Coryphia, in the Province they named Rosimer. To the North of Rosimer stood an intimidating row of mountains, separating one forest from another. The Elven people, learning that perhaps cities build entirely from wood was not a good idea, decided to hollow out portions of the mountains and transport them back to their settlements to reinforce their homes. What resulted was a tunnel, leading through the entire mountain pass, twisting and turning to avoid various beast lairs and magma rivers. Beyond the mountains was another forest, this one remaining on the whole untouched by the Elven people, and was instead used as a spiritual, cemetery-type place, for Elves did not bury their dead, instead encasing them within trees, becoming one with nature. They named the region Oakenheim, after the fallen capital city of their once beautiful island.

Among the survivors of the Demon attack on Nirndrelluin was a group of four powerful mages. Before the attack, they had each claimed to have artificially created a gemstone with enough power to control an aspect of the entire planet, keeping evil at bay, specifically keeping demons underground, as unlike the Isle, Demons roamed Oreldas freely, now that there were intelligent people there to summon them willingly, and corpses to possess and add to their armies. The mages, knowing the danger they would cause the common people with gemstones that would control the world, pleaded with the newly elected queen, Artemis Sibbil, a middle-aged elf who aided the construction of Coryphia, made decisions which shaped the development of the Province, and ensured the survival of the Elven people. She told them of an island below sea level to the East, of a mountain which stood so tall, protected by a circumference of lesser mountains providing a barrier from floods, one that could easily be hollowed out and hold within it an entire city for mages. The island itself resonated a deep, mystical energy the Elves wished to utilise.

The mages journeyed East, while in the North, tensions began to rise. For the first time, an Elven fisherman who drifted too far North during a nap in his small boat had landed in Niltay and was apprehended by guardsmen. Queen Artemis herself travelled to Marrivel, where he was being held prisoner, to publicly reveal the Elven people for the first time and strike a diplomatic treaty to keep the peace. Queen Artemis stayed in Marrivel, with it then becoming the mandatory home for every Elven leader after her. In return for peace, the humans requested aid from the Elves. Their wooden homes were proving difficult to maintain, and the mining skill of the people was not great enough to safely mine enough resources. Remembering the mages, Artemis opened a portal to the mining operation to the South, within the Rosimeris mountain island.

The need for finely carved stone changed the design plans for the mages' mountain drastically. Instead of carving from the inside out, with four towers surrounding the mountain city, an error in the Marrivel planning department meant the designs were flipped on their head. The Human miners, who learnt from the Elven miners, carved a funnel out of the mountain, with the four surrounding towers acting as support. The top of the mountain was flattened, every stone brick created being sent through a portal to the city of Marrivel to be used in the construction of better, stronger homes, and a separate palace for the Elven leader; The Rose Castle.

A city was constructed on the top of the mages' mountain, where every mage and Human who wished to be taught the way of magic and mysticism would travel for education, and to live among their gifted kin. The mountain was named Ald Rosimeris, and it became the hub of the magical world for centuries to come.

The only region which remained, for the most part, unchanged, was the region to the South-East, known as Greymire. This region, despite being, on the whole, uninhabited, is likely the most intriguing region of Oreldas. This land had no set inhabitant, it was, instead, mainly a swamp of ruins from a bygone era. Castles still stood, or at least what remained of them, and there were still the remnants of cities and towns, half sunk in the swamps and inhabited now by feared lizard beasts who weren't likely to give up their new homes so easily. Of course, there were some Elves who lived there, Elves who had bended a few of the trees to their will to act as homes, as well as Humans who had crafted small huts on stilts, or entire villages that stood on wooden legs. Those were, however, only in areas that were safe, it took a lot of trial and error before the right places were found.

The northern half of the region held countless cave systems, hidden by overgrown shrubbery and roots of trees which bent to conceal the entrances. It was here that travellers may encounter Wildlings. They were the offspring of Humans who had been outcast by Balmira's growing regime, men and women cast away for treason, murder, theft, or any crime. These Humans lived within the caverns and caves of Greymire, training their children to hunt and kill better than most Human hunters, their small frames and silent footsteps aiding their hunting abilities. The parents of these children would almost never leave the caves, they deemed the outside world unsafe and forbidden. They became almost feral from a young age, murdering and kidnapping travellers, some tribes going as far as eating whoever they captured, others simply robbing them of their possessions and throwing them back into the untamed swamps to be eaten by whatever lurked within.

Life in caves, however, became dangerous. With the completion of Ald Rosimeris, and the placing of the four gemstones in their respective towers, the dark Demons and Demonic Entities roaming the wilds diminished dramatically. The Diamond of The Bracing Winds made the fresh air of Oreldas toxic to these Demons, something the elves wanted to ensure, in the hope that there would not be a repeat of what happened in their homeland. Demons were driven deep underground, some of them turning to the Wildlings and their parents, manipulating them and possessing them to do as they wished. The surface world became, on the whole, safe, each gemstone providing magical security of their element. Along with protection in the air, the gems provided calm seas from the Sapphire, dormant volcanoes, never erupting, from the Ruby, and co-operative, peaceful flora and fauna from the Emerald. Though of course there were some species of beast which could never be tamed.

And so, society within Oreldas thrived and flourished. It continued for over a thousand years, into the lifetime of Gothwen Darkarrow, whose story would shape and change this world once again. Living in a time where civil unrest between the humans and the elves reaches a critical point, and the discontent Apostate mages held against the restrictions put in place within Ald Rosimeris sparks conflict on her doorstep, Gothwen must find herself, while seeing those before her as her allies, her friends, people she can trust. Alternatively, the darkness in her heart could consume her. For it is darker than any night sky, colder than any mountaintop, and deadlier than any predator within this magical world. Oreldas will test the strength of her soul.

CHAPTER ONE

Coryphian Morning

The midday woodland sun flickered through the leaves, shining through the thin, silken curtains onto the carved, wooden bed where Gothwen Darkarrow lay. She was awake. She had been for the past hour, watching the sun move slowly from the bottom of her bed on to her bare toes. She let out a moan, moving her feet out of the rays as though any more time exposed to the light would cause them to burn to ash. She lay on her side, bringing her knees to her chest, staring at the dressing table beside her bed. She knew she would have to get up eventually, though she did not see a point in doing so.

Gothwen's room was small. She was a young adult who could barely hold a job for more than a week without getting bored or messing something up. Her Aunt paid for her accommodation. All she could afford was a small flat in one of the smaller trees the Elven people of Coryphia had made organic, multi-story tower blocks out of. Gothwen's room had the essentials. Her essentials, to be specific. On one side of the room, under the window, was her bed; a carved log with a mattress stuffed with wool. The humidity of the forest meant only a transparent silken cover was needed, though Gothwen always kept a thicker cover in the cupboards along the back wall just in case the temperature dropped. Beside her bed was a nightstand. Carved from similar wood to her bed, it primarily served as Gothwen's medicine cabinet. She opened the draw, rummaging through it without looking. She knew exactly which vials held which medication. She pulled out a slender, glass vial of pink, delicious looking liquid. She cupped her palms together with the vial between them, counted to five, then opened them. The liquid had turned black and seemed to be much thicker than it was before. Gothwen sighed, and lay on her back again, staring at the ceiling until the liquid had returned to its original colour. She unscrewed the lid, and drank the contents in one gulp, wincing at the bitter taste of the deceiving vial. She threw it at the opposite wall to the window, striking the mirror of her dressing table which shattered the glass into shards which flew across her room. Gothwen turned to look at what she had done.

She sat up, her silver hair catching the sun, her fringe over her left eye. She had the typical look of an elf who had just woken up, her hair was sticking up in places, the eyeliner she was wearing the night before had run down her face, and what remained of the last meal she had eaten could still be seen as stains on her nightgown. She stretched her arms out, before standing up to the side of her bed. She caught a glimpse of herself in the mirror, a mirror which now had a crack running down the centre, what remained of the liquid she had just drank running in streaks down the surface. She had grown to detest her current self.

Gothwen stared at herself for a while, examining her body to see if she could find any evidence of what had caused her to become such a failure. She found nothing but a few spots and freckles, most of which out of eyesight for whoever would walk by her in the street. She shrugged, shuffling over to the chest at the end of her log bed. She kept her clothes in there, all folded in neat piles. One pile for shirts, one for pants and skirts, and one haphazard bundle stuffed between the piles for underwear. She kept her various pair of shoes underneath the bed. There were four pairs in total. One with heels, one without, boots for muddy days, and a pair of silver slippers for formal events. Gothwen chose her outfit for the day, laying them out on her bed-covers; a long-sleeved white tunic, a sleeveless, leaf green, twill jerkin which extended to her upper thigh, paired with tight, dark brown breeches and her black boots which climbed up her legs, almost as high as her knees. She had begun to take off her nightgown when she remembered the transparency of the curtains. Gothwen peered out, the tree trunk directly parallel to the one within which she resides was adorned with wooden windows of varying sizes and shapes. Shadows moved on the other side of some of the glass viewports. She clicked her fingers, and the thin, white silks began to fill. From the top, a tidal wave of white engulfed everything that could be seen through, giving Gothwen the complete privacy she needed to change her clothes.

Once she was finished, the curtains began to return to how they were. The transparent army fighting back against their opaque oppressors, until once again the curtains, flowing in the midday breeze, were almost as clear as daylight. All that was left for Gothwen to do now was sit at her dressing table and fix the mess on her face that was her makeup. This was the part of the day Gothwen hated the most. It meant she had to look at her own face for an extended period of time.

Gothwen dipped her handkerchief in the bowl of water she kept on the table. She used it to wash away the eyeliner from the day before, as well as the lipstick, and then to generally clean her own face. On the far corner of the table were Gothwen's various containers of differing makeup products in varying colours. She made them herself. Her favourite was her black eyeliner, which she made using a very specific charcoal dust and a small amount of water. She'd normally pair it with her lipstick of a similar colour, though she'd add monkey blood to her lipstick concoction to add a hint of red. The problem then being, as monkey dishes were a delicacy in the Rosimer forests, Gothwen would be tempted to lick off her lipstick halfway into the day, and she would then have to hunt her own replacement monkeys without being spotted by the hunting parties of the Coryphia High Count. Gothwen had already gotten into trouble with the City Guard on numerous occasions, 'accidents and misunderstandings' as she called them. It would be wise for her not to tangle with the High Count's personal guard.

With her makeup applied and her outfit, in her opinion, looking relatively fine, Gothwen turned her attention to the last item of clothing she wore. It was a circlet, forged from silver and given to her by her mother before her disappearance. In its centre, shining in the reflected light of the sun through her transparent curtains, was what Gothwen believed to be an emerald. Of course, it was highly unlikely that an emerald of that size was, in fact, real, and that instead it was a glass ornament. This was the tale woven by Gothwen's Aunt at least, who allegedly oversaw the creation of the circlet with her mother.

Gothwen sat back in her chair, staring at the emerald. Most days she never even wore the circlet, she grew tired of the whispers behind her back and the constant name-calling from those who walked by. Gothwen had grown to hate being called 'The Princess of the Rosimer Forest' simply for wearing an item of sentimental value. There were very little precious metal deposits in the forests, at least, ones that had been found. Jewellery such as the circlet would have had to have been forged miles away, most likely in the Niltay region far in the North, where the many mountain passes were mined in abundance by the local humans.

Gothwen swallowed her pride once again and picked up the circlet. She placed it on her head as she looked in her mirror. She hesitated, three times, before finally decided to leave it in place. She felt like an idiot wearing it. Though every day she felt drawn to put it on and leave it on for the entire day, only removing it to undress, she never understood why. Perhaps, she thought, it was because of her lost mother. The circlet was all she had to remember her by. Nevertheless, she twisted her face to make a fake smile, and with this she was ready to start her day properly.

Gothwen Darkarrow was a student of the Rosimer Regional College for Mages Gifted in The Arcane Arts. A mouthful to say the least, which was why, to the locals, it had simply been shortened to 'The Ark'. Gothwen never liked attending a College that forced her to control her magical abilities, she longed to use them to help anyone at risk of falling down a path that bore any resemblance to her own. Gothwen was a loner, a social outcast. Though to be perfectly honest that was how she liked it. It was by choice, if anything. Of course, she had a few friends in the college, good people who turned her frowns to smiles, real smiles this time. They included her in activities, they drank with her – a lot in Gothwen's case, she was an incredibly heavy drinker and had a high alcohol tolerance to match – and Gothwen loved them very much. They understood her. They cared for her. Though most importantly, her friends kept her from spiralling out of control. She was a complicated young elf. Over her teenage years her mental state had deteriorated. The cracks that formed from being an orphan, raised in a household by a woman not her blood relative, and being tormented by the students who found her story amusing were slowly filled with darkness and despair. Though the people around her, her isolation and inability to fit in anyway due to not knowing where she herself had come from were not the only things casting a darkened shroud over her mind. Gothwen despised her time at college, it did nothing for her mental health, she never knew why she didn't just stop attending, wandering into the wilderness of the world never to return. She wanted to be free, to be let out into Oreldas with no limitations and no boundaries, an opinion clearly shared by the Apostate Society of the college. These were a group of renegade mages who had become notorious for the constant protests on college grounds and frequent magical disruptions across the Rosimer region. Particularly on the streets of Coryphia where they would draw the most attention.

Gothwen was met by these protestors the second she left her home. A row of five mages, all wearing the same, tattered green robes were marching down the main road towards the Coryphia Council building, each of them with their palms outstretched as endless streams of gold coins flew into the air, turning to dust before they could fall back to the ground. Gothwen recognised the mage standing in the centre of the line; a rogue who went simply by the name Fillinel. A common name among the Rosimer people, combined with no surname, making her an incredibly difficult person to trace. She was, as Gothwen knew, the leader of the Apostate Society. There were not many outside of the college who knew what Fillinel looked like, as, to further conceal her identity and the identity of every member, the Apostates usually wore masks over their mouths and hoods, making only their eyes visible. Fillinel, however, did have a few strands of fiery, red hair cascading from her hood and onto her chest, making her easily recognisable by people like Gothwen.

Fillinel's eyes met with Gothwen's, she broke her line of protest to walk directly towards her. She had recognised the textbook Gothwen held and knew she was attending the college.

Fillinel hooked her leg around Gothwen's and forced her to the ground. "Conformist!" She pulled down the mask from her mouth and spat onto Gothwen's textbook. "You should not be forced to control your powers!" Fillinel winked, Gothwen knew the whole thing was staged. The two were once occasional friends at the college, and in their earlier years of studies, they would often cause magical trouble together. Though the two fell out of touch once Gothwen started skipping her classes and Fillinel turned her attention to her growing cause.

Gothwen looked up. For the first time in a very long time, she was looking at the full face of Fillinel. Her lips matched the red of her hair, her eyes a flaming orange. Both her eyes and lips sparkled in the sun. It must have been a new lipstick she used.

Gothwen did not have time to say anything. Fillinel outstretched her palms towards her face, and the stream of gold coins once again began, this time every coin hitting her like a cascade of little stones, before all turning to dust as they hit the ground again.

"This is what Ald Rosimeris does to Mages. They take away the riches they can rightfully make themselves, leaving nothing but dust!" Fillinel turned to address the crowd that had gathered on the street. "We mages can make gold, can distribute it to the poor! Though any form of currency we create is taken away!" Fillinel stepped away from Gothwen, allowing her to get to her feet again. "The mages of Ald Rosimeris control us. They limit our magic while they sit in 'Funnel Mountain' to the East." Fillinel threw her fist in the air, her robe revealing a pale, freckled forearm Gothwen had always found attractive. "Rise up, march with us, join our cause today! Riches for all! Not just the nobility!"

Gothwen dusted herself off, the coins had left a considerable amount of grey, sand-like powder all over her. Fillinel turned back to Gothwen. "You. You do not have to control who you are, suppress your desires, be someone you're not." A piece of paper, as though it was burning in reverse, appeared in Fillinel's hand. She thrust it towards Gothwen, who sheepishly took it. "Read it." She looked at the circlet and smirked. "I'll see you soon, Princess." Fillinel winked again as she retook her place in the centre of the marching line, continuing to spew coins from her palm as she walked.

Gothwen swore under her breath, hastily taking the circlet off and placing it in her satchel. She was not leaving it in her home.

Intrigued, she unfolded the paper, which she found to be a small poster advertising the Apostate Society, listing the times they met and the various locations. After a short while, the letters and various images on the paper began to change, rearranging themselves to read something else; an article titled 'How to Raise Piglets'. The paper was enchanted, to only show its true arrangement when Gothwen and only Gothwen was looking at it. She looked around and found the crowd of people who had watched the entire protest now had their eyes on her. The paper was smarter than she was herself.

She folded it back up and hid it in her satchel with her circlet. Of course, the satchel was enchanted too. It was bigger on the inside, meaning anything she could fit through the small opening of the bag itself could be stored within it. It was, however, only a limited illusion, her bag was not infinitely large and could not hold, perhaps, a person. Mainly because a person would not be able to fit inside the bag's opening, but also because any object added to the bag adds to the weight. Highest ranking mages or the richest students could afford a weightless, Unicorn leather model, but not Gothwen. Gothwen's was pigskin and heavy. Very heavy.

There were a few things Gothwen needed to take care of before setting off for The Ark, even though she was at least three hours late already. Missing classes never bothered her, she always put it down to her mental health, it was always good to take a day off if she needed it. An opinion not shared by her tutors, it seemed, though they seldom delved into a student's private, mental affairs, which Gothwen appreciated.

First on her imaginary list was a brief visit to her Aunt's home. She always loved visiting her Aunt. As a child, Gothwen would sit on the edge of her seat as she told the story of how Gothwen came to be orphaned. Gothwen had come to terms with her past, it was something out of her control. The fact she had such an interesting backstory was something she took pride in. This particular story was one she reminisced as she walked.

When she was little more than a few months old, her parents, Aringoth and Erinwen, two wealthy caravan owners who travelled between the elven city of Coryphia and the human city of Marrivel, were leading a cart of Human goods through the Rosimer forest when their caravan was attacked by bandits. Gothwen's parents had lost their lives, the bandits knew exactly where to position themselves to dispatch the guards one by one, before finishing off the owners without ever being seen. However, the attackers left Gothwen, sleeping in her basket. Evidently, they could not come to terms with the murder of an infant, instead allowing the forest to decide her fate. When Elaina, the woman Gothwen came to call her Aunt, found the smouldering ruin of the caravan on a hunting trip, she took in the helpless child before she was eaten by predators of the forest. Two pieces of the caravan were all that remained, from a side panel on which the names of Gothwen's parents were painted. All that remained were the fragments 'goth' from her father's name, and 'wen' from her mother's. Elaina combined the two, to create Gothwen. Her surname, Darkarrow, came from the obsidian-tipped arrow fired by a bandit which struck Gothwen's basket, narrowly avoiding her by inches. To this day, Elaina wears the obsidian arrowhead around her neck. One day, as she said, she would pass the amulet on to Gothwen.

Elaina's home was carved from the roots from one of the larger apartment trees similar to the one Gothwen lived within. In areas where the roots would soar out of the ground and arch like a serpent, the wood would often be carved into terraced houses, forming streets which wound like a maze to form a city. Gothwen's Aunt Elaina lived in one of these houses, she had done for longer than Gothwen could remember. She stood before the handcrafted staircase leading to the front door. In its old age it had become worn down, the wood in some areas replaced and nailed on to older planks. One of the stairs was broken, though Gothwen was just the right size to step over it and onto the next with ease. Though little over five feet tall, there were very few things Gothwen could easily hop over. She could remember climbing down these stairs as a child to play on the streets below. She always took her favourite toy with her; a hand-sewn doll made from the material of a disused sack, with buttons for eyes and golden hair from a horse's tail upon its head. Elaina had always told Gothwen that it was made by her mother, to always remind her of the way she looked, and the way she smiled. Gothwen's mother, like the doll, had a smile which seemed as though it had been sewn on. It never straitened or dropped, it always curved upwards, no matter what happened. Gothwen would play with the doll for days on end, taking it with her on adventures to the apothecary, or the baker. In many cases the doll would return to Elaina's home with Gothwen, smelling of her adventures, and as Gothwen lay in her bed at night clutching the doll, she herself would smile as she planned the next big journey they would take together. They were simpler times, days which Gothwen missed. She considered herself too broken to ever enjoy days like those again.

The doll was the first thing Gothwen always saw when she opened the door to her Aunt's home. Sitting atop the fireplace on the far wall, it always sat, slightly drooping, but always smiling. The contents of the room had barely changed in Gothwen's eighteen years of living here, topped by a further year of visitations when Elaina finally decided that, on her eighteenth birthday, Gothwen should move into her own accommodation, paid for by The Ark to aid her independent studies. Below the fireplace where her doll lay was the fire, almost always lit, surrounded by a brick wall, two blocks high at the front, though reaching to meet the doll's perch at the side. The smoke would rise through a chimney carved out of the root, lined with more brick to prevent anything catching fire. Elaina sat in her brown leather armchair facing the flickering flames. She was not old, Gothwen knew her to be forty-two, still relatively youthful for an elf, who had three times the lifespan of a human at least, though whenever Gothwen visited, she was always seated here, watching the flames burn as though she was expecting Gothwen despite the lack of notice that she would be coming. Gothwen's Aunt always kept her hair short; it barely fell below her ears. In the flickering light of the fire, those dark brown strands shone like a beacon. Though of course, to Gothwen, her Aunt *was* a beacon. She always knew that, no matter how lost she ever felt, she could always come home for a lavender-scented hug and a glass – no, bottle – of wine.

Gothwen took up her usual position, sitting in the matching armchair beside Elaina, separated by a small, round table upon which a bottle of wine rested, paired with a glass, half full of the deep, red liquid. Gothwen stared into the flames alongside Elaina, occasionally turning her gaze to note any changes in her Aunt.

"Your grades are suffering, Gothwen. You sit before me, while your seat in The Ark remains empty." Elaina turned her head, slowly meeting Gothwen's. She removed her rounded spectacles, pulling a cloth from beneath her and wiping away a few smudges. "Am I disappointed? Why would I be?" She smiled, offering Gothwen the glass of wine on the table. "Why are you not there?"

Gothwen swiftly took up the glass, wrapping her hand around the thin neck and pouring the wine in its entirety into her mouth. She wiped her mouth with her sleeve. "What's the point? The older I get the less interested I become. You never wanted me to go anyway." She placed the glass back on the table.

Elaina looked back into the fire. "Coryphia is too dependent on Magic. I wanted you to become what you always dreamed of becoming. An explorer, an adventurer." She continued staring into the flames. "Your eyes burn with a passion for the unknown. Ancient tomes, decrepit ruins. They are all waiting to be explored and understood. You always wanted to be the one to do it." Her words spoke the truth, she never even had to look into Gothwen's eyes to know that. "I never wanted you to waste your teenage years studying. All it brought you was torment and depression. It pains me, seeing the beautiful girl I raised become a prisoner to her own wavering mind."

Gothwen agreed, fumbling with her hair for a moment. "It's too late now, the damage is done. I am who I am, and I wish to be nobody else."

Elaina looked back at Gothwen, smiling. "Your self-confidence is admirable, dear. Among all the pain and sorrow in your heart, I am glad to see it flourish. If only you used it to land yourself a man."

"Or woman." Gothwen was quick to react.

"I believe finding someone to spend your life with will help you greatly, Gothwen." Elaina reached over the table, placing her hand on top of Gothwen's. The warmth of her skin brought back Gothwen's memories of her childhood. Whenever she was upset or mad, Elaina would always be there to comfort her. "Believe me when I say, it matters not who you bring home to me. There will always be a warm meal for the two of you prepared here. I keep your old bedroom clean for that reason too." Elaina winked, Gothwen turned a shade of red.

Gothwen looked back at her Aunt. "I'm nineteen, there's still so much of my life left to live. There's plenty of time to find someone."

Elaina nodded, looking back into the fire. "Until then, take these." She reached down the opposite side of her armchair, lifting three small vials, the same as the ones Gothwen drank from earlier. "Never run out of these. Never use them too much. Never rely on them." This happened every week. Gothwen always nodded, took the vials, then continued to stare into the flames alongside Elaina until she decided it was time to leave.

The Ark was a short, half hour walk from the outskirts of Coryphia, a walk Gothwen always loved, as it gave her moments to herself. Being alone with her thoughts probably wasn't the best thing for Gothwen, but it passed the time. Something wasn't right, however, and the source was coming from Gothwen's chest. She felt around for a while, cautious, of course, of what passers-by would make of Gothwen's apparent lewd act, until she found what was wrong. She pulled out a gold coin, much like the magically created ones Fillinel had thrown at her from her palms. As she rubbed the edges, she found the coin was, like all of the others, supposed to have disintegrated and turned to dust, as it had already begun to wear down. However, no matter how much Gothwen tried to break the coin in half, its original integrity remained. She examined the coin closely. It was exactly like a Coryphian Crown, the most valuable item of Coryphian currency available. It had an image of the High Elven Queen engraved on one side and, on the back, the crest of the High Count. The coin was genuine and had the weight of solid gold. Gothwen had never properly handled a Crown before, she had only ever dealt in Aiadems or Bloons, coins of lesser value, made of lesser metals. Gothwen found the Crown hard to believe, and a tidal wave of questions flooded her mind. At least now she had a perfectly reasonable excuse to speak to Fillinel again.

Despite this distraction on her journey, Gothwen eventually reached her destination. The Ark, a glimmering white college built around the largest oak tree outside of Coryphia, with walkways and staircases constructed out of the various twisting branches which towered above the elven-made building itself. The tree came first, the college was then constructed from the oak's hollow shell, much like many of the buildings in Coryphia itself. However, the stones used in the building's construction were of magical origin. They had been dipped in the Well of Abundant Magics within Ald Rosimeris individually before being transported via portal to the construction site on the outskirts of Coryphia, which gave them an eternal glow. The reason for that, as Gothwen learnt, was that it dispelled any evil, dark magics, with the intent of protecting young mages from dark influences. Gothwen always joked that this was the reason why the High Count could never enter the college. At least, she joked to herself about it. Gothwen didn't have many people to joke with.

What always confused Gothwen, however, was that on her first day of entering the college, the building refused to let her enter. Thinking about it, Gothwen came to the conclusion that was why she was always isolated, always alone. The students she studied with were afraid of her, of what she could be. Rumours even began to circulate that she was the Black Witch of Rosimer folklore, an elf who would burn Coryphia in a blaze of unnatural fires if tested to her limits. In reality, nobody knew why the college refused to let Gothwen enter, not even the professors, who dismissed the event as an 'Arcane Malfunction'.

Gothwen had been studying at the college for nine years, but even now she always took a deep breath and closed her eyes whenever she tried to open the door. Every time, the door opened without a problem.

Having passed Basic Magical Control, Gothwen was able to choose her own area of studies. She had chosen Mystical

Linguistics, combined with Old World Tome Studies. The past fascinated her, and she wanted to learn as much about the magics of the past and the languages of the past as was possible. However, she had begun to regret this decision, and wanted instead to travel the world and collect information of her own, using her knowledge of the languages of the Old World to read ancient, unknown texts nobody had ever seen before. Gothwen longed to be an adventurer, but she could not let her Aunt think she was a complete failure. As much as she disagreed with Gothwen's decisions to study, Gothwen felt as though abandoning her courses within The Ark would prove to Elaina that she was a complete waste of space, even though this was something he had felt about herself for a long time.

The interior corridors within The Ark were just as impressive as the exterior. The bright, white bricks were laid individually, each by hand and set in place, towering at least twenty metres high in the main corridors of the largest and grandest building. There were no stone archways on the inside of the building, however. Instead, the forest had seemingly been allowed to continue growing inside; the trunks of trees stood elegantly at equal intervals along the corridor, two on either side, bending inwards to meet at the top, where a glowing, bulbous tangle of vines and little spherical plant lights gave the halls a mystical, orange glow. Of course, these trees gave the corridors a natural smell, with the breezes which blew and gentle rustled the vines spreading the scent of nature, as though Gothwen was studying outdoors, in a forest.

Gothwen reached her classroom, after wandering the many corridors of the college, three and a half hours after the college day had begun. This time, she could at least think up an excuse that was relatively true, the old professor who taught her classes was not the meanest of mages. He had excused Gothwen's lateness and frequent absences many times before, dismissing them with a smile and the wave of his hand. Taking a deep breath, she opened the door.

Before Gothwen could even explain herself, she found her legs to be frozen in place. Her usual professor was nowhere to be seen, instead, a tall, thin, elven woman stood at the front of the class, pointing at Gothwen with the most elegantly designed wand Gothwen had ever seen. The wood was darkened and polished, curved like a hunter's bow, the grip was furred with what looked like a grey lion's mane above where the woman's fingers were wrapped. The grip itself, as Gothwen could make out, was a black leather, tied at the back by a silver string. Gothwen immediately recognised who the person was not by the face or the wand's elegance, but by its pommel. A clear glass ball was attached to the end of the wand and, inside it, was an emerald, frozen in place similar to Gothwen herself. Her eyes opened, and she found herself speechless. This woman was not a Professor of The Ark, she was a High Mage of Ald Rosimeris.

"You must be Darkarrow. Gothwen. Am I correct?" The woman consulted a sheet of paper on the desk, she twisted it with two of her slender fingers to double check, before pushing it back. Gothwen could hardly muster a reply before an enchanted quill had struck a line through her name.

Gothwen could only move her eyes. She let out a noise which, if her mouth wasn't frozen partially open, would have been a sound commonly meaning 'yes'.

The woman walked over to one of the windows lining the side wall, peering out at where the sunlight flickered in the leaves. "It is approximately twelve thirty. Class started three and a half hours ago." The woman turned to face Gothwen, who was still paralysed. "Where were you when this class started, mage?" With a wave of her wand, Gothwen became unfrozen. The unexpectedness caused her to fall to the ground.

Gothwen managed to pick herself up onto her hands and knees. She could feel the eyes of the class upon her. "I was held up by Apostates, they took me hostage and demanded I stripped naked and hand over all my belongings." Gothwen began to fake a tear. She had grown rather adept at making up stories. "I had to run home in nothing but a leaf and dress myself again!"

Gothwen found herself being forced upwards, onto her feet, a ghostly hand grabbing her by the throat and forcing her back up against the wall.

The mage drew her wand and extracted the tear Gothwen had fabricated. She balanced it on the tip of her wand. "Fake. An amateur's tear of sorrow. Not even the correct ratio of the Aquarius charm to emotional suffering. As every mage knows, if you wish to create a fake tear, it is essential that you get this ratio correct. A mage can easily determine how much genuine emotional pain goes into each one. This tear has none." The mage turned to face the class. "Take notes, it may not exactly be relevant to your course, but a good mage dabbles in more than just book work." The High Mage was not entirely incorrect. The magic of Oreldas was not solely based upon verbal utterances and the flick of a wrist or wand. Genuine emotion was key to the creation of spells. Destruction spells required an extreme level of rage and anger, conjuration spells required an advanced imagination, restoration spells would only work if the casting mage held significant compassion and empathy, and so forth. Meditation, a clear mind, and emotional stability were key factors in successful spellcasting. Of course, this was why Gothwen failed at casting higher level spells. She usually kept to lesser, easier incantations and abilities.

Gothwen was still pinned to the wall. Her feet didn't even touch the ground. "Who are you anyway? Why are you taking this class?" Her voiced was coarse and rough, the hand prevented her from both speaking and breathing clearly.

The mage turned to face Gothwen again, the look of disgust on her face. "You come in here, hours late to class, you lie to my face, you do not even bother wearing your college robe, and you dare ask who I am with that tone?" The mage lifted Gothwen higher, who was now grateful she had not chosen a skirt when she had dressed herself.

Gothwen hung on the wall for a while, her head almost touching the ceiling. Without warning, however, the mage let go of her spell, and Gothwen fell to the ground again. "I am High Conjurer Lucille Magelight of the School of Nature. I oversee all that occurs within the Emerald Tower of Ald Rosimeris and within its magical boundaries, specifically the Southern regions of Elven occupation; Rosimer, Oakenheim, and the Greymire."

Gothwen stood up once again. This time nothing forced her back or caused her to grow a tail or anything. She was how she should be. "Then I apologise, Conjurer." Gothwen performed a basic mess of a curtsy, to which Lucille responded by rolling her eyes and sighing.

Lucille addressed the class once more. "I believe a short break is in order. Go out, practice the incantations I have told you to read, and record the results. Miss Darkarrow." Lucille grabbed Gothwen's shoulder as she was attempting to be the first to leave the mess she had found herself in. "I need to speak with you. Your punishment must be discussed."

Gothwen sighed, watching as her classmates each left the room, some of them muttering to her under their breath, others barging into her. She sat in the closest empty seat to Lucille, who leaned herself back against the professor's desk.

Lucille directed her wand over her shoulder in the direction of the door. A slight breeze blew it shut, with an invisible hand locking the two inside the classroom. "Nine years ago, when you attempted to enter the college, what happened, Miss Darkarrow?"

Gothwen knew what Lucille was hinting at. "You mean when the door wouldn't let me in?"

Lucille folded her arms. "It was an incident that has been puzzling the High Mages for almost a decade. The magically attuned doors of this world do not simply lock for anyone. They do not 'malfunction' as we had your professors believe."

Gothwen rolled her eyes. "So, this whole thing was yet another mages conspiracy?"

Lucille let out a laugh, there were hints of nervousness in her tone. "I see you were not entirely lying when you said you were approached by the Apostates Society."

Gothwen slouched in her chair, crossing one leg over the other. "I met them, yes, but I'm also not naked so I wasn't *completely* lying."

Lucille continued. "We believe that, after nine years, we have the information we now need to fully understand this occurrence. Why it happened, what happened, and how we prevent what *will* happen."

Gothwen's face dropped. "What *will* happen? What do you mean?" Gothwen was suddenly genuinely intrigued.

Lucille glanced at the wall at the rear of the classroom behind Gothwen, where a portal whirled to life. Papers and various classroom objects were flung either into it or as far away from it as possible. "It would be easier to show you, Gothwen. Follow."

Gothwen, in shock at what was going on around her, couldn't stop herself from following. She found herself edging towards the fiery, orange hole in the wall, which seemed to lead to a dark, stone laboratory, where various liquids boiled, and a multitude of gasses were emitting from a plethora of bottles. The edges of the portal burned like a demonic flame, though as Gothwen stepped through it, it felt cold as ice, though that could simply be because of the room she found herself in.

Lucille followed after her, and the portal closed as quickly as it had opened. "You now stand in my laboratory, on the thirtieth floor of the Emerald Tower. Directly below us is the housing chamber for the Emerald of Natural Balance, the most priceless emerald in the entire mortal world."

Gothwen understood the significance of the Emerald. It was one of four gemstones, along with The Sapphire of The Unbridled Maelstrom, The Ruby of The Eternal Flame, and The Diamond of The Bracing Winds, which maintained elemental balance across the world, developed by Elves long ago on Nirndrelluin, the gemstones combined kept the darkness underground, and kept everyone in the world, not just Oreldas, safe. If one of the gemstones was used in the wrong hands, the unstoppable, elemental power of that stone would most likely destroy the world by corresponding natural disasters. Each corner of Ald Rosimeris had a tower which protected and studied the gemstones. Lucille was the highest-ranking Conjuration mage of the Emerald School of Nature.

Lucille gestured towards a vial of sentient-looking clear liquid which had been placed beside a comfortable looking chair. Above it was a shelf of countless other vials of the same liquid, the contents of each vial swirling and dancing as though gravity did not exist. Most of the vials had hastily-written labels, though Gothwen did not have enough time to pick them all up and attempt to translate Lucille's clearly illegible handwriting. "I need you to sit in that chair and drink this vial."

Gothwen had a look of confusion on her face. "I'm all up for drinking weird liquids in a comfy looking chair in a dingy laboratory that may or may not cause me to hallucinate, but just this once, I'll ask. What is it?"

"They're Liquid Memories. Each one is attuned to a day I've lived, since I first learnt how to extract memories from my own mind." Lucille demonstrated, placing her wand underneath her eyelid and pulling a tear from her own eye. She flung the liquid into the air and watched as it began to replay events she and Gothwen had experienced in the classroom.

Gothwen took this as enough proof of Lucille telling the truth. "You should teach me how to do that, I'll need it for when I sit my Linguistics exams." She sat herself down in the chair beside the vial. It was a luxurious, polished wooden chair with various wooden engravings and attached padding of red silks filled with feathers. It was entirely out of place in the laboratory. "So, what's the date of this vial?" Gothwen lifted the glass, shaking it and seemingly startling the liquid inside.

"That is the day you started at the college. When you walked face first into the door that did not open, this vial holds what was going on here."

Gothwen leaned back into the chair, unscrewing the lid from the vial. "I hope this works better than smoking Blackweed." She drank the liquid in one sip.

Lucille waved her wand at Gothwen, a spell that caused her to fall into a deep sleep. Or, it could have been the effects of the Liquid Memory. Gothwen would never know.

CHAPTER TWO

Liquid Memories

Silver spectres filled the emptiness of Gothwen's mind, Lucille's memories infecting every corner, reaching as far as was visibly possible. They were painting a picture, their silver inked tails darting left and right, up and down, forming a three-dimensional image which appeared to animate itself. The result was a grand, elegant hall, columns lining either side of a red carpeted walkway. On one end, an engraved, silver door, at least twenty feet high, which swung open as effortlessly as if it was made of cloth. A woman entered, her robe trailing behind her, her heels clicking against the stone was the only sound that could be heard, echoing against the walls as though the entire room was to be made aware of her entry. It was Lucille, visibly younger, her hair was instead tied up and, as far as Gothwen could tell among the slithers of silver which was still forming the image, was yet to begin turning grey.

Lucille began her journey on the red carpet, towards the end of the columned hall. As she moved, more silver spectres appeared, forming an image as though she was standing still, yet the world was moving around her. Eventually, she reached the end of the room, where a round, silver lined Oaken table sat, older mages than her seated around it. Some had long, silver beards they could, though some had already chosen to, wear as scarves. Others, mainly the female members, wore elegant robes and tied their hair in various, pompous styles.

Lucille seated herself in the one empty seat which remained, beside one man who was wearing his beard as a scarf, and a woman, whose grey hair was tied in hoops at either side, dangling onto her shoulders. Neither of them acknowledged Lucille, or even greeted her with a simple nod.

Each of the mages placed their wands onto the table directly in front of them, their tips pointing into the centre. They formed a circle, each quarter persisting of four wands with the same colour pommel; green, red, blue, and white. Lucille found herself between two green pommelled wands, matching her own.

The oldest looking mage stood up, taking his wand; a thin, bone-like wand with various notches and scratches, and a white diamond pommel. He struck the table with it, like a judge's gavel, signalling order. He spoke with a light, soft tone, which echoed through the hall. "I am sure you are all aware of the reason behind our summoning." He was met by brief mumblings. "It is an investigation we will conduct with upmost importance. An incident we will not let slip past us."

The old mage placed his wand back on the table, completing the circle once again. He waved his hand over it, and each of the pommels, in a clockwise motion around the table, began to light up. Lucille watched in awe, this part of the meeting always fascinated her, she wished she could make her pommel glow by herself.

An image appeared above the table, floating in mid-air, like a hologram. Gothwen recognised it, and it was clear Lucille, in her memory, could too. It was the entrance door to The Ark, closed shut. Attempting to push it open was a ten-year-old Gothwen, trying with every ounce of strength she could find.

Pointing to the image of Gothwen, the mage spoke again.

"This girl caused the enchanted door at the Rosimer Regional College to lock shut. At roughly the same time, I received word from the Protectors of The Well of a magical disturbance. The pool began to boil, and her name was spoken, repeatedly." The mage sat down in his seat. "I called you all here primarily to discuss what we are to do with her, until the reason why this happened is found."

An uproar of various, inhumane methods of torture and execution were what followed. Every mage coming up with a new, inventive way of executing Gothwen before, as they said, her powers could grow beyond pacification. Lucille remained quiet.

Once again, the old mage slammed his wand against the table, this time sparks of fire spouting in all directions. "We will not kill the girl. She could be influential in years to come; we need her alive! We do not yet know if this is a bad thing. It could signal the introduction of a great power for the forces of Good in the world." The room fell silent. No killing must have taken the fun out of the ideas the mages were coming up with.

Lucille stood up, she cleared her throat, nerves had gotten the best of her, for a brief moment. "Let me watch over the girl. Allow her into the college, I will ensure that no dark forces can touch her while she attends, and that afterwards, she is to be brought here, unharmed, and protected." The room remained silent.

The old mage spoke once again, stroking his beard. "If we have seen this event unfold, no doubt the darkness has too. Transmuter Marill, Illusionist Dorian," the mage glared at Lucille, "Conjurer Lucille, and Destructor Varen." The four pommels of The Emerald Tower wands lit up. "As this incident happened in your assigned territory, and seeing as Conjurer Lucille has willingly agreed to watch over the girl, I am tasking your tower with the investigation of The Darkarrow Incident. All resources, from the library to the

Well of Abundant Magics itself, are open to you."

Lucille bowed. Her three colleagues rolled their eyes. "Thank you, Conjurer Servius." The three Emerald Mages, along with Lucille, reluctantly stood and bowed. They each left, without her. They were followed by the rest of the table.

Lucille stood alone, in the empty, gargantuan hall. She looked around, there was nobody left in sight. She watched as the door closed behind the last mage, before turning to look directly at Gothwen, or at least, directly into the angle at which Gothwen was experiencing the dream from.

"I know you are watching this, Gothwen. That sometime in the future I bring you here and I give you this memory. When you wake up, I will be gone." Lucille began to pace around the table. "I have seen the events to come, I have looked in the Well myself. Every mage, on being rewarded a position on the High Council, must look directly into the Well of Abundant Magics, and allow it to read their destiny. It determines whether or not the mage is trustworthy enough to hold a position of power such as this." Lucille stopped, staring into nothing. "When I looked into the Well, I saw destruction. I saw pain, I saw death, and at the centre of it all, I saw you. Filthy and wielding my own dirtied wand. Around you, were the bodies of my loved ones. Lifeless. Motionless. I lay there too, paralysed and broken, able to do nothing but stare. Yet still, the Well allowed me to stay. It is my destiny, Gothwen, to save you from this path." Lucille picked up her wand. "Any mage can cast a spell, wand or not. I wield this one, custom made like every other Council mage's, because it serves as a focus. The spells locked to civilian mages are unlocked to those who wield a wand as finely attuned to Magic as one forged in Ald Rosimeris itself, and some of those spells are enhanced and empowered to those who wield them." Lucille flipped her wand, advertising the clear pommel. "The stone in the centre of each pommel was chipped from the much larger elemental gemstone we protect. That is what allows us to be more powerful, when we cast a spell through our wands, the gemstone amplifies our abilities."

Gothwen remembered what happened with Fillinel. The gold coins she was casting from her palms disintegrating and turning to dust. "Something draws us together, in the future. When I show you this memory, that day will be near, and you must learn how to use a wand carefully, accurately, and without blowing up both the wand itself, and your own hand. We High Mages, however, do not control what intensity of magic can be cast in the world, that decision is made by the Well itself. It is sentient and keeps a balance in the world that I know people wish to disrupt. I will not let that happen. I know you too do not wish for that to happen. I will not let the Society of Mages we have built disappear like...."

Lucille looked at the ground. "I knew the Elven Queen, Gothwen. I was her apprentice. Her closest friend. She was the former High Conjurer of The Emerald Tower. Nobody knows why she left, why she vanished without a trace, reappearing a few months later to forget her life with me and reclaim her throne. All she left was a note, assigning me as High Conjurer. I wish to go to her, to see her again like I know you would too. It is a lot harder than one would imagine to gain an audience with her. She is reclusive, antisocial. That, I will admit, was one of the reasons I agreed to watch over you, so that we can see her together."

She smiled to herself. "I have stalled you enough, Gothwen." The walls around Lucille began to collapse into a sea of silver. "Come with me, to her." The ground began to fall away around her. "Go to Marrivel". Lucille melted into a puddle of silver liquid, which broke off into clouds of silver gas.

Gothwen's eyes opened.

CHAPTER THREE

Black Magelight

Just as Lucille had predicted nine years ago, Gothwen awoke in an empty room. Even the various experiments which had been bubbling in the background had stopped. Lucille was nowhere to be found. Gothwen called out, a hint of nervousness in her voice.

"Great. Alone in this old place." Gothwen knocked over a few empty vials purposefully. Her attention turned to the ground as she watched them smash. Her satchel was torn in half, its contents scattered all over the floor.

"That's even better." Gothwen rummaged through the small pile of items on the ground. Luckily, her circlet was still there. "I guess I'll be wearing this then." She once again placed the circlet on her head and made her way to the door.

Gothwen found the door itself was open the smallest amount, as though somebody had left in a hurry and failed to close it properly. "Lucille must have gone this way. Trying to get a head start on me I see."

She squeezed through the small gap, opening the door a tiny amount to fit herself through. The corridor outside the laboratory was empty. A single torch lit the wall, pointless considering there was a window beside it letting in the early afternoon sun. Gothwen looked outside. She was definitely in

Ald Rosimeris. She was surrounded by the mountain range encircling the central, dominant mountain Ald Rosimeris and its children towers was carved out of.

Each tower served as a support column for the mountain itself, which had been carved to resemble a funnel, a mountain flipped on its head. The tip, the smallest point, being at the bottom, and the largest, flattest part was at the top. Gothwen had been told stories of what stood at the peak of Ald Rosimeris. It was mainly gardens, miles in diameter, surrounding various buildings and complexes. One building was said to house the largest library in all of Oreldas, holding every book known in the entire continent. Fundamentally, it was a city, every necessity of a prosperous civilisation standing at the mountain's peak. It was a haven built for mages, safe from the turmoil of the lands below.

Gothwen stepped away from the window, her heart racing from the sheer height. She turned, facing the stone staircase that spiralled up beside her. "I guess I need to go further up, see this city for myself."

She had no idea how far the climb was from Lucille's laboratory. In reality, it took her two hours of constant stair climbing to reach what she found to be the summit. That was, of course, not including the fifteen-minute break she took to catch her breath part way through.

The stairway, for the entirety of her climb, consisted of the same stone brick construction, the same stairs, the same torch sconce every thirty-seven steps, Gothwen had counted, and the same lonely window. Gothwen did, however, question the validity of the stone bricks. Were they genuine bricks? Was it stone carved from the mountain itself made to look like bricks? Or were they even a combination of both? Every so often, Gothwen would run her hand against the stone, feeling its course coldness against her skin and wondering where each brick had come from.

At the top of the staircase, Gothwen was met by a grand,

dark wood door, with a golden doorframe and shining golden door handle on either side of the central split. This, as Gothwen could tell by the breeze blowing through the slight crack between the two doors, must lead outside. There was a thin strip of light shining through, another piece of solid evidence that led Gothwen to the conclusion that this was, in fact, the top of the mountain.

Gothwen pressed her palms against the left door, it was warm, in comparison to the cold stone she had been used to. She began to push it open, forcing herself against it in an attempt to push it even the slightest amount. Gothwen was short, as was typical for the woodland elves, meaning the door provided a worthy challenge for even her to overcome. Her feet slipped against the stone, the door gave way only slightly. Eventually, however, she managed to push it open enough so that she was able to slip herself through. The door slammed behind her again, the sound resonating both down the stairway she had just climbed and in front of her, across her new surroundings.

Before Gothwen now stood what looked like endless spires reaching even higher than the peak Gothwen found herself upon. Towers glowing as white as the stones all over The Ark, gold accents separating the stone walls from the roof tiles, the windows a multitude of colours, their reflections bouncing off every surface, some of them landing besides where Gothwen currently stood. However, it wasn't the buildings Gothwen saw that struck her the most, it was the sudden realisation that, despite all the magnificent architecture, the beautiful, stained glass windows, and the cobbled streets, the city itself remained wholly empty. There was not a single mage anywhere in sight, the leaves which had fallen from the trees beside the road had piled up, dead and brown, even blocking some doors. The roads were overgrown, grass seeping through the cracks between the cobblestones. The lower windows of buildings were covered in vines, some of the natural tentacles had even penetrated holes in the broken glass. The entire city was devoid of both human and elven life.

On closer inspection, Gothwen found that a lot of the lower windows dotted around the towers were, in fact, broken. The glass, in some cases, was still in broken shards among the grass in the street. She could only imagine the splendour of the city in its prime, bustling, the roads filled with mages and carriages pulled by horses. Though none of that remained. The streets were empty. Silent. The only noise was the howling of the wind through the open mouths made by broken windows.

Crouching, Gothwen investigated the ground. The leaves were dead, the roads were falling apart. Gothwen ran her hands through the grass rising through the cobblestone, it had been untouched for years. There were no corpses, no skeletons, no sentient being had made its lair among the ruins. Gothwen, however, didn't want to take any chances. She remembered a spell to be used in precarious situations such as this. A spell which resonated the heartbeat of any living thing through any obstruction, directly into Gothwen's eyes and ears. She whispered the spell, *Cardilus Reviliere*. At first, there was nothing. Gothwen turned on her heels, scanning her surroundings. Then, she heard it. A heartbeat. Calm and slow, the person was in no shock or discomfort, and the beat was either human or elf, so at least a Mountain Minotaur or some kind of beast wasn't using the city as their home, lurking behind a building ready to pounce and swallow Gothwen whole. It was coming from the central tower of the Mage's fortress, a marble spire which extending farther than any of the surrounding towers and buildings. It looked to be dead in the centre of the city, various walkways and bridges extended like stone legs down equidistant openings in the walls. A few of these bridges had, expectedly, fallen apart, with some looking as though they would fall at any moment.

Gothwen nodded at the tower. "That must be Lucille." She

shook her head, the sound of the heartbeat faded away. She took a deep breath before continuing to walk ahead. She had more of a desire for answers than rest. Her feet, however, seemed to disagree.

Despite the pain in her feet, Gothwen continued along the road, her heels echoing through every open door and window. She began to regret wearing her heeled boots. If there were undead creatures lurking in the shadows of the abandoned buildings, her spell would have been unable to detect them. Their hearts were completely dead, the corpses were possessed instead. Considering there were no corpses anyway, the chances of Gothwen walking directly into a Dread Ghoul nest was likely. Dread Ghouls. Gothwen shuddered at the thought of them. She had only ever seen one from a distance, before an entire squadron of Coryphian Elite Guards almost knocked her over in an attempt to kill it. They shuffled aimlessly like zombies; their brains had rotted away from their Darkworld influence until all that remained was a husk with a remote connection to the demonic hive mind via a sentient lump of slime which had taken the brain's place. A specific group of Ghouls were connected to a specific Demon, said Demon using the lifeless husks as avatars, as they were unable to survive on the surface. The perfect air of Oreldas was poison to them. So long as the Diamond of The Bracing Winds remained within its tower, it would continue to keep the darkness underground. Many of them remained in groups, the Demon controlling them like little armies, feasting on the life essence of any who stood in range of their touch.

Gothwen was now afraid of the shadows, and what they could hold. She began to pick up her pace, breaking out in some parts into a jog until she reached the golden doors of the central tower.

Like the one she saw in Lucille's memories, it towered over her, looking as elegant as it was large. She took a deep breath and held her hand out to open it. What she received was more of a surprise than anything she had experienced today; an electric shock, which forced her backwards twenty feet, falling on her back in a pile of leaves. There she lay, disoriented and confused, until the sound of a cloister bell far above her brought her back to reality. The noise was like a chapel bell following a wedding, though it had less of a merry beat to it, it was more of an alarm, a warning.

As abruptly as they began, the bells stopped. Gothwen's eyes ran down the tower, until they too stopped at the door before her. It had begun slowly opening, as though the tower itself was showing reluctance in letting her pass but was doing so anyway out of pity, seeing the poor girl lie among old leaves.

Gothwen managed to stand back on her feet, just as the doors opened enough to allow her to pass. She squeezed herself through yet again, into a room she was all too familiar with; the room from Lucille's memory. It was, of course, different to how she remembered it. The columns had crumbled, some of them in better shape than others, the red carpet leading ahead of her was torn, dusty, and stained, and the table was broken, snapped in two by what looked like a chunk of stone from the ceiling. What struck Gothwen, however, was the figure sitting casually at the table, their feet propped up against what remained of the Oaken meeting table. Gothwen immediately recognised who it was.

"Gothwen Darkarrow." The figure crumpled up the paper in their hands, tossing it behind them. "I believe it is you I should thank for bringing me here. It isn't what I expected, but I'm still impressed."

Gothwen's breaths became shallow. She could only let out a whisper. "Fillinel. How did you…"

Fillinel held up her finger, silencing Gothwen's already softened voice. "You don't think I let anybody walk away with an enchanted pamphlet, do you? It's a tracker, the Magic we used to create it emits a powerful aura we use to track your every movement. You entered The Ark and after a while you vanished." Fillinel lifted her legs, placing them on the ground. The click of her heels resonated through the empty room. "So, I activated it's secondary protocol. To act as a teleport focus." Fillinel grabbed another piece of paper from her pocket. The pamphlet she had given to Gothwen. It looked alive, various Arcane runes floating effortlessly around the paper. "I thought the magic of the college had blocked me, we originally planned on using you to get inside the place unseen and paint a few walls, but when you brought me here, and I realised where I was, I just *had* to kiss you."

Gothwen began to turn a shade of red. The thought of missing her first kiss with Fillinel brought her down. Her heart sank, she felt her face begin to drop. She realised she had dropped her vials.

"I apologise for what happened to your satchel, Gothwen. I had no idea I'd be teleported *inside* your bag. I guess it wasn't big enough for me." Fillinel stood up and began to walk rather seductively over to where Gothwen was standing. "There was a receipt in that satchel, Gothwen. From the Coryphian Apothecary. It was an old one, but I knew what it was for." Fillinel reached out, her pale, slender hand cupping Gothwen's cheek. She felt cold, but Gothwen soon felt her warm up. She looked into Gothwen's eyes. "I know how I can help. These mages must have had an Apothecary of their own."

Gothwen began to feel light-headed, her heart racing. She reached up, holding Fillinel's hand against her cheek. For a moment, she held her new friend, a single tear running down her opposite cheek. Fillinel reached up with her left hand, wiping away the tear, and placing both her hands on Gothwen's shoulders. Gothwen's head dropped, she found herself looking at the floor. "I'm too weak, Fillinel. Worthless, unimportant." She looked back up, more tears forming. "You can have far better friends than me."

Remembering what ailed Gothwen, Fillinel took the downtrodden elf by the hand, and began to lead her out of the door she had come from. "It's worse than I thought, we need to move as fast as possible." She looked at Gothwen. "For your own sake."

The road Gothwen had come from seemed to have been what was once the main road. A marketplace of sorts, with different buildings on both sides where a Mage would be able to purchase anything they needed. Gothwen had not realised this before, she was focused more on reaching the tower. There were various different signs above broken, dilapidated doorways, some swaying in the breeze, their metal chains groaning as they moved, others had already fallen to the ground. Eventually, however, the couple did find a sign that looked as though it must lead to an Apothecary. A symbol of two vials, frothing at the top and overflowing various wild, vibrant colours. Or at least, it looked as though the colours once were vibrant and wild.

Fillinel sat Gothwen on an overgrown chair, one that, in its prime, looked as though it was an elegant armchair made from the highest quality materials. By this point, Gothwen was staring into complete nothingness, a blank expression on her face juxtaposing the numerous tears streaming down her cheek and turning her eyes a bloodshot red. Fillinel threw various vials and potions across the room, cursing when one she found seemed to contain an entirely different concoction to what she thought. She did, however, pocket a few she found to be useful, or at the very least, she considered useful.

Fillinel let out a celebration. She pulled out a vial containing the same pink liquid Gothwen had drank when she woke up, one which, when Fillinel placed in Gothwen's hands, turned a version of black she had never thought was possible. It felt as though it was a black hole in a glass vial, sucking Fillinel's joy from every crevice on her body. The liquid returned to its pink state, which was the exact moment

Fillinel unscrewed the lid and threw the liquid directly into Gothwen's mouth, as though she was putting out a tiny flame on her tongue.

Gothwen's eyes lit up, and a smile began to form on her face. She laughed, her eyes meeting Fillinel's. She threw herself up, off the armchair, and wrapped her hands around Fillinel, giving her the most passionate hug she had ever thought of. Gothwen dragged out the embrace as long as possible, she never wanted to let go of Fillinel who, fortunately, looked to be enjoying it as much as her.

Eventually, however, Fillinel managed to pull herself from Gothwen. "Liquid Laughter. Gothwen. I…"

Gothwen pressed her finger against Fillinel's lips. "Some people cope in different ways, Fillinel. Medication helps me."

Fillinel sighed. "If you are sure it helps you, Gothwen." She wiped a tear from Gothwen's eye, one that had somehow managed to creep down her face without Fillinel realising. It had almost reached the corner of Gothwen's perfect smile. The once silent, distraught face now beaming with light and happiness. Fillinel found it hard to believe that this was, in fact, the same woman. She slipped a couple more vials of medicine into Gothwen's pocket. "It's best you carry these, Gothwen."

Gothwen frowned, as though she had just remembered something she really shouldn't have forgotten in the first place. "Fillinel, did you see another woman around? Blonde hair, tall, elven?"

Fillinel shared Gothwen's frown. "I haven't seen anybody here other than you, and I have thoroughly explored as much of these ruins as I could before you showed up." Fillinel managed to release herself from Gothwen's grasp. "Which reminds me. For a city of mages, this place is eerily deserted. Why? Where *is* everyone?"

Gothwen looked around, as though she had only just begun to see the ruin of the Apothecary they were standing in as a ruin, and not an intact, bustling hub of herbal remedy trading and potion brewing. "Disappointed you can't spout a stream of gold in someone's face or something?" Gothwen remembered the coin in her pocket. She kept it to herself.

Fillinel rolled her eyes. "Kind of, but that's not the point. If there's nobody here, then who or *what* is controlling our Magic?"

"The Well of Abundant Magics." Gothwen remembered what Lucille had told her about the Well. "That's what controls all the Magic in the whole world."

"The Well? I just thought that was some kind of 'All-Seeing Eye' or something. They never taught us what that *actually* does." Fillinel played with her hair as she thought.

Gothwen tried to remember what else Lucille had told her in her memory. "It's a sentient Well of Magic that acts as a type of Overseer for all things Magic related. It controls what Magic is used and helps keep the balance between light and dark Magic."

Fillinel began to pace back and forth. "Then if we were to find a way to shut down the Well, we will be free to use whatever magic we desire!"

Gothwen didn't like the thought of this idea. "It keeps a balance, Fillinel. If we disrupt that balance, who knows what could happen."

Fillinel, by this point, had become lost in a world of her own self-righteousness. "Imagine the good we could do for the entire world, Gothwen." She paused for a moment and turned to face her frowning companion. "And please, call me Filli." She smiled, a smile so beautiful Gothwen tried, and awkwardly failed, to mimic.

Gothwen gave in. "I suppose we could at least try to see what we can do about the Well. If it can even be tampered with. Or if it will actually let us tamper with it." In truth, Gothwen mostly wanted to see the Well for herself.

The room the two were in had begun to turn a golden,

orange colour. Fillinel looked up, there was a hole in the ceiling that poked all the way through to the outside world. "It's getting late, Gothwen. Perhaps we should rest. There might also be some food around. I don't know about you, but I'm pretty hungry."

The mention of food made Gothwen's stomach growl. The only things she had consumed today were the various potions and liquids she had been given. As well as the wine her Aunt had given her. "I believe we should, Filli. There has to be at least one intact restaurant or grocers in this whole city. Perhaps a place with a nice bedroom too." A shiver shot down Gothwen's spine. The thought of spending the night with Fillinel made her heart race, even if it was entirely for resting purposes.

Fillinel turned to face what remained of the vials lining the wall behind the counter. "You go ahead and find somewhere comfortable, I'll see if I can find, or maybe even make, any more Liquid Laughter for you." She scanned the shelves she hadn't yet destroyed in her mad search.

Gothwen made her way to the door, turning one last time to admire the view of Fillinel from behind. Despite all she had been through today, she had never been happier.

"Hello, Mother." Torril tilted her head. "Come to gloat? Tell me I've been a bad girl? Or are you simply here to give me a slap on the wrist."

Lucille looked down on her daughter from the safety of the iron bars before her. Her face held a look of disgust, combined with disappointment. "Why, Torril?" Lucille shook her head. "Your own sister." Lucille paced the length of the bars up and down, repeatedly. Torril never broke eye contact.

"I finally have dear Mother's attention then?" She placed her hands on her knees, staying perfectly still in her central position within the cell, cross-legged on the cold, stone floor. "Ethril was such an annoyance." She smiled, biting her bottom lip and bearing her pointed fangs.

Lucille punched the bars of Torril's cell. "Your own sister, Torril!?" A tear fell down Lucille's face. "Poison? Is that really the fate she deserved? At fifteen years old?"

Torril tilted her head in the opposite direction. Her tongue slid out of her mouth, caressing the piercing in her lip. "Slow and painful. I should know, I watched the whole thing." She held out her arms, a welcoming gesture to Lucille. "This, Mother dearest, was worth it for the look on her face as she choked on a concoction of her own blood and wine. I would have celebrated with a glass of her blood myself, would it not have killed me too."

Lucille turned cold, bitter. A resentment boiling inside her in the segment of her heart which once held love. Love for both of her daughters. "You murdered her. Out of spite!" The guardsman standing beside her nervously grasped the hilt of his blade.

Torril scoffed, rolling her eyes. The first time she broke eye contact with Lucille, which resumed immediately after. "Murder? I like to think of it as an assassination. An art I've been mastering over the past few years." Her gaze felt like daggers, piercing Lucille's soul. "Not that you would know what I've been doing."

Lucille's heart snapped. Her wand slid out of her sleeve as she raised her arm, pointing it directly at Torril. An invisible, ghostly hand grabbed her by the throat, forcing her backwards and against the wall. The guardsman flinched, unsheathing his blade in a panic.

Torril managed to form a sentence, broken by deep, frantic gasps of breath. "I never imagined you'd be the next woman to do this to me, Mother."

Lucille raised her wand, toying with Torril as though she was attached to a string. Like the wand, Torril too rose, onto her feet and higher still, until her legs dangled, unable to touch the floor. "You deserve to be executed for what you've done. Hung, drawn, and quartered. You should be fed to the Dread Ghouls!"

The guardsman inched towards Lucille. She turned her head, looking into the terrified eyes of a man who had clearly never seen such use of Magic before. *Typical for the common people of Marrivel,* she thought. *I need to remember how sensitive to Magic these people are.* Lucille released her grasp. Torril fell to her knees, struggling to get back her breath.

"Keep your Magic away from me, Witch." Torril took back her cross-legged position in her cell. "I don't care who you are. The next time you do that to me, you'll get an up-close inspection of my dagger at your throat."

Lucille lowered her arm. Her wand disappeared up her sleeve as quickly as it appeared. "You're my daughter, Torril." Their eyes met. "I still do not understand why you would do this."

Lucille's eyes burned Torril, forcing her to look away. "Practice, Mother. I needed practice." Realising Lucille's gaze was elsewhere, Torril began to stare again. "Gothwen Darkarrow." Lucille gave Torril a look of shock and fear. "A pawn on the chessboard. One I shall knock down in the least amount of moves possible."

Lucille shook her head in disbelief. "I have sworn to protect her. There is no way you can reach her. Not where you are now."

Torril bore her fangs again. "You underestimate me, Mother."

Lucille wrapped her hand around one of the metal bars. "You cannot cast any spells to get out of here." She tried to shake them, testing their sturdiness.

Torril shot up onto all fours, crawling like a primitive, barbaric creature to where Lucille stood. "I'll get out." She stared at Lucille, making her feel uneasy. "You know I will. You've seen it."

Lucille forced herself back, out of Torril's psychotic reach. "I have seen a lot of things. Some of them come true, others I change."

Slumping back down onto the floor, Torril sighed. "Make it more fun, Mother. Make it so I have to at least put some effort in my escape."

Lucille's head dropped. "Where did I go wrong, Torril?" In reality, Lucille knew exactly where she went wrong in the raising of her children. Something Torril then reminded her of.

"You went wrong when you left me with Father. What sort of a life did you leave me in? Did you know what we were doing? Did you not think perhaps it wasn't a life for a child?" Torril showed no emotion, while Lucille was showing enough for them both.

"I loved your father, Torril. More than anything. I trusted him with you, like I would have trusted him with Ethril afterwards!" Lucille fell to her knees, her face pressed against the bars.

Torril joined her, reaching her hand through the bars and holding Lucille's face. For a moment, Lucille closed her eyes, hoping that Torril would repeatedly smash her face against the iron until nothing remained but a bloody pulp by the time the guard could tear her away. Instead, she stroked her face, wiping away the multitude of tears. Lucille opened her eyes. Torril was staring directly into her soul again, the hand she had just used to wipe the tears now in her mouth. She was eating Lucille's tears.

It was at this point Lucille decided it was time to leave. She stood herself up, and handed the guardsman a small purse of gold, to keep quiet about the spell she had cast on Torril. Drying her eyes on the ends of her sleeves, she left, saying nothing to her incarcerated daughter.

Fortunately, Lucille had rented a room a short distance

from the Marrivel Barracks. A city at ground level seemed so much different to the city in the clouds Lucille was used to. The stone walls of Ald Rosimeris were replaced here by wooden, bent structures, some looming over the streets looking as though they would collapse at any moment. In the gutters lay various drunks, homeless people, and used prostitutes thrown out of homes once their services were no longer needed. It was clear to Lucille that some of them had been drugged, voluntarily or by force, she could not determine. The night was still young, Lucille could barely imagine how busy the streets got at night with drunks stumbling around. Every other step Lucille took either covered her silken slippers with manure or stagnant street water, the roads were not cobbles or elegant marble designs, they were as though they had not yet been constructed, strips of dirt acting as a lane for carriages and horses, a thin line of grass in the middle where the wheels of the carriages never touched.

Tired and frozen, clutching herself to keep warm, Lucille found herself at the front door of the Inn, a charming den of drunkards by the name of *The Backwards Mage.* A fitting name for Lucille, to say the least, it was why she had chosen this one. Once Gothwen arrived it would be easy to locate her. Gothwen would barely have to use her brain, something Lucille knew could be potentially dangerous.

She gestured a nod to the innkeeper, who returned the nod as he juggled countless drinks orders and settled down the rowdier few at the back of the inn. Ensuring she was not followed, Lucille made her way upstairs, the floorboards creaking as loud as the yelling and merriment downstairs.

The fourth room on the left. That was Lucille's. The very last room on the corridor. One of the biggest, though she knew it had to be. She opened the door, looking once again for anyone following her, before swinging herself around it and locking it shut. Lucille sighed, her back against the door, her eyes fixed on the summoning circle on the ground. She drew it herself.

Lucille lit the candles manually; it was better for the ritual this way. Once the last one was lit, she took several steps back. The flames shot upwards, like beams of pure light. Falling again, they revealed a portal. A cave. Lit only by a single candle, inhabited by one man, dressed in the torn remains of a noble's clothes and hunched over a makeshift desk. His hair was shoulder length, unwashed, greying in parts yet still a deep brown in others.

He turned his head slightly, revealing the edges of a beard. He kept his back to the portal, to Lucille. "Is she safe?"

Lucille's breaths grew heavy. She looked at the ground. "She is fine." Lucille looked through the liquid glass-like portal. "I will keep our daughter safe." Lucille took a deep breath, looking up at the bearded man again. "There is something I need to ask of you, my love."

CHAPTER FOUR

The Escapes

A diamond. Carved into stone. Split in two. One half, a backwards 'G', the other, a 'D'. The mark of Gothwen Darkarrow. Wherever she went, whatever she wrote on, she always marked it with her mark. This time, it was difficult. Gothwen did not want to move, Fillinel had fallen asleep with her arm wrapped around Gothwen, as though she was her toy defending her from the terrors of the night. The two had decided that, for warmth, it would be best to sleep together instead of separately. The rooms were not heated, and the holes in the wall created a breeze which blew chilled air through the room. She carved her initials from an awkward position, as not to wake her. At first, the whole experience of sleeping together almost made Gothwen's heart jump out of her chest, it was so loud and quick Fillinel had even commented on it herself. The only bedroom they could find that still provided them with four walls, a roof, a floor, and a door that locked was a single room, a teenager or a young adult's room, an apprentice, perhaps, of one of the many workers who must have lived within the city. The blacksmith, the two had predicted, judging by the tools and small, crafted weapons strewn around what remained of the room. It was only a single bed, Gothwen feared they would have broken it.

She had no idea how strong the wood was by this point.

Gothwen slept in her clothes. Fillinel had removed her robe. Fortunately, underneath she wore a thin vest and loose, comfortable breeches, which she had chosen to sleep in instead. Gothwen stared at the clothes on the floor, trying to think up a humorous yet slightly sexual explanation for it all. The various tools, weapon hilts, and Fillinel's robe gave Gothwen a story that made her blush, and desire her more. *One day*, Gothwen thought, *that might come true.*

Fillinel stirred, holding Gothwen tighter. Her eyes began to flicker, and she awoke, realising where she was and who she was with. She swung her arm back from over Gothwen, and lay staring at the ceiling for a while. Fillinel let out a yawn, a nervous yawn, trying to keep her mouth closed as much as possible.

Gothwen cleared her throat. "You should put your robe back on, I'll check if the streets are still safe." Gothwen stretched, her arms touching the wall at the head of the bed, the tips of her bare feet poking out from the bottom of the blanket.

Letting out another, much larger yawn, to which Gothwen, on impulse, copied, Fillinel sat up, clutching the blanket to her breast as though underneath she was naked. "I haven't slept that well for a long time. Do you think these beds are enchanted?"

Gothwen swung her legs over the side of the bed, the spring in her step an indication that she too shared a night of good rest. "This is the City of Mages, Filli. I'd say it's highly likely. While I'm out, you should try and find a blacksmith's, and a tailor's. There has to be one around. I don't see myself wearing these clothes all day every day, and I'm sure that robe can be replaced by something more practical for the journey."

Fillinel stroked her hair, trying to set it back in the same place she had it the day before. "I saw a tailor a few buildings down the road, I'm not sure what we'll find in there, this place was built for mages after all." It was pretty clear by both of their builds that it would be essential to find separate outfits to wear. Gothwen was at least two sizes larger than Fillinel, her chest also being significantly greater. Fillinel was a couple of inches smaller than Gothwen, and she was a lot thinner. Almost every aspect of her body was smaller in comparison to Gothwen. There was no way the two would be able to comfortably share clothing.

By now, Gothwen had turned to unlock the door. Just as she placed one foot in the threshold, Fillinel called out. "Gothwen." She sighed. Gothwen knew what was coming. "I know we've been getting pretty close, and we shared a bed last night, but please, don't think about... Us... Too much, okay?"

Smiling, Gothwen turned. "There isn't a single person in Oreldas who could tame this hopeless mind. The ones who thought they could, turned and ran in fear of who I am deep inside. I wouldn't expect you to stay anyway, Fillinel." She looked away from her partner, and continued through the door, hiding the tear rolling down her cheek.

The bottle bounced off the brick, into the air. It smashed on the ground ten feet from where it originally stood. The arrow, landing with a clatter, fell a further ten feet in the opposite direction. Gothwen was pleased with herself. Even though she was taught to use some of the most powerful spells to defend herself, her skill with a bow was unmatched in the entire Rosimer forest. Or at least, she liked to think it was. Elaina had taught her the basics of using a bow and arrow, in an attempt to get Gothwen to see how much better and more rewarding life without magic could be. Training with a bow was one of her favourite sessions, there were countless others, including sword-fighting, cookery, farming, all without the use of any spells or enchantments. At least, when they could be avoided. Countless times Gothwen's Aunt had wanted her to earn her keep as an apprentice or become one of the Coryphian hunters. Nothing she tried ever worked, magic just seemed to always be the easier option.

She sat down, one of the bottles she found still contained some form of alcohol. It tasted foul, bitter, nothing like the sweet orchard cider or wine she was used to at home, but she drank it. She tossed the bottle, which smashed at Fillinel's feet.

"Drinking already?" She looked at the sky. "It's barely midday." Fillinel had ditched her robe. She was still wearing the same clothes she had slept in; the difference this time was a silken jacket she had clearly found lying on the ground. It was burgundy, torn and covered in dust. The sleeves looked at least one size too big, but Gothwen knew it would have been better to move around in than a robe. Especially one emblazoned with the Apostate logo, with them being in Ald Rosimeris. Besides, for someone as small as Fillinel, finding clothes would prove to be incredibly difficult. "I found the tailor. I think the stuff in there suits you more, I only found this that was remotely my style."

Gothwen stood up, brushing away the dust that had blown onto her, and swinging the bow she found onto her back. "The blacksmith is down there." Gothwen nodded to the left, "you should pick up a dagger or two, maybe a sword. Nothing too heavy, no matter how enticing it looks." She moved past Fillinel, towards the tailor. "I'll change, if I find anything."

Fillinel called out to her. "Feel free to use my satchel, a change of clothes, your old ones, any supplies, I can fit it all in there." Gothwen thanked Fillinel with a simple smile, before walking away, shaking her head.

The door fell off its hinges. Gothwen stood, frozen in the doorway. At least Fillinel was right. The collection of clothes within which still looked wearable was the line of short skirts and low-cut tops Gothwen liked the look of. Clothes designed for the warmer climate of the southern regions, which Gothwen filled her chest of clothes with back home. She rummaged through the various drawers which Fillinel seemed to have overlooked, drawers which were filled with women's underwear, clearly hidden from customers who weren't in the interest of purchasing them. A few of them seemed a little too sexual for adventuring, others just downright made Gothwen cringe in disgust.

Gothwen removed her clothes, checking occasionally in the doorway and the windows for Fillinel, mainly out of privacy concerns. She looked at herself in the mirror for a while, checking everything was still in the right place. Fortunately, everything was. She tried on a few of the more comfortable, relaxing outfits first, merely to entertain herself. She thought she looked pretty good, surprisingly. A few adjustments to the breasts and Gothwen would have been tempted to take a few home with her.

Gothwen realised what she was doing. She had begun trying on outfits to impress Fillinel. A flood of guilt and regret washed away every other thought in her head. She tore off the clothing, pulling and tearing the fabric off her skin. She was thinking about Fillinel too much. The dread of losing her already engulfed her mind. She fell to her knees at the pile of her clothes on the ground, rummaging through the pockets Fillinel had placed the potions in. She found the vial she was looking for and drank it whole without taking a single breath. She collapsed, broken down in tears.

The Liquid Laughter took a few seconds to take effect. This one seemed to be less potent than the one Fillinel had fed her. Gothwen sat herself back up, laughing and brushing what remained of the fabric off her shoulders and from around her waist. Turning back to the rest of the intact items of clothing, she resumed her search, as though nothing had happened. She chose a normal, green skirt, furred at the bottom, and a low-cut, long sleeved top to match. She found a pair of green leggings and black boots buried under piles of bricks and wooden beams, along with a belt and a strap for over her shoulder. She picked up her old outfit and emptied the pockets. There were four small vials left, ones Fillinel had prepared for her a short while ago, minus the one she had just drank from. She slotted them into the conveniently sized potion pockets in her new shoulder strap.

Her outfit was almost perfect. It was, of course, missing a few pieces of protective gear. Specifically, shoulder plates, arm bracers, and weapons. Fillinel was, as far as she knew, investigating the blacksmith, Gothwen decided to check there. She slung the bow she found back over her shoulder, picked the tattered quiver back up off the ground, and left the building. Gothwen could hear the sound of metal clashing against stone and wood as soon as she left. It only got louder the closer she got to the blacksmith. Fillinel must have found a supply of weapons and was testing their durability. Gothwen quickened her pace.

At least the dagger didn't shatter when it hit the support beam, this time. The past three tries, any attempt at a killing swing Fillinel made resulted in the complete destruction of the blade. She was unsure whether the blade was crafted from bad metals or she was swinging too hard. Most probably the former.

Gothwen entered the blacksmith, the heels of her new boots signalling her arrival. "Did you find any armour pieces lying around here Filli?" She took a look around, the many swords and daggers giving Gothwen an exciting feeling which churned her stomach. She took an odd liking to blades; she found the patterns and engravings on custom designs fascinating.

"There are some enchanted metal plates around. I think those are what you need. The smith kept most of them in a pile." Gothwen gave Fillinel the look of someone who had no idea what enchanted metal plates were. Fillinel sighed. "Enchanted metal feels like leather and can bend to suit the wearer's movements. However, it keeps the strength and appearance of heavy metal gear." Gothwen seemed to understand a lot better now.

Fillinel laughed. "Had you never heard of enchanted metal? I suppose I never saw you in Magical Craftsman Class. It wasn't a course that you enjoyed?"

Gothwen rummaged through the pile of armour pieces on the ground. "I preferred books over crafting weapons and armour. As much as I like a good sword, making them seems like too much effort. I'd sooner pay a master crafter to forge a beautiful weapon with the most elegant designs than make one myself." Gothwen picked up an elegantly patterned shoulder plate. As Fillinel said, it bent and twisted as Gothwen moved it, yet it felt almost like cold rubber. "Learning about how things were before our people moved here was what I enjoyed more, I suppose."

Gothwen began to closely inspect the shoulder pad she had found, it consisted mainly of multiple pieces of silver metal shaped liked tear drops layered upon each other. Swirls and curves were engraved on its surface. Fillinel helped her attach it to her right shoulder. "I never thought about how life was before Oreldas. I guess everyone has their own area of interest." Gothwen attached a matching right bracer herself. "I take it you're right-handed then?" Gothwen tested the flexibility of the metal. Fillinel tossed her one of the blades lying on the floor beside her. "How about a competition? Whoever gets hit first has to make lunch." She waved her free hand, bending her fingers as she moved. Both their blades turned partially transparent.

"You want a duel?" Gothwen took up her fighting stance, Fillinel copied.

Fillinel spoke in a hushed tone. "You wouldn't hurt me.

You couldn't." She winked at Gothwen, before lunging herself forwards. Gothwen twisted her hand, bringing her own blade horizontally in front of her. The ghostly blades clashed as though they were still solid metal. Fillinel pushed herself black, twirling her blade in her hand. It was Gothwen's turn to make an offensive move. She spun in a circle, making sure that, in the brief moment she had her back to Fillinel, she could let go of the sword, gripping it with her twisted left hand and bringing it to Fillinel's stomach. She was able to take a step back, sucking her stomach in to ensure the blade did, in fact, miss, retaliating with another swing of her own. Gothwen pulled a tiny dagger from her sleeve, catching Fillinel unaware. The blade was still solid, Fillinel had no idea Gothwen had concealed it. It cut her hand, causing her to lose her grip and drop her own sword. As it hit the ground, the blade turned solid again. Gothwen's did the same.

Fillinel's cut stung. She grabbed the wrist of her injured hand. "That was cheating. That actually hurt!"

Gothwen concealed the blade up her sleeve again, spinning the other before sheathing it in her belt. "Are you going to say that when the Demon you fight does the same? When the squad of Human guards we anger pull bows on you while you stand there with a dagger? Or maybe when the horde of Dread Ghouls we find decide to use their teeth instead of facing you one by one in a swordfight?"

Fillinel moaned out of a combination of pain and annoyance. "Point taken." She flapped her hand loose. "Consider yourself lucky you didn't chop off a finger or something."

Laughing, Gothwen inspected the wound. "It's nothing but a paper cut, you'll be fine. If I wanted to hurt you properly, I would have."

"It was still cheating, Gothwen." Fillinel did not sound too impressed. "A deal is a deal though. What would you like to eat?"

"Raw meat? Again? Did you at least throw some salt on it this time?" Torril stared at the chunk of flesh which had just been thrown in front of her. She lifted it, inspected it. It looked like horse. She smelled it. Definitely horse.

The guard took his usual seat in the old, wooden chair parallel to Torril's bars. He was the usual spectator of her cell. It was all he did, day after day. "It's been seasoned, don't worry. The chef prepared it especially for you." He briefly took on the role of a waiter. "Presenting horse's arse marinated in spit and piss." He leaned forward in his seat. "Only the best cuts of meat for a fine murderer such as yourself." The guard howled in his seat, his stomach jiggling as he laughed.

Torril stared at the guard. "So, you carried a hunk of raw meat drenched in body fluids to my cell? I'm not sure who comes out of this worse off." Her gaze stared into his soul. It haunted the guard, tormenting him so much he stopped laughing and sat back in silence, slumping back in his seat like a schoolchild in trouble.

The guard still, however watched her every move. She took a few bites of the meat, scoffing at the taste, her eyes watering slightly. After a few minutes, Torril clutched her stomach. Groans as loud as a shuffling Dread Ghoul echoed through the cell, coming from both Torril's mouth and her stomach. She fell backwards, curled up in a ball. She began to froth at the mouth, turning on her back in agony.

The guard sprung up from his chair. He fetched a medicinal potion from the emergency shelves beside the stairs, before rushing back to the cell where the sick girl lay. He fumbled with the keys, there were at least twenty cells in the dungeon, each with their own key, not to mention the keys to various other areas of the jail all kept on the one ring. Eventually, he found the right key, bursting through the cell door and falling on his knees by Torril's side. She had stopped moving.

The guard leaned closer, listening for a heartbeat. For a few seconds, there was nothing. Then, there was one beat. The guard barely had time to spring up and reach for his weapon before he felt a cold, sharp metal at his throat, twisting and being pushed deeper and deeper. His head was forced backwards, and he found himself lying on the stone floor of the cell, Torril now on top of him. She put her finger to his lips, despite his inability to shout out anyway. He felt the life fade away from his body. The last thing he felt was a cold, wet slab of meat being dropped on his head. His final smell was of horse flesh and human excrement. The last thing he heard was the devilish cackle of Torril as she began her escape of the confines of the jailhouse.

Torril stole the guard's dagger from his belt before she left. She skipped down the candle lit halls of the jailhouse, tossing it in the air and catching it again, perfectly every time. Any guard who got too close got a swift slice at their throat and left to bleed to death where they fell. The final room Torril found herself in was the entry hall. A room full of guards drinking and playing cards for each other's wages.

Torril stood in the doorway. Thirty feet ahead, on the wall furthest away, was the last door. She could see the midday light shining underneath it. Every guard had turned to face her, drawing their swords and forming a line. She counted six of them. Torril sighed.

She performed a successful forward roll, ending in the sliced shins of two of the guards. They both fell to grab their wounds, giving Torril the perfect opportunity to stab out one of their eyes and chop the ear off the other. One of the guards attempted an uppercut, which only ended badly for him. Torril was able to bring her dagger down on his wrist, cutting it clean off. She grabbed the sword with her free hand, shaking off the severed body part. With two on the ground nursing their pain and one already dead from his injuries, Torril was already halfway through the bloodshed. Two of the guards came at her at once, though she was able to quickly sidestep the attacks from both, impaling one of the guards from behind on her new sword. She swung her human shield to block the next attack, the guard instead slicing off the arm of his comrade. That was what killed her shield. She let go of the sword, allowing the corpse to fall forwards by itself onto the ground. The guard who had killed his friend fell to his knees, dropping his blade and calling the corpse's name as though he was merely asleep. Torril decapitated him with his own sword as he mourned. The final guard, who had done little more than watch, gave up his blade willingly. Torril forced him against the door to the street. She pierced his eye socket with the cold steel of his sword, leaving him hanging on the door, his feet dangling in pain. She waited, watching them and laughing until the movement stopped and the blood began to drip off the guard's boots. That was when Torril left the jailhouse, leaving the door wide open for the entire street to see. She took a breath of fresh air. She was free.

Torril had taken little more than a few steps before she realised something was not right. The streets had gone quiet, bone-chillingly cold. Even the sun itself had cowered behind the clouds. Torril saw why. It was Lucille. She had ditched the mage's robes she wore when she visited Torril the day before, instead wearing loose, white breeches sewn together with a golden thread. She was wearing a matching white corset, more golden thread holding everything in place, with frills in places, specifically on her wrists as part of her gloves, adding a sense of prestige and sophistication common in anything Lucille wore. She was gripping her wand in her right hand, the tip pointed to the ground. She stood fifty feet ahead of Torril, enough of a distance, as Torril knew, to cast whatever spell she needed to subdue and incapacitate her again.

Torril sighed, her hand flirting with the hilt of the dagger wedged in her belt. "This can only go one way, Mother. Step aside or you'll be seeing Ethril again."

The mention of her lost daughter caused Lucille to raise her wand with one swift swoop. "I won't let you hurt anyone else I swore to protect."

Raising her arms, as though she was surrendering, Torril began to inch closer to Lucille. "Fine, I'll leave your precious protégé alone. If I walk free." She smiled, bearing her fangs once more to Lucille. She leaned forwards. "I know how much you like her. I wouldn't want to get in the way of Mother's Mistress fetish."

Lucille flicked her wrist; a fireball flew directly at Torril. It wrapped around her as though she was stone, until it disappeared into the air behind her. Torril stumbled onto one knee. "Mother! That one was pretty good." She brushed her stomach as she regained her balance. "Though, I'm afraid you'll have to do better than that."

Confused, Lucille cast three more balls of fire at Torril, each one wrapping themselves around her daughter, while Torril stood, with her arms outstretched, cackling a laugh which echoed throughout the entire street. None of them had any severe effect.

Lucille changed her tactics. She moved her wand in a circular motion, seemingly building up some sort of force which became visible in front of her. The air in front of Lucille had become distorted, as though a bubble of liquid was forming before her. With both her wand and her left hand, she released the ball of energy at Torril. She raised her arms in a cross to block it. Nevertheless, Torril was pushed backwards, remaining in the same position, as though she was being pushed by a large object. Her feet built up a mound of dirt as she was forced back, though her body itself never left the ground.

"Impossible. That spell alone should have shattered every bone in your body and tore you limb from limb." Lucille threw her wand to the ground. "Never has my magic failed me." She outstretched and lifted both her arms halfway up, clenching her fists. In her hands, two silver, elegant blades appeared, trailing golden dust as they grew. Torril, meanwhile, had returned to the door of the jailhouse, pulling the blade of the guard pinned to the door itself out of his eye socket, and wiping it clean on her tattered shirt. The corpse fell to the ground.

"You want a traditional fight then?" She smirked. "No magic. Nothing below the belt."

The two of them stood, now a couple of metres apart. They stood in silence for a while, mother and daughter, thinking up ways to kill each other. Gothwen's life depended on the outcome of the fight, though she was not around to witness it. It had begun to rain, the ground beneath them had turned wet and muddy.

Torril lunged forward first, her blade aimed directly at Lucille's face. Lucille caught it, crossed between both of her own silver blades. She pushed Torril back, spinning and striking her in the cheek. She drew blood. That only enraged Torril. She struck back again, letting out a war cry that almost deafened Lucille. She blocked every strike, first from the left, then from the right, then an uppercut from which she spun on her heels and attempted to blind Lucille with dirt from the ground. Every attack was blocked and dodged, usually receiving, in retaliation, a clash of blades from Lucille. She was training Torril. At least, that's how it felt. Lucille had begun to enjoy herself, despite the fact Torril was attempting to kill her. She encouraged Torril, which made her angrier and even more volatile. Torril pushed Lucille back, against the wooden posts of one of the stalls. Lucille picked up a basket of fresh apples, flinging the whole container at Torril. It gave her the brief opportunity to move behind her and strike her back. Torril yelled in pain. Lucille's blades were almost always enchanted. They often hurt three times as much as standard swords. Eventually, however, Lucille slipped up. Torril struck her left hand with enough force built up from anger that Lucille lost the grip of her blade and it fell to the ground. Torril pushed Lucille back, rolling towards the blade and picking it up, before springing back towards Lucille to continue her attack. Lucille was now fearful of the outcome, Torril outnumbered her in terms of blades, and her fighting style significantly changed and became even more unpredictable with her rage. Eventually, Torril crossed blades with Lucille again, though this time she used her second blade to slice Lucille's hand almost clean off. Lucille fell to her knees in pain.

Torril stood over her. Victorious over her mother. "I can't make any promises that Gothwen will be safe, Mother." She kneed Lucille in the face, forcing her on her back, lying in the dirt. Her pristine, white clothes now filthy, and soaked through.

The cold, soft rain hit her face, mixing with the blood now coming out of her nose. Torril stood over her. One of the drops of liquid on Lucille's face felt warm and thick. Torril had spat on her.

Torril balanced the blade on Lucille's stomach. "Tell Ethril I said hello." She sunk the blade deep inside Lucille, through her body and into the ground underneath her.

Lucille kept her silence. She remained alive as Torril sunk the blade through her, her breaths becoming quick as it fell deeper. A single tear mixed with the rain fell down her face. It was wiped away by a slender, pale finger. Lucille, though her head was frozen in place, turned her gaze. A golden haired, freckled elf knelt beside her. The rain had no effect on her, she looked as dry and beautiful as she remembered. Lucille's blue eyes had, for the last time, met the similar blue eyes of her daughter, Ethril. Lucille drifted out of the mortal world, her spirit walking hand in hand with her youngest child once again.

Torril, soaked and muddied, wiped the blood from her cheek and spat out a concoction of spit, mud, and blood. She limped over to Lucille's wand, the furred handle brown with dirt. Torril picked it up, inspecting it. She looked at her fallen mother, before launching the wand down the street, out of her sight. The rain poured heavier than it had ever poured in the history of Marrivel. The sky itself was in mourning.

CHAPTER FIVE

Leaving the Mountain

"I didn't know you could cook so well, Filli." Gothwen sat back, letting out a quiet burp. Fillinel had kept her word. After her defeat, she had prepared the two of them a full three course lunch, made from whatever was left in the ruins of a local tavern. From whatever wasn't covered in mould, however.

Fillinel wiped her mouth with a torn piece of tablecloth. "Don't get any ideas, Gothwen. You're cooking the next meal."

Gothwen smiled, leaning forward in her chair, resting her folded arms on the table. "So, what's our next move? Lucille told me where I needed to go, but is there anything you still wanted to do?"

Leaning back, Fillinel disappeared into her own imagination. The entirety of Ald Rosimeris was at her disposal, empty and there for the taking. She remembered what she wanted to do. "I wanted to see the Well of Abundant Magics, remember?"

Gothwen had hoped Fillinel had forgotten that venture. "Are you sure? Do you not think it's a bad idea for us to tamper with the untamed well of Magic?"

Fillinel rose from her chair, brushing off the crumbs from

the bread she had made herself. Much of the edibles in the tavern had been remarkably well preserved, as though the food itself was enchanted. "I just want to see what it is, what it does. If it really does limit what magic we can use, I want to destroy it." She picked up her plate, Gothwen's too, taking them both back into the kitchen. There was no point in washing them, the dishes they had just eaten from were cleaner than most of the furniture.

Gothwen had followed her, holding the bottle of wine they had shared in her hand. Gothwen had, for the past half an hour, decided to ditch her wine glass, drinking from the bottle instead. She took another sip. "I won't let you destroy it. It's there for a reason, it might do a few bad things, but it does them to protect us, to protect all of Oreldas."

"You might be right, Gothwen." Fillinel sighed, leaning back against the counter. "We can still see it though, right?"

Admitting she too was curious as to what this Well looked like, Gothwen nodded. "Then we need to get to Marrivel, somehow. I'm sure Lucille will meet us there." They both remained quiet for a while, before Gothwen realised. "Do you know where this Well is, anyway?"

The main tower, where Gothwen had found Fillinel, and where Lucille's memory had taken place, luckily held a map, of sorts, to various parts of Ald Rosimeris. The library, situated halfway up the tower itself, was the first place Gothwen and Fillinel decided to look. They found the map among various other plans and blueprints, as well as books dating as far back as the construction of the mountain itself. Gothwen wanted to keep a few of these books for herself, until she remembered Fillinel tore her satchel. She felt uncomfortable loading Fillinel's with unnecessary items anyway, so she decided to leave them where they were, occasionally glancing at the diagrams and writings within.

"The Well must be here." Fillinel pointed to a large chamber in the heart of the mountain, the plans detailing a huge, open space held up with carved stone support beams and lit with the largest chandelier the two had ever seen. The map was incredibly detailed. The room was, however, apparently lacking a door.

"Filli." Gothwen looked up, slowly. "How do we get into that place, there's no entrance."

Fillinel already had her nose in a book. An old book, one of the ancient tomes from the time the mountain was being constructed. She looked up, back at Gothwen. "Apparently the mages teleported in and out of there. Only those with clearance to access the chamber could successfully enter." Fillinel realised the problem. "I guess with none of the mages around there's no way we can get in."

Gothwen scratched her head, then made sure her circlet was still firmly in place, perfectly flat on her forehead. "Luci had clearance, but without her I can't think of any other way we can get in." A sense of relief took over Gothwen. "I suppose there'll be no tampering with the well today."

The disappointment in Fillinel's face was enough to make even Gothwen feel a shred of sympathy. "To Marrivel it is, then." She stood up, closing the books she was reading. A cloud of dust overwhelmed the pair as Fillinel closed one of the older tomes.

"I suppose the easiest way to ground level is down one of the towers?" Gothwen didn't really want to take the journey of a million stairs again. "Please tell me you know a teleportation spell?"

Filli's eyes widened. "No, but I have an idea."

Fillinel had shot up and ran out of the library the second she finished speaking. Gothwen struggled to keep up, she must have been in better shape than her. By the time Gothwen caught up, Fillinel was kneeling by the table on the ground floor of the tower, inspecting the scrunched-up pamphlet which had brought her to Ald Rosimeris to begin with.

"I can throw this over the edge of the mountain, attach it to a stone or something. Then, I can activate the portal held within it."

Gothwen had to admit, she never would have thought of using the paper. "Impressive, but the walls are thirty feet high, and made of the mountain's own stone."

Fillinel signalled her to be quiet. "I saw a place where I can climb up, in the Gardens." She was clearly growing exited to put her plan in motion.

Gothwen had to begin chasing her again, as she had begun to run as quick as before over a much larger distance.

They were outside, among the crumbling ruins of the city again. Fillinel was running between buildings, down alleys and over fallen pieces of wall. A few times Gothwen lost her, having to resort to using the same spell she used to find her in the first place to locate and give chase again.

Eventually, the buildings gave way to a Garden. Surrounded on three sides by what looked like houses, the fourth, furthest wall was a wall of stone, clearly part of the mountain. On the left side of the wall, near the edge of the Garden, a tree had fallen, leaving behind a dead trunk. Fillinel was climbing it, her arms outstretched as though she was walking a tightrope. In her hand, she held a large stone, attached by a piece of string to the pamphlet. By the time Gothwen had caught up with her, she had reached the top of the tree and was now balancing herself on the wall.

Gothwen struggled to catch her breath. "Filli, be careful up there." She threw herself onto the ground, exhausted.

Fillinel had sat on the wall, shuffling herself along carefully, clearly standing was now too dangerous. Gothwen couldn't see how thin the wall was. "I'll throw the stone over, then count to a hundred. After that, I'll cast the spell, and we can teleport to the paper."

Gothwen managed to regain a portion of her strength. She joined Fillinel up the fallen tree and onto the wall, where they both sat, legs dangling over the edge. Gothwen could barely see the ground, or the rest of the mountain. It curved inwards, giving Gothwen and Fillinel the impression they were sitting on a floating island. Gothwen's companion tossed the stone, they watched as it fell, shrinking smaller and smaller until it seemingly vanished into the abyss below. Neither of them spoke, they instead enjoyed the view of the mountains beneath them, and the feel of the wind in their hair.

"One hundred!" Gothwen almost jumped so much she fell off the wall. "We can teleport now, Gothwen."

"If you're sure the paper fell far enough, Filli." Gothwen swung her legs over the wall, Fillinel did the same.

The red-haired mage withdrew another piece of paper, one similar in design to the one Gothwen owned. She threw it towards the ground, though halfway into the gardens below it stopped, and began to unfold. It unfolded bigger than the paper was supposed to be, seemingly duplicating its size at every fold. Eventually, it reached its maximum size, and a circular, fiery portal opened. The edges crackled in flames, fires which hardly affected the paper itself. Gothwen could see through the portal. The other side held clouds; it was as though she was looking into a deep mist below her.

"The paper hit the ground. The problem is, once we pass through, gravity will pull us back down. We have to be quick and careful." Fillinel began to shuffle herself forwards. Gothwen copied her. "One, two, three, jump!"

Gothwen jumped at the same time as Fillinel, falling through the portal at the same time she did. The sensation she felt after passing through was one she never hoped to feel again. The second she passed through, she felt gravity pull her back, like she was being flung backwards and forwards. Luckily, before they fell back through the portal, to be stuck in a sickening loop of falling up and down, even though Gothwen at this point had no concept of what was, in fact, up or down, the portal they had come through sealed shut, and Gothwen found herself falling onto the stone floor which had appeared in its place. She landed on her stomach, Fillinel almost landing on top of her.

Gothwen managed to stand herself back up. She was dazed and slightly confused; she had never travelled through a portal like that before. She took in her new surroundings, the bottom of Ald Rosimeris, the mountain itself towering over her, expanding above her head. "I guess your plan worked, then. We seem to be at ground level." Gothwen could not see the top of the mountain from where she stood.

Fillinel brushed herself off and rubbed her forehead. She had landed on a small rock; her head was bleeding slightly. She examined her bloodied hand. "I'm starting to actually feel a little jealous of your circlet, Gothwen." She wiped her hands clean on her breeches. "So, which way to Marrivel now?"

Looking around, confused and trying to get her bearings, Gothwen scratched her head and adjusted her circlet. "We should go North, through Oakenheim. Eventually we should reach the river. After that I'm sure someone can help us."

Gothwen had barely taken one step, before she felt some magical force lift her into the air and warp the world around her. She seemed to be moving faster than any living thing she could imagine, the entire world nothing but a blur beside her. Then, she realised, Fillinel was gone. In the rush she was no longer beside her, most likely hundreds of miles away by now. The sudden event was too much for Gothwen. She started to scream.

The whole magical abnormality lasted for around thirty seconds. Gothwen had, by that point, closed her eyes, still screaming out of panic. She was eventually thrust forward, her journey had apparently come to an end, finding herself, now, in an elegant, half organic, half constructed hall. The tree the building was clearly constructed from could be seen curving around the corners of the room, branches protruding from various points of the wood. The organic corners met in the middle of the ceiling, from which hung a majestic chandelier of glowing, bulbous plants attached to hanging vines. There was a table in the centre of the room, a large, oaken dining table made from the same wood and in the same style as the furniture in Gothwen's own room. The chairs around the table, however, were a lot more elegant to the carved stool she was used to. Still made from the same wood, the backs of these chairs interwove with themselves, creating a beautiful design similar to that of the vines hanging above. There were twenty-one chairs in total, ten on either side of the grand dining table, placed perfectly facing the chair opposite, with one, taller, comfier chair on the farthest end, padded with emerald green cushions and matching emerald arm rests. Gothwen somehow recognised the room, though once again teleportation, which was what she had deduced just happened, had obscured and disoriented her.

Gothwen remained on the floor, she was too dizzy to stand and, if she did, she felt she was likely to throw up. Fillinel was nowhere to be seen, which concerned her. Had she been teleported elsewhere? Or was she still at the base of Ald Rosimeris? Luckily, she wouldn't have to wait long for answers.

Two men entered the hall, to begin with. Guardsmen, clearly, by their armour and spears held upright. They both stood at either side of the entrance door, the only way in and out of the room. Neither of them looked at Gothwen, though she had plenty of time to examine them and figure out who they were. Their breastplates held the answer. They both wore the crest of the Coryphian High Count. Gothwen's face dropped. She knew where she was.

During her first week in The Ark, Gothwen and her classmates were treated by the scholars to a tour of the High Count's palace. She hated the trip, spending most of it at the back of the group, alone, talking to herself. Gothwen had seen the beautiful design of the door from the other side and decided to break off from the group. She had entered this room, sat in one of the chairs, satirising a meeting which would have taken place over a grand meal, then ran back out, laughing to herself. Now, she was back, and completely at the mercy of whoever walked through that door next.

Unfortunately for Gothwen, the next person to enter was someone she recognised. Not from the Ark, or from home, but on every coin she had every picked up, from posters on every wall, propaganda, artwork, and some graffiti, though those were usually in compromising positions. It was, to Gothwen's shock, the High Count of Coryphia.

"Miss Darkarrow, I presume?" He stroked his grey, bearded chin as he looked down on Gothwen, looming over her like a tower of deep green and silver silk. He wore a circlet, oddly less elegant than Gothwen's, though it held much more gemstones than hers. Rubies, emeralds, sapphires, and one diamond wedged in the centre to complete his golden crown.

Gothwen remained silent. She had always resented this man, mainly for his anti-human policies within Coryphia. Laws which, of course, were never fully enforced, limited only to establishments which followed the Count indefinitely. The same could be said in Marrivel, with anti-elf laws. Both halves of the continent, it seemed, were at each other's throats behind closed doors.

The Count strode elegantly past Gothwen, towards his seat beyond the far end of the table. Passed the farthest chair, there stood one more, much larger seat, a throne of sorts. From it protruded clear tubing, connecting to a large, brass container to the throne's rear. The Count sat within, attaching the various pieces of tubing to his arms and legs, connecting the final piece to the back of his neck. Gothwen didn't move, she didn't stand. She could hardly breath. "Are you going to sit there, on the floor, for this whole afternoon?" He gestured to the closest seat at the table. "Please, do sit. We have much to discuss." He gestured to one of his servants, who had shuffled, almost unnoticed by Gothwen, to a lever beside the container. With a single pull, the contraption came to life, pumping a deep, red liquid through the tubing and into the Count's body. He closed his eyes, sighing a sigh of relaxation as his body filled with the liquid. The servant silently left the room once again.

"Ah, Miss Darkarrow. Excuse this tangled mess of tubing and equipment. You see, I was born with no apparent link to the mystical side of our world. Something the elven people are not wholly aware of. Every few days I am required to, recharge? Perhaps that word fits, yes? I must recharge my ability to use magic. This." He outstretched his arms, advertising to Gothwen the hellish device he was sitting on. "This keeps the magic running through me."

Gothwen remained silent. Her gaze pierced the flesh of the Count, like spectral daggers, twisting themselves deeper as she stared longer.

The Count cleared his throat. He moved on. "Lucille Magelight is dead. I thought you might have wanted to know that."

Gothwen's eyes opened wider, her mouth stuck open. He had, as much as she hated it, got her attention.

The servant brought a silver platter through the door, placing it on a tray which had extended in front of their master's lap. They lifted the lid. A monkey's head sat within, the lifeless eyes staring back at Gothwen. "Have you ever eaten monkey head, Gothwen? The brains are quite delicious." The Count removed the top of the skull, like a fleshy teapot. He inhaled deeply through his nose, taking in the smells of his delicacy. "Now, will you sit?"

Gothwen managed to stand, maintaining eye contact with The Count. She grabbed one of the chairs at the farthest point of the table to him, dragging it along the stone floor so that the wood made a deep groan as she pulled, until it was at the end of the table, directly opposite to her rival. She sat with all her weight, slumping into the chair, in silence.

The Count took a spoonful of the monkey brains, his pristine silver spoon now bloodied and filled with what looked like grey jelly. "Murdered. By her own daughter, no less. It seems she has been on a killing spree. She had broken out of the Marrivel jailhouse after murdering her own sister, merely to kill her own mother." He tossed a newspaper down the table, it landed upside down before Gothwen. "Tomorrow's edition of the Marrivel Crier. Look for yourself."

The front cover of the paper was emblazoned with the headline *Missing Mage Meets Muddy End*. Gothwen turned the paper to get a clearer view. There were three drawings below, one of Lucille, that much was clear to Gothwen, one of another female who shared a few similarities to Lucille, which must have been her daughter, the middle drawing was of the scene of Lucille's death. She was lying, impaled by a sword, in the wet, muddy streets. It was definitely Lucille. Gothwen pushed the paper away, shaking her head in disbelief despite the evidence laid out before her.

The Count swallowed another mouthful. "As it turns out, High Conjurer Lucille Magelight was one of the last of the Rosimeris Mages. Nobody knows where they all went or why they left. With the only one showing her face in public dead, Ald Rosimeris is free for the taking." The Count smirked, wiping the blood from his mouth with a napkin.

"What does that have to do with me?" Gothwen felt now was a good time to finally speak.

"Well, you and the Apostate have already been there. You know what it is like. Besides." He licked his bloody spoon. "There is something about you, Gothwen. Lucille knew it, she came to me to ensure you'd be protected." He smirked again. "I of course declined her constant insistence. I wanted to throw you in Blackirons and throw away the keys."

"Is that because you were afraid of what I could be? No,

what I *will* be?" Gothwen stood up. "You'd rather throw me in Magic negating chains than see me become a rival to your regime?"

The Count looked up, without moving his head, staring at Gothwen through his brow. "I would watch your tongue, girl. Or Fillinel will not be the only one in Blackirons by the end of the day."

"Fillinel? What did you do to her?" Gothwen started to piece things together. Fillinel must have been teleported elsewhere.

"She is safe. For now. The leader of the Apostate Mages was just too easy a target to pass up. We left her in Blackirons in the dungeon until her execution. We cannot have such an unruly soul causing an uprising when I need the people's support now, can I?" The Count appeared to realise another key point he wished to discuss. His eyes lit up. "Miss Darkarrow, it has just dawned on me that there is another story I do so wish for you to read. Please, turn the page." He gestured to the newspaper before Gothwen.

Sheepishly, she turned the page. She looked in horror at the story unfolding before her. She read it aloud, through a voice filled with fear. "Psycho Arsonist Gothwen Darkarrow murders abusive Aunt before torching her own apartment?" Gothwen continued to read. "In a sex-fuelled rage stoked by the seductive nature of the harlot rebel leader Fillinel, once innocent student of The Ark Gothwen Darkarrow murders her own Aunt for not supporting the Apostate cause, before torching down her own apartment to prove to her newfound lover that she has completely rejected her former life?"

"A brilliant story! Do you think? It is a shame she had to die, really." The Count smiled a sinister grin.

Gothwen threw herself out of her chair, running towards The Count. She was immediately thrown to the side, crashing against the wall, with one simple flick of the villain's wrist. The Count laughed a laugh which boomed throughout the hall. He sighed. "I was once like you, Darkarrow. A reject. A nobody. I was a Majless, born without the ability to cast even the simplest of spells." He lifted his arms, the red tubes lifted with them. "You see these? I concocted an approximation of elven blood. A liquid which gives me a focused affinity to Magic, blood more attuned to Magic than any Rosimeris Mage." He lowered his arms again, leaning forward towards Gothwen. "I almost feel bad for you, child."

Managing to get herself onto her hands and knees, Gothwen stared back at The Count. Her eyes narrowed; she had begun to hate him even more. "What are you planning, Count?" She hoped at the very least she would get an outline of his plan.

"Let us say Ald Rosimeris will be staying in Elven hands, and those gems?" He pointed to his crown, "I have a new one, with four holes each the size of one of the stones. With all four, I control Oreldas. Not just the people, but the land itself."

Gothwen shook her head. "That will never happen, I will make sure of it. Me, Fillinel, the rest of the Apostates, and anyone who resents you will stop whatever you're planning to do to get those gems."

Gothwen's head began to burn and, with it, a stinging pain pierced her forehead. She put her hand to her skin, feeling underneath her circlet. The pain vanished.

"You will not be going anywhere, girl." The Count lifted his hand and gestured it towards Gothwen. Black chains flew at her, clamping themselves around her neck and her wrists.

A scream came as a response. "Blackirons!" Gothwen could feel the magic drain from her. "You're an idiot if you think these will stop me!"

The Count smiled, nodding to the guards by the door. "Throw her in with the Apostate. Prepare the engines for our attack."

CHAPTER SIX

Imprisoned

"Another. Now." Torril was drowning her sorrows. She had begun to regret killing her own mother. A part of her had begun to feel some sort of emotion.

The barkeep slammed another glass bottle in front of her. "When are you going to pay for these?" He examined the twenty bottles already amassed on the bar.

"I told you, my mother will pay for it. She'll be here later." she took a seemingly endless gulp from the bottle.

The barkeep sniggered. "Yeah right, no more until I see coins." He began to walk away.

Torril slammed her dagger into the bar. "There's no gold, but unless you want me to sink this steel in your palms instead, I suggest you keep them coming."

The barkeep threw three more bottles in Torril's direction, before disappearing back through the door behind the bar.

Picking up the bottles, Torril sighed. "Great, now he's going to get the guards. Time to move I guess." She stood up, having to balance herself slightly, before disappearing out of the door.

She sank the bottles in the saddlebags of her horse. Stolen, obviously, it was a jet-black Courser with a matching mane and tail. The owner must have taken a liking to black everything on a horse. It was nightfall in a few hours, at least then Torril would be able to move without being seen. If the horse was good for anything, it was blending in with the night.

Before she left Marrivel, Torril had raided an Enchanter's store. Killing the proprietor, Torril had stolen various objects of importance that would have helped with the search for Gothwen. One of those objects was a glass ball. Torril hated magic, with a passion, her elven body was infused with human blood, this tampering with her genetic code making the learning of magic and casting spells impossible for her to practice. Fortunately, glass balls were a human creation, they didn't require any significant magical talent to use, simply patience and the correct thought. Torril thought about Gothwen, where she could be, and, before her, the image of the elf appeared. She was tied in chains, black chains, and had been pushed into a cell with a redhaired elf wearing the same metal. Torril recognised the crest on the guard's chest. Coryphia. Torril had been travelling South, to Ald Rosimeris. That was where the ball had told her she was. Now it seemed she had to change course.

"Useless ball of junk." Torril threw the glass ball on the ground. It shattered, releasing a cloud of mystic gasses.

Torril mounted her horse, Coryphia was at least a twenty-day ride from where she was now, two miles from the southern riverbanks of Niltay. She started South, hoping that Gothwen stayed where she was this time.

"We aren't going anywhere, are we Gothwen?" Fillinel was sitting against the back wall of the cell, her legs outstretched.

Gothwen paced around the cell, looking for any weaknesses in the walls or the bars. "Apparently not, but we need to get out."

Fillinel looked at Gothwen, a tear forming in her eye. "Of course we do. They're going to execute me, Gothwen."

Kneeling by her side, Gothwen tried to comfort the weeping elf. "That's not going to happen, ever. Not while I'm around." The guards at this point must have left for a meal, there seemed to be nobody outside. "Filli, we'll get some rest tonight, then see what happens tomorrow." The small window to the outside world let in a slither of golden sunset light. It caught Fillinel's wild, red hair. Gothwen stroked it. Fillinel held her hand, moving it away from her head. "Not now, Gothwen." They simply smiled at each other.

Gothwen had felt her blood run colder. Without Magic running through it, she felt defenceless. That was the mystical properties of Blackiron, a metal which somehow managed to negate magic, both in a physical form and within a person. The process didn't hurt, it just made the wearer of any Blackiron feel cold, much colder. Both Fillinel and Gothwen were shivering, despite the temperature in their cell being no different to the temperature elsewhere.

Gothwen fell beside Fillinel. They both sat, holding themselves, shaking. Neither of them knew how they would escape the cell. The sun had begun to set, the golden light turning into darkness. They both saw this as a good enough time to at least try and get some sleep. Fillinel slumped onto her side, closing her eyes. Gothwen did the same, in the opposite direction, so that their feet touched, nothing else.

Neither of the two could sleep for too long. There was no comfortable bed, no covers, and the chains around them made finding a position to sleep without getting some sort of cut or bruise in was near impossible. Eventually, however, the sun did rise on a new morning, heralding what must be the first daily meal.

A single wooden tray was slid under the bars of their cell, with nothing on it but a hard slice of bread and some form of grey porridge with curious black lumps. Clearly Gothwen and

Fillinel were expected to share meals.

They ate what they could, not saying a word to each other. They split the slice of bread in half, at the very least. The sound of chewing echoed through the cell. Neither of them spoke, not even after their meal. Though after an hour, Fillinel decided it was, perhaps, time to end the boredom.

"What is it with you, Gothwen?" Fillinel sat with her knees at her chest, her arms wrapped around her legs. "What makes you so special? I remember when we both first started at The Ark, and the door wouldn't open for you. I saw what it did to you, mentally. How you fell into a pit of loneliness and depression." Fillinel rubbed her eyes. "Why did the world pick you?"

Gothwen was lying on her back, one leg bent, pointing to the ceiling. She had been counting the stones that made up the top of the cell. "I like to think it has something to do with my circlet." She turned her head to look at Fillinel. "My mother had it made for me. I believe it has some magical connection to her. Something so strong The Ark itself feared it. I wanted to find her. I still want to find her. I *will* find her."

Fillinel was intrigued by Gothwen's desire to find her mother. She moved herself closer to Gothwen. "When we get out, we'll go to Marrivel. If anything, spreading word of my cause across Oreldas is a good idea. I ought to raise awareness across all civilised lands. Plus, you can find your mother." Fillinel lay with Gothwen, resting her head on her stomach. She was a lot more comfortable than the stone floor. "We can find Lucille too, I suppose." Fillinel articulated the words through gritted teeth. She didn't want to seek the help of such a powerful mage.

It was clear Gothwen felt some deep discomfort. Fillinel felt her sigh so hard her head started to sink deeper into her stomach. Fillinel frowned, running her hand along Gothwen's leg to comfort her. "That won't be necessary, Filli. She's-" Gothwen felt another sting in her head, like a tiny electric bolt had been forced inside it. "-fine. She's... Fine. We just don't need her anymore, she has more pressing matters to attend to." Gothwen hastily changed the subject. "Filli, why do you do what you do? Why do you fight so strongly for Magical freedom?"

This was a subject which had clearly gotten Fillinel's attention. She sighed, lifting her head from Gothwen's stomach and instead shuffling up to lie beside her. Fillinel reached for Gothwen's hand. They both stared at the ceiling as Fillinel began her story. "I had a sister, Gothwen. A few years younger than me. She was a lot like you, relying on frequent doses of Liquid Laughter to get through the days. I remember one day, we had run out of vials. We needed them, desperately, but we had no coins to pay for them, and none of us were skilled apothecaries, we had no idea how to create them ourselves. My sister got worse, until she no longer spoke to any of us. She would lock herself in her room for days, no sound coming from within, save the sound of whimpering every so often. One day, the crying stopped, and she no longer left her room even for food. My parents were both distraught. I remember eventually, my father burst into our home brandishing the shovel he used to clear the streets of fallen leaves, as was his job. He pried open the door to my sister's room with it, and there she was. Hanging from the vines on the ceiling. She had taken her own life, and none of us knew about it. The next day, stricken with grief, I burst into The Ark, demanding why we are not permitted to freely create coins or medicines in the palms of our hands, should we need it, even though the Fabrication Charm can create anything imaginable. My sister died because not one member of my family had the skill to create a vial of the medication she needed, and we were so poor that we could not spare the extortionate amount to buy them, unlike you." Fillinel turned her head, looking at Gothwen, who returned the stare. "I fight so I can protect the people like you, so the people out there who share my story can protect those who need it too. We have the ability to fabricate anything we desire, though those mages who lived in Ald Rosimeris believed we shouldn't. They are wrong." Fillinel's eyes narrowed. "Gothwen, I never asked you. What do you think? Am I right?"

Gothwen knew she had to think carefully. "I agree, Filli. Though you must understand, there are those out there who, with complete magical freedom, would use the Fabrication charm for their own villainous ends, to do evil in a world that, even now, is incredibly unstable." Fillinel's story had moved Gothwen. The thought of her sacrificing her education, her position as a student within The Ark solely to benefit those around her made Gothwen smile, though Fillinel was no longer looking in Gothwen's direction. She was staring at the ceiling, the tears in her eyes creating a glossy sheen. Fillinel had begun to stroke Gothwen's hand. For a moment, she stopped, grasping it again. She rolled over to face Gothwen, gently kissing her cheek. "Thank you, Gothwen. For listening to me. It had been so long; I didn't know if I could still trust you."

Gothwen knew what she had to say. Her heart began to beat quicker. The palms of her hands had begun to sweat. Swallowing the lump in her throat, Gothwen spoke up. "Fillinel. I lov-"

She never finished her sentence. The wall at the back of the cell burst inwards with a floor-shaking roar. One of the bricks struck Gothwen on the forehead and she fell, unconscious against the stone.

CHAPTER SEVEN

The Highest Society

Gothwen awoke in what seemed to be an old elven ruin. She had read in her studies that much of Coryphia had been blocked off over the years, sealed by Treeshapers who would cover entire districts in trees and shrubbery, hiding them as though they never existed. The room Gothwen found herself in seemed to be an old meeting hall, perhaps the previous city hall which had gone unused since The Count ordered the construction of his new, elegant and sophisticated palace. The new residents seemed to have cleaned much of the hall up, even allowing new illumination plant bulbs to grow from the ceiling. There were banners draped down every wall, hand-painted banners bearing a symbol Gothwen knew. It was of a ring of hands, each one connecting with another at the forearm, encircling a cross of interwoven lines on a background of more curving, weaving strokes. At the heart of the cross was a circle, many of the artists choosing to add their own interpretation within, be it of a face, of what looked to be a star, or something personal to them. On the largest banner, at the very back wall of the meeting hall, Gothwen could make out the image of a face within the circle. She knew whose face it was. The smiling face of Fillinel, within the logo of The Apostates.

Gothwen stood up, her head still ringing from the blast. She had been given a simple cot to recover in, it seemed. Beside it there was a rather old looking oaken dresser with a cracked mirror on it. Gothwen looked in the mirror. Her circlet was gone, in its place was, instead, a bandage. It was bloodied where her head was still throbbing, which was to be expected, what lay underneath must have been a ghastly cut. She touched it, some of the blood had seeped through, the cut must have been deep.

There was the distant sound of footsteps in the background. It was the only thing Gothwen could hear, the hall was eerily quiet. The near silence was broken abruptly by the door behind her swinging wide open, revealing a young elven boy who must have been no older than nine.

His eyes widened at the sight of Gothwen. "Miss! You're awake!" He no longer looked as excited as his footsteps sounded, instead showing caution as he approached Gothwen. "I'm Norel. I have no parents. I live here. I love to do magic. I'm also blonde, see?" He pointed to his head. "Now tell me who you are. Fillsi wouldn't tell me. Neither would Vorn or Gretch. You look pretty." He stopped to catch his breath. Gothwen took this as her chance to speak.

"I'm Gothwen. Gothwen Darkarrow." Seeing someone so full of life made Gothwen smile. "Look, my hair is white." She pulled a strand from over her eye, crouching down to make herself level with Norel. She began to laugh.

The young elf looked confused. "No, you're blonde. Like me. That's why I told you I was blonde too. We're hair friends." Norel touched Gothwen's hair. The area around his hand rippled like water, changing from white to blonde, until the new colour had completely engulfed Gothwen's head. "See, blonde. I knew you were the second I saw them carry you in. That's why I was so excited to meet you. That's also why they put me on Watching Duty, they knew I was so excited to say hello. Everyone else with hair like mine is always so busy. Or they hide it behind funny colours, like you do." Norel removed his hand. Gothwen's hair began to return to its dyed white, the same way it changed in the first place.

Gothwen had no idea what had just happened. She knew her hair had changed colour, at the very least. She could see her fringe over her left eye change. The reasons how and why still eluded her. "How did you know that? What spell did you just cast?" It had dawned on Gothwen that she was asking a child how they performed a spell. She suddenly felt embarrassed.

"I was born with this magic. Fillsi likes to play with me. She said if I could guess the hair colour of all the elves that followed her here, I would get to stay here with them forever. I did. Now, whenever I get it right, she gives me some chocolate. We need to find her now. She owes me more. She said I'd get two bars if I got yours right."

Gothwen held out her hand. "Alright then, Little-Leaf. Show me where Fillsi is and I'll make sure she gives you chocolate." The elf smiled and jumped up and down as he grabbed Gothwen's hand and dragged her out of the hall. He was much faster than her, there were a few moments where Gothwen thought she would trip over herself; she was failing to keep upright.

Norel stopped outside a set of old double doors. There was a lot of noise coming from the other side, though Gothwen couldn't make out what was being said. "Here we are. Fillsi is in here, along with everyone else. They seem to be talking about something really important." Norel looked up at Gothwen, as though he was expecting something.

Gothwen didn't know what to give him in return. "I don't have anything Norel, I'm sorry. You've been a good little guide though, thank you." Gothwen bent forward, kissing the boy on the forehead. He touched the kiss and smiled.

"That was a better gift than any chocolate, a kiss from a

pretty girl. Thank you Gothy!" Norel ran further up the corridor laughing to himself. When he was nothing more than an echo in an empty hallway, Gothwen turned to face the door. She took a deep breath, and pushed it open with all the strength she could muster.

Within, there seemed to be another form of meeting room. Though this one was laid out differently to the one Gothwen had awoken in. This room was a semi-circle, chairs half-encircling a podium at the centre, directly in front of Gothwen. The seating here was layered, rising five times before hitting the back wall, each layer consisting of three rows of seats. Half of the seats in the room were taken by various robed mages, a lot of them, as Norel had told her, sported exotic hairstyles and colours Gothwen would never imagine seeing in the outside world. That, she thought, must have been why they hid under hooded robes. What interested Gothwen the most was the peculiar seating arrangements. There were three large groups of mages, each of them separated around the entire room, none of them seemingly wanting to communicate with each other. They all looked roughly the same age, a similar age to Gothwen. They did have one thing in common, however, they were all looking directly at her. The mage who was standing in the podium even turned to face Gothwen. Dressed once again in her Apostate robes, she found herself making eye contact with Fillinel.

"Gothwen, I'm so sorry for what happened." Fillinel jumped down the steps to the podium, holding Gothwen tight again. "I didn't plan for that to happen. None of us did."

One of the mages, an elven male with greased, black hair and a stubbled beard, spoke up. "The guy never told us there was two of you." He stood from his position in the centre of one of the mage groups, walking towards Gothwen in an effort to introduce himself. "Vorn Blackthorn. Founding member of The Apostate Society." He reached out his hand, offering Gothwen to shake it. As she did, he brought it to his lips and kissed it. Gothwen blushed. Vorn saw the change in Gothwen's facial colour. He responded with a wink.

"Don't let him seduce you, Gothwen." The next mage to step down was a woman, from the group of mages consisting mainly of women similar in appearance to her. Her hair was a deep brown which matched her skin, it was shaved off on one side, with the other cascading down the left of her head. The tips were twisted upwards and dyed a deep purple. Gothwen lost count of how many piercings she had. "Malina. One of the *other* founding members of The Apostates." She nodded her head, a much more solemn greeting, to which Gothwen matched. Malina gestured towards the third group, who continued to say little. "That is Gretch. He isn't one of the founding members." Gretch grunted a noise which Gothwen roughly translated to 'hello'. She waved cautiously.

Fillinel spoke up again. "Gothwen, we were discussing this." She lifted a letter, advertising it to Gothwen. "It was addressed to the High Count. I'll read it to you." Fillinel unfolded the paper, sitting comfortably on the steps to her podium. "To the exceptionally kind and generous Count Vlastoril the Seventh of Coryphia, I write to you now from my office within the Emerald Tower of Ald Rosimeris, regarding the threat of The Apostate Society and their mages. These terrorists plot the downfall of the civilised world, disguised behind their veil of righteousness and compassion. These traitors to the magical world must be stopped, and their position within The Rosimer Regional College for Mages Gifted in The Arcane Arts must be eliminated. In doing so, the people of Coryphia will become exceptionally more docile and will be much less likely to question their suppressed magic. I will be willing to offer yours truly a position within Ald Rosimeris, within the tower of your choosing, should you successfully cut off the head of the serpent, so to speak, and capture the mage Fillinel, apparent leader of these Apostates, and bring her to us for questioning. I trust you will fulfil our request and bring us what we desire. Should certain events transpire that result in my untimely demise, I leave the fate of Fillinel and her associates to you. You may do with them as you see fit. Yours Faithfully, Lady Lucille Magelight. High Conjurer of The Emerald Tower." Fillinel folded the paper again. She slammed it against the steps, burying her head in her hands.

Malina spoke for Fillinel. "Basically, it means we are no longer a society protected by the rules within The Ark. We are now Terrorists, as this mage puts it. Rebels. Revolutionaries. We're a rogue group that The Count will surely hunt down and kill. This bitch of a mage has basically given The Ark permission to cut our ties to them and toss us into the mouths of the Dread Ghouls."

Vorn spoke next. "So, we decided to split up. For now, at least. I will remain here with those who choose to join me." He gestured towards his greasy-haired group. "It's the most dangerous choice and will most certainly get us imprisoned or killed, but I'd want to go out as a hero anyway. Malina will ride to Marrivel with her group. There aren't many mages there, but she can surely find people interested in aiding our cause, the promise of infinite money should gain us the support of merchants and the upper class at least. Gretch and his crew are tough, I mean, look at them." He gestured to Gretch, who demonstrated his power by snapping a chair leg in half. "They will leave for Balmira City. They can handle the mean streets up there. They could even get us in touch with Black Market traders and connections too. We could certainly use those"

Clapping her hands together, Gothwen spoke up. "So, you have a plan, you know what to do. What was with all the arguing I heard from outside the door?"

Fillinel looked back up, wiping a tear from her eye. "I don't want this, Gothwen. All of us separated. We were like a family, I treated Norel like he was my sibling." She stopped, looking into the empty nothingness before her.

"Filli." Gothwen immediately knew what was wrong, she sat beside her. "You can't protect everyone everywhere. The mages need you, they'll still be around, they'll be spreading your cause all over Oreldas. Isn't that what you wanted?" Gothwen wiped Fillinel's tears away. Fillinel leaned against her shoulder, placing her hand on Gothwen's knee.

She sighed, brushing her fiery hair out of her face. "Malina, Gretch, go. You have my permission to spread the word of The Apostates across the land. Go North, find whoever you can, and bring them to our cause." Fillinel wiped her nose on her sleeve. "Malina. Take Norel with you. He needs to get as far away from here as possible. Let him play with the other children in Marrivel. Let him have the life he deserves." Malina nodded.

The two groups of mages left together, presumably to gather their belongings. Vorn ordered his group away too, to watch the main entrances for any guards. The five of them were left alone together, one last time before they left to spread Fillinel's cause.

Malina offered to help Fillinel stand. She outstretched her hand, pulling her up, before pulling her close and holding her tight. "Until we meet again, Sister. Don't go dying on me with your new girlfriend here just yet." Malina winked to Gothwen. "Keep her safe, or you'll have me to answer for." Gothwen smiled back. It certainly wasn't the thought of being called Fillinel's girlfriend that caused a beaming grin.

Releasing her grip, Malina walked away, following her group. Gretch was next. "You're the strongest woman I know, Filli." He grabbed Fillinel's hand with his bone-shattering grip. Fillinel tried to hide the pain. Quiet squeaks were coming out of her mouth. "Don't let anyone beat you down. Or *I'll* be the one to beat *them* down." He left too, almost having to duck to get through the door.

Gothwen and Fillinel looked at each other again. Before Vorn came between them. "I hope Malina was joking when she said you two were together." He laughed, mostly to himself, before turning to Gothwen. "I hope to get to know you better. We can see where the night takes us."

"Buy me dinner and a couple of bottles of wine and I'll be yours." Gothwen laughed, hiding the fact that she really did just want a good meal and a lot of alcohol. If she had to go on a date to get it, it was a sacrifice she was willing to make. She thought for a moment on whether that made her a bad person. Her face dropped.

Vorn temporarily got lost in Gothwen's leafy green eyes. "I should leave you two alone, allow you to catch up on what's gone on the past couple of days." He winked at Gothwen before leaving himself. Gothwen stared as he left.

Her attention turned to Fillinel. "I was asleep for two days? Why didn't you do anything? Why not try to wake me?" She rubbed her head. The periodic stinging she had felt days before seemed to have gone. It had now been replaced by the throbbing of the cut on her head. "Where is my gear, anyway? I really don't think any of your clothes will fit me, I need my own again. This vest I'm wearing smells like sweat and is covered in dried blood."

Fillinel stood up, moving over to the podium again. She fumbled around her neck, withdrawing a key attached to a chain. She knelt by the oaken object, turning her key in one of the holes. The entire podium opened up. As soon as the cabinet door had finished, the side panels fell back, until all that remained was the back of the podium itself, outstretched four times as long with the addition of the other three panels. Hung from holsters within were the daggers Gothwen had carried at Ald Rosimeris, confiscated by The Count on their imprisonment. Sitting on the bottom was Gothwen's circlet, which looked to have been cleaned since the last time she saw it. On the opposite panel to her daggers, Gothwen made out her various pieces of armour plating, stacked together and hung by their straps on wooden rails outstretched from a high midpoint within.

"Your armour plates and daggers are here. I kept the bow that had been confiscated from The Count in my quarters, along with that quiver you picked up. I'm sure we have a few arrows lying around somewhere if you want to refill it. Gretch was pretty good at forging weapons, it's likely he would have made a few."

"Filli, how did you get all this back from inside The Count's palace?" Gothwen began to re-arm herself. The strap she had found in Ald Rosimeris to attach her quiver and store vials in was laid out beside her circlet. There were still four vials inside, though now one of them was empty. Gothwen needed the help of her medication.

"We have a couple of people working on the inside. They told the rest of the mages I'd been captured and was awaiting execution. In the commotion following our escape they managed to steal back our confiscated gear and get it back to us. Your circlet, however, we needed to remove to treat your wound. I don't know why The Count didn't confiscate such a valuable item too. I would have expected him to sell it or keep that emerald for himself."

Gothwen placed the circlet over her bandage, completing her outfit again. "He must have had more important issues. He told me what he plans to do, Filli." Gothwen sat back on the steps, Filli sat beside her. "He's planning an invasion of Ald Rosimeris. He mentioned something about Engines."

"Engines?" Filli thought for a moment. "I heard stories from our agent within the palace. He mentioned some form of magical device the top scholars were constructing. They say it has the power to turn the trees themselves into soldiers. Men of vines, living wood, groaning and creaking as they move, wielding weapons of solidified sap and bearing armour of the same make. They already know the spell, it was just a matter of converting it into a device of some sort that could be focused and aimed at a tree. You know, one tree is said to produce at least twenty soldiers. The tallest ones being able to make as much as fifty." Fillinel stroked her chin. "I'm sure there were others too. The Count is trying to utilize the different wands from the different Mage Schools. Destruction, Conjuration, Illusion, Transmutation. Each one doing something big and scary." Fillinel stopped to think. "I'm not sure what exactly the others will do, but warriors of wood created to fight will be far more powerful than the living soldiers of Humans. I'm certain they'll fight for Ald Rosimeris too. The Humans would do anything to gain the ability to use the spells we use ourselves."

Gothwen looked Fillinel in the eyes. "Then we need to be there when that battle unfolds, to stop both sides from taking over."

Fillinel stood up, brushing herself down. "We should prepare for what lies ahead, then. Malina told me she left you some hair dye and make-up in my room. You should freshen yourself up, take a bath too, perhaps." Fillinel leaned closer, smelling Gothwen. "You certainly need it. I still smell the wine you drank excessively in Ald Rosimeris. Along with a lot of Blackweed. Since when did you have the time to smoke that?"

Standing up almost instantly, Gothwen blushed. "I'll... Go and freshen up." She quickened her pace as she left, hiding the embarrassment on her face.

"Oh, and Gothwen?" Fillinel stopped the embarrassed elf before she could leave. Gothwen turned on her heels. "You should talk to the others afterwards, before you come and see me. Get to know them a little." She smiled. "I'm sure they like you already."

"I'll ask again. Where is she? What do you know about her?" It was too late. The dagger Torril had put to the guard's throat had already sunk into his flesh. He bled out on the spot. She let him fall to the ground, dead. "Oh piffle. Now I need another one. That's the fifth guard today. Why are they all so weak?" Torril's lust for blood never helped. She would rather see a man bleed out than walk free. She dragged the corpse behind the tavern. Thankfully, the people inside were too drunk or stupid to care about what was going on outside. She threw the corpse into the cellar, hopefully nobody will go in there until she was long gone.

Torril had been riding for three days now. She was on the border between Oakenheim and Rosimer, at a tavern called *The Forest's Edge.* She didn't understand why it was called the *edge* of the forest; the border merely provided a separation between two woodlands. She explained this to the proprietor, before he banned her from ever entering again, out of sheer confusion. He was most likely reviewing the name of his tavern. Torril had found a guard patrolling outside, and, after sticking the tip of her dagger to his abdomen, she had led him to the side of the stone and wood amalgam of a building to interrogate him with the least amount of interruptions. She did not, however, accurately judge the distance between her blade and his throat after she backed him against the wall. He died within a couple of minutes. This had gone on for some time, half of the day at least. Torril would lead guards away from their patrols, question them with as much scare tactic as was possible, then prematurely dispatch them before they could reveal any information she needed. She thought that, after killing Lucille, her bloodlust would have subsided. It did not.

She wiped her blade clean on her shirt, which was by this point covered in various red streaks, marks of her failed attempts of interrogation. She closed over the door to the tavern's cellar, jamming the door shut with a plank of wood between the handles. At least this way, if the corpse managed to walk again, it wouldn't be able to get back out. Torril lifted her hood over her head, before setting out once again on horseback to find any clues to Gothwen's location.

Fortunately, as she was about to leave, Torril was stopped by a man in a matching dark robe to hers, covering his entire body. His face was obscured by a large, grey beard, he didn't seem to be a threat. He began to speak; his words had grabbed Torril's attention.

"You ask about a mage girl. Gothwen Darkarrow." He stroked his beard, his hand almost getting lost in its bushy mess.

"Who's asking?" Torril drew her dagger.

"Someone who knows. She was taken captive by The Count of Coryphia. She escaped. With her mage friend Fillinel, and the help of The Apostates."

"How do you know about this?" Torril dismounted her stolen stallion.

"A mage sees all. One as powerful as I can see all, even in the darkest of rooms." His eyes seemed to shine in the light of the setting sun. "There are old ruins. To the North of Coryphia, ruins of the Old City. She is there, I see her." The old man grinned. "She appears to be bathing." He continued to stroke his beard, smiling a gap-toothed smile. "She is preparing to leave. You must move with great haste, Black Magelight."

Torril stopped. Her heart skipped a beat. "What did you call me? Black Magelight?"

The old man laughed. "Yes! Murderer of The Golden Mage herself. Her daughter, spawn of darkness, executioner of the unworthy, the weak, the feeble. The elf with a heart so black magic refuses to run through it." His eyes narrowed. "Though that could be because of your father too, could it not?"

Torril slapped the man with a backhand of such force it knocked him to the ground. "Never speak of my father. He's dead and buried, like my mother. I never needed them. It was time to move on, time for the mages to die."

"That is why you hunt her, is it not? She threatens what you want. The end to all mages, the end of the order your mother held so highly. So very highly. Above even you."

The old man barely had time to finish his sentence before Torril had placed the tip of her blade at his stomach. "Watch your tongue. You know nothing, old man."

He laughed, staring Torril directly in the eyes. It was as though he was staring into the black void of death itself. "I know enough. I know why she hired you. I know why you want to kill Gothwen. I know what you've done. I know where your father is."

"You know nothing!" Torril kicked the man to the ground, pinning him down with her blade now at his throat. "Tell me your name before I kill you. Let me know whose blood I spill tonight for the thrill of the kill."

The man, coughing and laughing, spoke his name. "Servius Amalgor." He smiled at Torril. "High Conjurer of The Diamond Tower of Ald Rosimeris. I was the Head of The High Mages Council. I knew your mother." The old man, knowing his fate, lifted his head. He flung his arms up, a large, flaming orange portal forming above him. "Here my pretty little Psycho. This will get you to your destination quickly. Do what you must, I welcome my end."

Torril thought for a moment, before coming to her senses. With all of her rage, she pierced the mage's chest with her dagger. Raising her arm and bringing it back down again. She stabbed at his flesh repeatedly, while Servius did nothing more than laugh as blood filled his lungs and began to run from his mouth. Torril continued, never stopping, relentless in her murder. Fifty times her blade met the old man's flesh, until Torril had worn herself out. She wiped the blood from her face with her sleeve, before walking away, reluctantly holding her breath and stepping through the portal the old man had made. In the distance, the light of Coryphia shone.

CHAPTER EIGHT
Silver Lining

Lucille could never get over the elegance of the realm she had found herself in. The walls gleamed a pure, untainted white, reflecting the light of the blinding rays of some sort of supernatural force outside to every corner of the room. The glass door to the balcony leading outside was wide open, the silken curtains blowing in the breeze, a breeze which Lucille could neither hear nor feel. Every object in the room was white, brighter than anything Lucille had ever seen before. Some objects were lined with gold, such as the table, the chairs, even the frame of the animated painting above the hearth behind them. The artwork seemed to depict the Rosimer forest, though the leaves moved and glided with grace within, and wild animals appeared to roam freely. Lucille sat opposite Ethril, who sipped tea from a white-gold teacup. She wore a matching white gown to Lucille, though hers was seemingly smaller to match the difference in their age. Her hair was exactly how Lucille had remembered it, like golden blonde silk cascading down her back. It was braided at the front, one braided strand falling down the right side of her head. She was seemingly oblivious to the supernatural setting around them.

"What do you think, Mother?" Ethril looked around the room. "I wanted you to feel at home here, I missed you ever so much."

Lucille watched as Ethril took another sip. Her eyes

scanned the room. "It is beautiful, my dear. Though I cannot stay. You know this." She grabbed her stomach, it still stung from when Torril had sunk her blade inside her.

"I know, I could feel it. The mortal world pulls you back with warm hands. Though it seems those ghastly claws have given up on me. I belong here now." Ethril picked up a white, gold-lined handkerchief with her initials sewn into it. She held it to her mouth, coughing into it. When she pulled it away, Lucille saw the white had been tainted by the red of blood, and the green of something vile. "The affliction which brought us here remains, Mother." She folded the handkerchief up. "We wear the causes of our deaths like you wear an amulet. Or to put it more accurately, like you flaunt a scar."

Lucille's gaze remained fixed on Ethril's bloodied handkerchief. "You have only been dead for two weeks, Ethril. If I was to learn what Torril used to end your life, I could still bring you back. Your soul could return!"

Ethril stopped her Mother's scheme born from hope. "No, Mother. Like I said, I feel no pull back to the mortal world again. I am sorry, but there is no way for me to go back." Ethril's hand dropped, her teacup spilled onto the table. Her eyes began to close, as though she was tired. "Poison. Sister knew what she was doing when she plotted my death. She wanted me to suffer." Ethril began to weep. "My eternal sleep has been thwarted, Mother. I cannot find rest in a body that refuses to be at peace with itself! Every waking moment is pain, every step I take I risk collapsing. When I close my eyes and try to sleep, even in this world, my body will not accept rest. She poisoned me, destroyed me from the inside out. Even now, Mother, it hurts. It hurts so much."

"I'm sorry, my love." Lucille knew there was nothing she could do to help her daughter. Eventually, her potion would wear off, and the illusion of death she had created would end. Lucille would wake up, back in the mortal world, fully healed.

Though she would remember everything that was going on around her now, from the moving painting, to the silent breeze, to the blinding light. Lucille would also remember the teary, sky blue eyes of her daughter, in horrific pain from the method of death Torril chose for her, helpless and afraid, alone in the realm of existence beyond the mortal world. "I will find a way to bring you back, Ethril, I promise." Lucille thought for a moment. "If not, then I will ensure your sister pays for the crimes she has committed. If your soul cannot find rest, I will make sure hers suffers twice as much."

Ethril gasped. "Mother, I would not want you to turn to Necromancy. Spells to bring the dead back to life are forbidden, unspeakable." She looked down at the table, stained with spilled tea. "Would a life as a reanimated corpse be any better than what I endure now? Like the tea on this tablecloth, I would be a blight on the world, a scourge that countless people would want to clean with blades of steel." She looked at Lucille. "Your reputation-"

"My reputation means nothing now. I am dead to the world, and so are the High Mages." Lucille's outburst caused Ethril to cower back in her seat. "Many of the mages had abandoned Ald Rosimeris long before Gothwen's incident. After it happened, the last of the mages fled. Even those in the Inner Circle, my colleagues who were supposed to help me, fled without word of where they were going. That was why I had you moved to Marrivel too. The city was no longer safe. I fear it never will be again."

Ethril shook her head. "That is not true, Mother. The city will be safe. Dark times may lie ahead for the place we once called home, but Gothwen, the girl I've seen you with, she will make it right again. I know it."

Lucille could feel herself being pulled back to reality already. "Ethril. Our time together grows short. The pull back to mortality grows stronger." She began to feel herself fade, the light around her intensified.

"I will miss you, Mother. I shall wait for your return. Everything will be as you remember it." Ethril grew tearful again. She outstretched her arm to Lucille, who reached back, hoping to touch her daughter again.

The light engulfed Ethril, until all that remained was her outstretched hand. Lucille never got the opportunity to hold it again. She felt the light overpower her, and she began to fall. Back, through the light she fell, only gathering speed as she plummeted down into never-ending nothingness until, with no warning, everything around her stopped, and she opened her eyes again.

The air was tight, there was barely enough room for her to move. It was dark. Blacker than night and twice as cold. Though it was not the casket Lucille found herself in that was cold, it was her own body. Her heart still hadn't started working again, only her brain was functioning. For a few brief moments she could only stare, paralysed by her own concoction of literal death-defying aptitude. Of course, she knew she was to return, which was why, prior to her skirmish with her daughter, Lucille had paid the closest undertaker thrice his usual cost to swoop in while her corpse was still warm, like a vulture attacking its near-to-death prey, to simply store her temporarily lifeless body among the rest of the more unfortunate dead, the ones who were not likely to come back. Lucille needed to see if her plan had come to pass, or if someone had tampered with it, and she now lay buried, dead to the world, in some stone tomb, a testament to her facade of greatness.

She had, in her brief moments of semi-lifelessness had the opportunity to reflect on her life. After her fight with Torril and seeing how Ethril suffered in the Realm of The Dead, Lucille began to realise, she was not a good mother. She had understood the fact that siblings often quarrelled with each other, bearing witness on numerous occasions where Torril had turned to physical violence against her sister. The sound of a loud slap and a body hitting the floor came to be a regular occurrence within the walls of the secluded Magelight holiday home. Lucille had thought, hoped, that she could have a family. A loving, caring community consisting of herself, the father of her two daughters, and the children themselves. Though Lucille knew leaving Torril in the hands of her father, who unintentionally allowed her to be taken in by a group of murdering, seductive outlaws, would only lead to a household of troubles. She found solace in the thought that Torril bothered to show up to these planned 'family gatherings', albeit it being solely for the purpose of bullying and teasing her sister over Lucille's attention. The pair's father never showed up, though Lucille knew that was probably for the best.

As her body began to warm once more, Lucille began to review her own life. Her troubles began seventeen years ago. She was a young woman of twenty, recently promoted to the role of Apprentice to the High Conjurer of The Emerald Tower. Her mistress was a soft, golden haired goddess of a woman, whose emerald eyes shone whenever she made a magical breakthrough in her school of Conjuration. She went simply by the name Aastere, nobody ever questioned her lineage or where her family had even come from. All the mages knew was that she was a fine Conjurer, one of the best in Oreldas. Lucille recalled that she and Aastere were given a task of upmost severity in Marrivel, and that a portal would open, and remain open, in Aastere's quarters for their mission. The two passed into the city of Humans on numerous occasions, until Lucille made the mistake of falling in love. She had met a human male by the name of Torick Morden, one of the best, and possibly most underrated alchemists in Niltay. He sold Lucille potions and poisons almost every day, sometimes throwing in something extra, such as a rose or chocolate, to get her attention. On one visit, Torick gifted

Lucille a necklace. "An Amulet almost as golden and beautiful as the hair on your head", as he told her. That night would be the night Lucille would regret for the rest of her life. It was the night Torril was conceived.

Though ashamed and embarrassed at her own disregard to Ald Rosimeris sanctions on love and procreation, Lucille was able to hide her pregnancy for a while, though as the months passed her stomach began to swell, and she could no longer pass her child off as simple weight gain. Aastere took pity on Lucille, who waved her pregnancy off as the result of 'basic elven emotions', something she joked the High Council never understood. As mistress and apprentice, the pair could take time away to focus on their studies, secluding themselves from the outside world until their studies were complete. Or, in this case, until Lucille's pregnancy ended. She eventually gave birth to her first daughter in Aastere's quarters with the help of a bribed midwife of Marrivel, silenced with a coin purse of riches, while Torick watched through the portal, waiting to see his child. She named her Torril, a combination of her parents' names. Lucille held Torril for a few brief moments until she was handed to her father by the midwife, who both watched as the portal sealed shut behind them. It would not be the end of their relationship, however, as the couple communed frequently for a number of years afterwards.

Two years after Torril's birth, Lucille was with child once again, a child fathered also by Torick, yet another creation of mixed race who would have no magical affinity. Lucille gave birth to her second daughter, Ethril, deciding instead to swallow her pride and admit her misconduct to the Council, having her live in her Ald Rosimeris home, an upbringing which, in Lucille's opinion, would result in the largest rift ever created between siblings in the history of Oreldas. Afterwards, Aastere fled. She left Ald Rosimeris for a better life elsewhere with her own daughter, though Lucille never knew where, or even when Aastere had actually given birth. Aastere left a note for her, stating simply that the position of High Conjurer would be passed on to Lucille, an apprentice who showed more promise than any she had taken on. After a few long months of tedious paperwork and rituals which came as standard with her new position, Lucille finally realised both where and who Aastere was, after reading a note from Rose Castle itself, on the return, election, and coronation of Queen Aastere Sibbil The Third of The Elven People of Oreldas. There was no mention of a child travelling with her.

Lucille knew where she had gone wrong in her life. She had left her infant daughter in a city hostile to inter-species relationships. Torril was born a Majless, a being of elven appearance whose flesh was filled with Human-tainted blood. There was a chance she could have been born with the ability to cast spells and use magic, though her father's genetic makeup was so strong within her that it cancelled out any connection she had to the magical forces of Oreldas, replacing it instead with a bolstered resistance to any form of spell. Only by frequently consuming concoctions in which elven blood was the base substance was a human able to tap into the forces of magic. Torril lived with her father for half of her childhood life, living in secret and in seclusion from the outside world. This peacefulness was, unfortunately, temporary. Eventually, the people of Marrivel found the truth, that Torick had committed the unspeakable act of engaging in sexual acts with an elven mage and conceiving a cross-species child. A horde of Humans who wanted only pure-blood humans within the city walls stormed Torick's home, forcing him to flee, a young Torril behind him. They left Marrivel, falling in line with a group of outlaws who used Torick's ability as an alchemist to brew the purest possible drugs, the strongest sedatives, and cures which could heal almost any ailment. A group of outlaws, however, was no place for a young girl to grow up.

Lucille stopped her recollection of her life. Her fingers began to twitch. She was beginning to move again. She clenched her fists and began to move her feet. Exercise was what was required to bring her strength back, though stuck in a casket left her options of movement severely limited. With all of her strength, she threw her body to the left, then to the right, repeating this process until, eventually, she felt her entire wooden world crash down onto the surface below. The lid fell open, and Lucille rolled out onto the cold, stone floor of the funeral home.

CHAPTER NINE

Passion and Potions

The sound of Gothwen's damp feet echoed through the corridor of the Apostate leaders' quarters. She had taken the most comforting bath she had experienced in a long time, now finding herself doing exactly what Fillinel had recommended; she was visiting the Apostates, wearing little more than a towel around her chest, with a second in her hands as she scrubbed her hair dry. This was not how she imagined making a good impression on them would be like, though she was certain that, as Fillinel had said, they liked her already.

Four doors stood before her, two on either side of the corridor. Each one was painted to match the style and personality of the leader within, from the elegant, purple swirls on Malina's door, to the vibrant flowers hand-painted onto Fillinel's. Each of the doors were unique, hinting at a similar possibility for what lay within them. Gothwen could not wait to see the diversity of each of the rooms themselves. Fillinel and Malina lived within the two rooms on the left side of the corridor. As she was to see Fillinel last, she decided it would be a good idea to visit Malina first.

She knocked three times on the first door. "It's Gothwen, I wanted to have a chat, get to know you better." The door swung open by itself.

Malina lay on her back on an elegant, purple couch wide enough for three. There was a book floating above her, leaving her hands free for snacks. A bowl of what looked to be nuts rested on her stomach. She wore a white vest and a pair of deep, purple shorts which almost matched her furniture, her robes sprawled across her floor in front of the couch. Clearly, she had not long settled down for the evening. Malina turned her head to face her door, taking off the glasses she was using to read and placing them on the table beside her couch.

"Ah, Gothwen." She swallowed her mouthful of snacks. You want something to eat?" She gestured to another, larger table pushed against the wall.

"I haven't eaten much, thank you!" Gothwen walked quickly to the food, to examine what was laid out. Malina joined her.

There were at least five plates on the table. Two of which were empty, though recently used. Malina reached for a third, there were a few pieces of meat left on it which she picked up and dropped into her mouth. Gothwen picked up the fourth plate of various meats and cheeses of different colours and aromas.

"What brought you here hun?" Malina licked her fingers, wiping them dry on her shorts.

"I wanted to talk, get to know you a little better." Gothwen adjusted her towel with her free hand.

Malina smiled. "I take it Filli sent you, huh? Just like meeting the in-laws." Malina winked at Gothwen, before throwing herself back onto her couch. "I see she didn't donate any of her clothes to you. Though then again…" She eyed Gothwen up and down. "I don't suppose anything *she* has would fit comfortably on you. Even her robes would probably be a little too tight."

Gothwen looked down at herself. She agreed.

Malina nodded over to her dresser. It was dark brown,

polished oak, with, unsurprisingly, a purple blanket draped over the top of it. "Take a look in there. Second drawer. You can borrow one of my vests and a pair of shorts, you look to be a similar build to me. I can't guarantee it would be comfortable, but it's better than visiting the boys in nothing but a towel."

Gothwen opened the second drawer, folding one of the white vests and a pair of light blue shorts over her arm. She looked around for somewhere to change.

Malina laughed. "I won't judge you! But here, if you need comfort." She waved her hand. The plate that was in Gothwen's hand lifted into the air, landing on the table beside Melina's couch. One of the vines which hung low on her ceiling lowered and stretched. The blanket which had been on top of the dresser came to life, gliding upwards, unfolding, and moving towards the vine. Three pegs marched in the air above the vine, before snapping down, one, two, three.

"Thank you, that's a lot better." Gothwen dropped her towel in comfort, putting on the shorts and the vest before pushing the blanket aside to show off her new look.

Malina clapped. "That looks better on you than it does on me, sister!" She picked up one of the nuts out of the bowl, signalling to Gothwen. She threw it upwards, in Gothwen's direction, who caught it perfectly in her mouth. Gothwen bowed.

"Here, come sit with me." Malina patted the seat next to her. Gothwen joined her. Bringing her knees close to her chin. "You've known Filli for a few years, haven't you?"

Gothwen nodded. "Mhm." She reached for the plate, taking a few pieces of cheese. "We used to be close. We'd pull pranks on the professors, on the Dean, we did a lot together."

Malina nodded. "I know, I was there."

Gothwen looked confused. She swallowed the cheese as she thought. "The only other person who was ever with us for things like that was Nialam. I didn't see him much though. I don't know whatever happened to him, he seemed to just disappear."

Malina scratched the shaven part of her head. "Filli told you why she founded the Apostates though, right?"

Gothwen nodded again. She remembered the story Fillinel told her.

"Each of us has had experience with magical limitations like her. We've all felt neglected by the mages, disappointed in their disregard for the people."

Gothwen tilted her head. "Do you mind me asking what yours is?"

Malina looked at Gothwen. "Of course not. Do you want to know what happened to Nialam?"

Gothwen's eyes narrowed. "I don't have the faintest idea what happened to him. One day he was there at the college, then the next, he was gone." Gothwen shrugged, taking a piece of cheese and wrapping it in meat.

Malina sighed. "That's because he's me. I'm Nialam."

Choking on her food, Gothwen could barely managed to say "what?"

"Yeah. On my eighteenth birthday I made the journey to the Palace of The Lost Souls."

Gothwen nodded. "I've heard of that place. It's the only place left in Oreldas that openly practices live transmutation."

Malina raised her hand, offering Gothwen a high-five, which she took with a giggle. "Correct. Where 'lost souls' go to find and understand who they are. Slowly but surely the mages have been phasing out any study into live transmutation. The ability to alter a person's appearance; their face, their body type, even their gender. Funnel Mountain banned research into it. Said it was 'horrific' and 'morally wrong' to toy with something like that."

"So, the mages who *did* practice it set off on their own, to found their own place where they can study and cast without ever having to worry about answering to anyone else."

Gothwen understood.

"Correct again. You're pretty well-informed." Malina patted Gothwen on her knee. "The process is incredibly painful. Especially when you go through the entire procedure like I did. Altering my whole body, inside and out, changing my whole appearance. I could feel bits of me falling off, my insides rearranging, my bones stretching and contracting."

Gothwen had a stunned look of horror on her face. "I'm glad I've never had to go through that. But at the same time, I understand why you would."

"I'm far happier this way. I'm far more comfortable with who I am. The man I was just wasn't that." Malina sighed again. "Though there are a few people who believe that it doesn't matter whether or not we feel that way. Who we are is who we stay, according to them. That's why they begun to phase out live transmutation."

Gothwen agreed.

"Nevertheless. I still return to the palace. The process is so painful and tiring for the body. Many of those who go for the ritual and up leaving out of fear. They're terrified the pain would kill them. It's usually up to me to help them understand if it's something they really need. The looks on their faces when they come out of those doors a week later, a brand-new face, a brand-new body, the person they know they were destined to be, is always something I love to see."

Gothwen threw herself forwards, wrapping her arms around Malina. A tear fell onto Malina's shoulder. "Clearly, there are still good people in this world. You are one of them, Malina." The two embraced for a short while, before a pat on Gothwen's back signalled it was time for them both to get up. Teary yet smiling, Gothwen left Malina's room, finding herself back in the corridor.

"Gretch and Vorn usually hang out in Vorn's room at this point in the evening." Malina nodded towards the door painted with blue swirls and crude swords. She smiled one last time at Gothwen, who smiled back. Malina stepped forward, kissing Gothwen's cheek. "I was serious, Princess. Keep my sister safe, or next time I won't be so nice." She waved, closing the door behind her.

Gothwen took a deep breath, then exhaled it with a long, hard blow. She knocked three times again, this time on Vorn's door. Though before she could say anything, the door swung wide open. The layout of the room was similar to Malina's. The was a couch in the centre of the room with a small table next to it. A much larger dining table was pushed against the wall, a dark dresser was placed diagonally across the corner, and a window at the back provided the room's inhabitant's with fresh air and a view of, well, a view of overgrown vines. The only difference was the lack of snacks. Everything was neat and clean, the tables were polished, the couch had been picked clean of any pieces of dirt, the stone floor had been mopped, and there was a scent of lavender in the air which filled Gothwen's nose the second the door opened. It stung her throat and caused her to cough. That was what got the attention of the two already in the room.

"Gothwen! A pleasant surprise. Though really I was expecting us to be alone for this." Vorn laughed, looking at Gretch, who was standing by the window. He had begun to lose interest in Gothwen before Vorn had even finished speaking. His attention seemed to be on a ladybird crawling down the glass.

"Hm. Don't mind him." He waved his hand at Gretch, while standing to greet his guest. He sauntered over to his door where Gothwen stood, wrapping one of his arms around her lower waist and leading her into his room. Gothwen could have sworn she heard Malina laugh from the other side of her door.

Vorn led Gothwen to his couch, where he offered her a seat. He remained standing. "Would you like something to drink?"

Gothwen nodded. "Yes, please. I had plenty to eat with Malina, I could use something to wash it all down."

Vorn's gaze was on Gothwen's chest. "Yes, I see Malina has been at our cheese supply again, judging by the pieces on your vest."

Gothwen brushed the small pieces of cheese off herself, an action met with painful groans from Vorn. "Not.... On the floor.... Ah well." Vorn shrugged, turning towards a neatly organised cabinet. "Wine? Gothwen?" He picked up two glasses from inside the cabinet and placed them neatly on the top.

Gothwen smiled. "Oh yes, I'd like that more than anything right now."

Vorn grinned as he poured two glasses at exactly the same volume. He turned to Gothwen, looked for a moment, before turning back to the glass. Instead of putting the bottle away, he carried it with her glass, setting them down next to each other on the table beside Gothwen.

"Filli says you can handle your drink. And you love a good wine." He outstretched his arm towards the bottle as he returned for his own glass. "Give this one a try. If you like it, the bottle's there."

Gothwen took a sip. It was fruity and sweet, yet not sickly. She enjoyed it a lot. She drank the glass effortlessly, pouring herself another. Vorn removed the suit jacket he was wearing, hanging it on the wooden coat rack beside his door. He stretched his arms as best he could, given his limited mobility, as he was still wearing the silk, blue vest and white shirt of the suit, along with matching blue silk pants. Gretch was wearing something similar. Though his suit was a leaf green and smaller in parts than it should have needed to be. There were tears all over his vest and pants which had been stitched back together. Though every time Gothwen looked at him, another tear seemed to have formed.

"My guess is Filli sent you." Vorn slumped back into his couch beside Gothwen. She nodded while gulping another glass of wine. "If she's told you her story, I'll tell you ours."

Gretch grunted. He turned away from the window, falling back into the armchair in the corner of the room. It creaked and groaned as he put his tremendous weight within it.

"Let's start with that big oaf there." He nodded to Gretch, who nodded back. "He's not one for talking much, especially around new people. He finds them intimidating."

Gothwen gave Gretch a look of confusion. Who could possibly intimidate him?

"Gretch was born a little different from the rest of us. Something wrong with his brain, you see? Doesn't matter what he's doing, or where he is. He can't do things like me and you. It's because of that, he was never accepted by the college. They don't allow people with abnormalities in, the main door won't grant them access. We found him on one of our marches one day, eating discarded food from the ground behind a tavern. We took him in, I took him under my wing, and we became best friends. Despite, of course, the entire foot height difference, the brain problems, and his inability to cast any spells."

Gothwen stood up, walking gently to Gretch. There was definitely a look of fear in his eyes, combined with anger at the people who had cast him aside. Gothwen stroked his arm. It was completely solid from the size of his muscles. She couldn't lie, she was impressed.

Gretch stood up, letting out a high-pitched noise of fear. Gothwen calmed him, continuing to stroke his arm. The look of fear had begun to subside, and a smile began to creep across his face. Gothwen lifted her other arm, moving in to hug Gretch. His entire torso was as solid as his arms were. Gretch patted Gothwen on her head, stroking her hair and toying with her pointed ears. She seemed to have gained his trust.

Vorn was amazed. "It took me three months to even get him to touch me. He's stroking your hair after three seconds. Remarkable."

Gothwen's voice was muffled by muscle and patched suit. "Hugs make everything better."

Once Gothwen had manged to convince Gretch to let go of her, he let out a large, open-mouthed yawn. Still tugging at Gothwen's hair, he started to leave Vorn's room. Gothwen realised she was going with him. She tried to resist but his grip was too strong. She grabbed his arm in an attempt to force him into letting go, but she had already found herself in the corridor. Gretch's door was no longer on a hinge, she could guess why. With one small push, it fell to the ground. Gothwen thought this would be her end, smothered to death while he slept. She had begun to accept her fate when Fillinel's door swung wide open. Her nightgown flowed with the force she had pulled her door, she stomped barefoot into the corridor making direct eye contact with Gothwen.

"GRETCH." Fillinel screamed a high-pitched shriek to get his attention. Malina's door opened slightly, she looked on out of curiosity.

Gretch stopped to look at Fillinel, who stood with her hands on her hips. Her gaze pierced Gretch's, who had begun to realise what he had done.

"Fillsi. I'm sorry. She was just so nice to me. And she smells pretty."

Gothwen threw herself at Fillinel the second her hair was free from his grasp. She stood behind Fillinel; her hands grasped firmly at Fillinel's waist.

"I know, she's very pretty. But you can't drag *all* the pretty things into your room, can you?"

Gretch bowed his head, shaking it. There was a look of regret in his face.

Fillinel walked towards him, stroking his arm as Gothwen had done. "You did well letting go of her though. Thank you."

She kissed her hand, using it to caress his cheek. "Hey, tomorrow, how about I let you pick one pretty thing out of my room to keep?" Gretch smiled and nodded.

"Thank you Fillsi." Gretch picked up his door and placed it back in its original position.

Vorn, who had been leaning against his doorframe, yawned. "It's getting late, I suppose I should head off to bed. We'll talk another time, alright Sweetleaf/" He winked at Gothwen, before spinning around and closing his door behind him. Malina's door closed with a quiet click.

Gothwen hugged Fillinel from behind, wrapping her hands around her stomach. "Thanks for that, I thought that was the end."

Fillinel smiled. "I'd never let anything bad happen to you here. Ever"

They both retreated back into Fillinel's room to retire for the night.

Gothwen and Fillinel had spent the night together again. Fillinel had told her the night before that she felt safest while holding her as she fell asleep. Gothwen's heart skipped a beat, and she had begun to sweat. It began as an awkward evening, with Gothwen fearful that Fillinel would find out the truth of how she felt, and she would never want to be with her again. The bed they had slept in was almost as comfortable than the bed they had slept in the first time they shared a sleeping space. It seemed the Apostates valued their comfort as much as they valued their cause. Fillinel did as she said she would in sleeping with Gothwen, she drifted away with her arm wrapped firmly around her stomach, breathing on her neck. Gothwen knew exactly when she had fallen asleep, as the breathing had increased severely, and her grip loosened slightly. Gothwen took this as an opportunity to hold her hand, the one on the end of the arm holding her in place, bringing it up to her lips and kissing it, softly as not to wake her.

They slept until the sunlight of the next morning poured through an open crack in the window of Fillinel's quarters, caressing Gothwen's face and forcing her to wake up. Fillinel had, unfortunately, moved out of her position, and was now lying on her back, sprawled across the majority of her bed. Her hair was a curled mess of a mane, covering the entire pillow she was lying on. Gothwen looked at Fillinel, smiling. This was what she wanted to wake up to every morning for the rest of her life. She continued staring, until Fillinel began to show signs of waking up. Her eyes began to flutter, before finally opening. By now, Gothwen had decided it would be best to close her eyes again and pretend to fall back asleep.

"Gothwen?" Fillinel's tired voice was enough to make Gothwen's eyes open again. She found herself staring into Fillinel's orange eyes. "I know you weren't asleep."

Gothwen smiled. "You just looked so peaceful when you're sleeping."

Fillinel threw the covers off herself, she too was smiling. "I've never heard that one before. A little creepy, don't you think?"

Gothwen began to turn red. "It's true! Don't blame me for your sleeping cuteness." She too had gotten out of the bed now.

Once they were both dressed, they sat down together at the small table to eat and discuss their plan. Fillinel gave Gothwen a bowl of grey sludge. A porridge of some sorts judging by its appearance. "Today, Gothwen, will be our last free day together. After today, there will be no turning back, no returning to this quaint little home of ours." A corner of the ceiling collapsed, covering Fillinel's dresser in dust and a few bricks. "As we speak, two hundred of The Count's private army are resting for their journey to Ald Rosimeris. We will join them."

Gothwen had taken a mouthful of the grey substance. She

tossed it around her mouth before sheepishly swallowing. "How do we travel with The Count's private army undetected? Won't they be looking for us both? And why does he need a private army in the first place? Won't his transfiguration engines give him enough soldiers?"

"I'll answer your questions, Gothwen. Just don't question me when I say we have a plan. I have reliable sources within the palace itself, and they're telling me that, just in case something goes wrong with The Count's engines and the sap soldiers turn on their master, he needed a force of enough loyal, skilled individuals to cut them down."

Gothwen spoke up again. "But how do we get inside that army? They'll be looking for us."

Filli gestured to her alchemy table. "Perceptiplasm. The two-person potion that alters how other people perceive us. It'll change our hair colour, our jawline, our eyes, it'll even make these stupid freckles fade away."

"I like your freckles." Gothwen almost choked on the mouthful of food she was eating.

"I... Thank you." Fillinel smiled. "We'll need something taken from both of our bodies to ensure the potion works. Saliva, sweat, a strand of hair, anything. It will bind the potion to us, so only we will see each other for who we really are." Fillinel narrowed her eyes. "Just remember we have to drink it every twenty-four hours so take something that tastes nice, okay?" Fillinel smiled. "I'm joking, there's no way this will taste anywhere near as good as you think."

Fillinel finished her meal and made her way over to the alchemy table. She began to toy with a few ingredients, Gothwen recognised them. She decided to join her. "It needs a stem of milkweed, a splash of sugar water, a couple of chunks of glowy fungus..."

"Don't forget to crush all the milkweed." Gothwen noticed the little chunks in the bowl. "I don't really want us to turn into jelly piles." She took the ingredient herself, ensuring all that remained was a thick paste.

Fillinel looked impressed. She had no idea Gothwen was competent in alchemy. She flicked through her book of potions, mixing all of the ingredients together. "Next, we have to heat the potion slowly." Fillinel snapped her fingers, a tiny fireball appeared in her palm. She threw it towards a candle placed perfectly underneath a tripod, upon which she placed the bowl. Without a word, however, her face dropped.

Gothwen realised Fillinel had stopped. "Filli? What's wrong?"

Fillinel gulped. "I completely forgot. The only ingredient that remains is the binding agent. Samples from our bodies. I lit the candle too early. If we don't get it now the whole concoction will fail, and I don't have spare ingredients."

Gothwen's breaths increased. "I have an idea. We can add our saliva." She gestured to her cheeks.

Fillinel looked confused. "But we wouldn't be adding *both* of our saliva at the same time."

Her emerald eyes shining, Gothwen smiled. "Then kiss me."

Looking at her concoction, then looking back at Gothwen's beaming face, Fillinel sighed. "That could work." They turned to face each other, moving their faces slowly together. It was here that Fillinel realised this was something she wanted as much as Gothwen did. Their lips touched. Gothwen never imagined this would be how their first kiss would take place, though she imagined something similar to this happening at some point on their journey together. It was, as she had felt, something which was inevitable. Fillinel fumbled around her alchemy table for the bowl she had made the potion in, Gothwen held her by the waist in an attempt to steady her, though really, she just wanted to touch her. Fillinel pushed herself away, gathering as much saliva as possible from her moth and adding it into the bowl.

"You're a pretty good kisser, Gothwen." Fillinel smiled.

"How many people have you tried it on?"

Gothwen smiled back. "I've wanted to do that since our first practical joke on the college Dean."

Looking at the ground, Fillinel moved closer to Gothwen again. "How about a real one, then?" She held Gothwen's hand, locking her fingers between each of Gothwen's own digits.

Leaning closer to Fillinel's ear, Gothwen brushed aside the red lock of hair in her way and whispered. "I have a better idea." She stared longingly into Fillinel's eyes, pulling her closer to her bed. Their lips touched again as they fell back.

Torril had been riding all night. Upon leaving the portal she had ran towards the nearest source of light, a small homestead used as a farm. This time, she decided to skip the murdering and moved straight away to stealing the inhabitant's horse. She had reached the main gate to Coryphia late in the morning, a gap in the organic vine wall which encompassed the city itself. It stood indestructible and unscalable, any attempt at doing so would result in the wall itself coming alive and strangling the life out of the assailant. Torril was not afraid of the wall, or the city itself. She still had the physical appearance of an elven woman, the elven cities did not make her fearful, she was treated in the southern regions as though she belonged. Nothing did, and anything that did make her afraid she would cut to pieces. A solitary guard stood vigil at the gate, another creation of wood and vines. There was nobody coming in or leaving, which seemed odd for the capital city. Torril could see inside, the entire city itself made her sick. It stood as a testament to the magical ability of the elven people, every stone that was placed, every tree that was bent, was done so by some mage a few hundred years ago.

The guard slammed his wooden staff on the cobblestones. "Who enters this city? From where do you hail? Speak now."

Torril sighed. She knew if she was going to enter the city,

she needed to act the role of innocent little schoolgirl. "I come from a college in the North. I got separated from my tutor and classmates and found a horse. I followed the road, I didn't know where I was going." She began to fake a tear. "Please, I don't know where I am. I'm so hungry and thirsty and tired and I need a place to stay until my parents can find me."

The guard bought her story. "How old are you, pumpkin?" He helped Torril off her horse.

Torril sniffled, wiping her nose. "Seventeen." She looked around; a sense of fake fear filled her eyes. "Where am I? How far am I from home?"

The guard held her shoulder, guiding her into the city. "You're in Coryphia now, child. Safest city in Oreldas. One more question, love. What's your name?"

Torril cosied up to the guard. "Ethwen." She held him tight, shaking. "My name is Ethwen Filligoth." The thought of such a ridiculous name almost made her burst out laughing.

"Ethwen? That's a beautiful name, child." The guard signalled another nearby patrol to take his position.

Torril's eyes darted around the city, a strategic scan of her surroundings for vantage points and shortcuts disguised under a veil of fear and vulnerability as she held the guard tighter. It almost made her throw up. "Can you tell me where places are? Where I can eat? Who I can talk to?" Torril thought for a moment. "I met a girl from here once. Maybe I can stay with her. She was called Gothwil I think. Gathwed? No! Gothwen! Do you know where I can find her?" She looked up, her tearful gaze meeting the guardsman's.

The colour left his face. He sopped walking. "Gothwen?" He swallowed a lump in his throat. "I'm afraid I don't know her. One of the other guards might." His eyes moved side-to-side; he couldn't make eye contact with Torril any longer. She could tell he was lying.

They reached a bulbous, organic structure, sculpted to look like the fruits of one of the trees or, from another perspective, a bloated, oversized amalgam of tree and sentient spherical beast. The sap had been solidified and acted as windows, the door was one of the largest leaves Torril had ever seen, covering a branch-framed doorway with numerous other, much smaller leaves protruding from irregular intervals.

"Here we are, little Ethwen. The barracks. Head inside, get some food in you, and rest up." He let go of Torril, who nodded as she cautiously climbed the organic oaken steps to the leaf door. The guard followed her, brushing aside the leaf to let her inside.

Wooden beds carved from logs encircled the room, a matching table with six chairs around it took central place. There was food on it, Torril had no idea where it came from, there was no kitchen or cooking fire. She sat in one of the chairs, Torril had to admit she was pretty hungry from her journey. She tore the leg off what seemed to be a poultry animal of some sort, finely cooked and golden. She sunk her fangs into the flesh, tearing chunks of the meat away and stuffing her mouth with any piece that fell off. A bottle of wine was on the table. She picked it up and washed down the dry meat with one gulp. Torril never found the need for glasses anyway. As Torril ate, three more guards entered the room. They watched as she ravaged the meat, whispering among themselves. Eventually, there was no more meat left for Torril to feast on. "I should rest." She eyed up one of the beds, standing up and cautiously walking over to one of them. The guards never stopped looking at her.

"Perhaps that is a good idea." The guard who had escorted her spoke up.

Torril lay on her side in the bed, facing away from the guards. She began to fake the sound of snoring, making it seem as though she had already fallen sleep. The guards began to talk louder. So Torril decided to eavesdrop.

"The girl claims to know the one who escaped." The guard she met first spoke.

A second followed. "The flat-chested redhead or the busty one?"

"The second one. The busty girl. I told her I had no idea who she was."

One of them laughed. "You're a complete idiot. There are posters of them all over the damn city!"

The third guard was most intriguing to Torril. "I'm telling you, they're in the ruins of the Old City. There's been a lot of Apostate activity there."

The last guard, a much smaller man, spoke next. "That's ridiculous. They haven't been seen there for weeks. They're in the Apartment Oaks somewhere."

"Doesn't matter where they're hiding, I'll find them, I want that one with the big tits." Three of them began to laugh.

"You take her, I prefer mine with a bit more bite. The redhead will do me perfectly."

The first guard spoke up again. "Watch your tongues. We have a situation here that needs our attention." He nodded to Torril.

"Nothing wrong with a bit of practice I suppose." Torril grabbed the hilt of her dagger. She was prepared to slice off whatever part of that guard touched her.

"Don't be ridiculous. We need to take care of her. She knows about Gothwen, and she could lead us to Fillinel."

"Now." One of the guards unfastened his breeches. "That still doesn't mean we can't have some fun with her."

The second the guard's hand touched Torril's shoulder, she swung herself back around, hacking off the one thing the guard needed to continue, like a butcher slicing meat. She threw herself out of the bed, rolling into the middle of the group, and, as she stood, swung her dagger with one strike, slicing two of their necks. It was the smaller, rounder guard who made his advance on Torril, he was now knelt clutching the bloodied remains of his crotch. She threw her dagger between his eyes, before pulling it back out and watching as he fell face-first onto the corpse of his comrade. The only guard who remained was the one who had helped her, currently on his knees staring at Torril with a look of terror in his eyes.

He held up his hands to surrender. "I don't work with them, please. I'm a double-agent. I work with The Apostates. I know where they are. I know where Gothwen is!" He pointed a trembling finger to one of the guards. Or at the very least, the bloodied mess of the guard on the ground. "He. He was correct. They are in the ruins to the Old City. Please let me go. I don't wish to fight you."

Torril flipped her dagger in her hands, before licking the blood off the blade. "You know, there isn't a single living being who could beat me in combat." She sniggered. "All I get to face are the weak ones." She too knelt down, at eye level with the guard. "The world can produce more victims for me, though I hope eventually I'll get a challenge." Torril stroked the guard's hair as she spoke, before resting it on the back of his head. She thrust her knife into his throat, pulling his head closer with her other hand. The blade pierced the flesh on the back of his neck, creating a hole straight through. She pulled the dagger back, flicking the dripping blood off it. As the twitching corpse fell to the ground, she kicked it out of her way. "I'll find the Old City myself."

CHAPTER TEN

Spells and Spies

Gothwen and Fillinel were still in bed. Half the day had passed, and the couple showed no signs of moving. For the past hour, Fillinel had lay holding Gothwen, her arm wrapped around her chest, and her face buried in her neck. Every now and again she would kiss it, a soft, sensual kiss that made the hairs on Gothwen's neck stand. The next kiss was different. She pulled herself on top of Gothwen, leaning closer to her face. Fillinel caressed her cheek, before biting at Gothwen's lip. Then, she kissed her again, her hands still on Gothwen's cheeks. Every instinct Gothwen had was telling her to disappear under the covers with her new lover again, though they both knew they had more pressing matters to attend. They needed to infiltrate The Count's secret army, a mission that required such delicacy Gothwen was afraid their newfound love would surely ruin it. She wanted to stay in bed. Just for another hour. It was that mindset that would probably get them both killed.

Fillinel started to kiss Gothwen's neck again. "Nobody has ever made me feel like that, Gothwen." She could feel Fillinel's breath against her skin as she spoke. "You know we should get dressed. The fate of Oreldas rests on us and we've been lying here all morning."

The thought of what the couple had done sent a shiver down Gothwen's spine. "I don't want to ever leave this bed." She held Fillinel's chin, moving her lips closer to her own again. "That was a lot of built up passion, Filli."

Her new lover smiled. "I could tell." Fillinel sat upright on Gothwen's stomach, stretching her arms to the side. "Now, we really should prepare ourselves. We can do this again when the whole Vision thing has passed, and we get time to ourselves again." She leaned forward, and kissed Gothwen's nose, before rolling off the bed to find her clothes again.

Gothwen followed Fillinel out of bed, searching for her own clothes too. Once they were both dressed, they decided to plan for their mission. Fillinel led Gothwen to a room within the ruins that The Apostates must have been using as a sort of planning room. There was a table in the centre of the room, which was a lot similar to Fillinel's quarters, only larger. The organic corners of the walls met with the artificial, stone construction, and, like many of the rooms, a chandelier of glowing bulbs hung from above. On the table was a map, a map which Gothwen recognised as a map of The Count's palace and its grounds.

Fillinel positioned herself at the opposite side of the table to Gothwen. There was a shine in her eyes Gothwen had somehow always missed before. She placed her index finger on one of the buildings on the map. "This is where we need to go." She smiled at Gothwen, who returned a grin back at her. "We enter the grounds here." She moved her finger to a portion of the fence near to the building she has initially pointed out. "The wall itself is pretty structurally weak, a few ghouls apparently knocked a part of the fence over there. It's been boarded up with planks until The Count can be bothered to fix it, most likely after his Ald Rosimeris campaign."

Gothwen thought for a moment. "What about guards? If a section of the wall has been knocked down, surely a few extra guards will be posted to defend it."

Fillinel nodded in agreement. "Vorn has offered to help us with that one. The guards know his face, he has agreed to act as a distraction. He'll wave a torch a few metres away, telling them all who he is. With any luck, they'll all follow. Any who don't will probably run to get reinforcements." Their eyes met. "That, my sweet, is when we infiltrate the grounds and enter the barracks, before this private army awakens. We had better hope they haven't memorised the faces of all of their members."

"I heard somebody say my name. Was it one of you lovely ladies?" Vorn stood, leaning against the doorframe.

"We were discussing the plan. Is everything set, Vorn? You know what you have to do?" Fillinel needed reassurance, Gothwen could tell by the tone in her voice.

"Relax sweetcheeks, everything will go as planned." Vorn turned his attention to Gothwen, who was now running the word 'sweetcheeks' through her head. "Nice to see you recovered completely from your little injury. He rubbed Gothwen's head above her circlet, before running it through her fringe which sat over her eye. He was moving closer, though Gothwen was too hypnotised by his chiselled jawline and deep brown eyes to notice. "Promise me you won't get yourself hurt now, will you?" Before Gothwen could react, Vorn had moved in, kissing Gothwen's lips. She let out a high-pitched squeak, his stubbled face felt a lot different to Fillinel's soft, warm mouth.

Fillinel decided when enough was enough. She pulled Vorn away before he could finish, leaving a stunned Gothwen, frozen in place. Fillinel stared into his eyes, a look of anger enveloping her gaze. She slapped Vorn across the face, most likely an attempt to remove Gothwen's taste out of his mouth through sheer force. "She's mine, Vorn. No more of this nonsense around me." Fillinel wrapped her arms around Gothwen's waist. She was still unable to move. She buried her head into Gothwen's shoulder.

"I see. Then I apologise." Vorn stopped rubbing his sore cheek, raising his hands as though surrendering to the mage's wishes. He backed away from Gothwen. "So *that* was what I heard earlier, then? The two of you solidifying your relationship, so to speak?"

Gothwen and Fillinel looked at each other. In truth, Gothwen was picturing her naked again. It was highly likely Fillinel was doing the same. "You should go and prepare yourself, Vorn." Fillinel ushered him back out of the room. He didn't say another word. She turned around, facing Gothwen again, smiling as she walked closer. "We should get ready too, we have a lot to prepare for." She kissed Gothwen's nose again, to which she received the same kiss back.

Gothwen hesitated for a moment. "Fillinel, I need to see something before we begin. You don't mind, do you?"

Fillinel shook her head. "Of course not, my love." They both drew a vial from the bowl of liquids they had created earlier and took the first drink together.

Lucille examined the slip of paper nailed to the lid of her coffin. She rubbed her shoulder; it had begun to ache after she fell out of her wooden box. "Miss Magelight, I regret to inform that your wand was not found anywhere near to your alleged corpse. I do not have the ability to undertake a search for an item of such value without raising suspicion. A dead mage's wand has as much use as a piece of kindling, though I mean you no offense." Lucille scoffed and rolled her eyes. "Well some taken!" She continued reading. "For an undertaker to launch an expedition to find it would certainly raise a few eyebrows. I have taken full payment for the completion of my job and have left the funeral home for twenty-four hours, as was the agreement. My thanks for the gold, Undertaker Maxus." Lucille placed her hand on her forehead. "No wand? How can I face Torril again without my wand?" She stopped, taking a deep breath. "No, Luci. Her resistance to my spells is too high. I must lure her into the open, overcome her through numbers, not skill in combat." She was disrupted mid-thought by an almighty noise coming from outside.

The bulky, crimson curtains of the funeral home were drawn shut, as not to arouse suspicion when Lucille seemingly rose from the dead. She decided to take a peek through one, the light of day outside temporarily blinding her before her eyes could adjust. There seemed to be a parade marching down the streets outside, citizens of Marrivel throwing flowers and petals from their upstairs windows and their balconies. At ground level, people were waving, gathering huge crowds either side of the road. Beyond them, marching down the road itself, Lucille could make out armed soldiers, clad entirely in combat metal and bearing glistening blades and flowing banners bearing the crest of Niltay. Lucille knew she could not leave without someone recognising her, so instead, she decided to do what any mage would do, she opened a portal. She knew exactly who she had to speak to.

The flaming amber ring gave way to a damp, stone cave, the same cave she had summoned an impassable portal to in her Marrivel Inn room. This one, however, was different, she was able to step through without hesitation, though every movement she made she knew she would regret. She looked around, the cave was dripping with rainwater, it seemed to be raining heavily outside, juxtaposing the sunny warmth of Marrivel she had previously experienced. There was nobody around. "As usual, never around when I need him so desperately." She turned to walk back through the portal, though as she did it began to close once again. Lucille could not get to it quick enough, the entire burning doorway was shrinking into the air before her, that was when she realised, she was not alone. Standing on the other side of where the portal once stood, completely soaked and holding a dead elk draped over his shoulder was Torick, Lucille's former lover, and father to Torril.

"You needed me, Sunflower?" Torick threw the elk in an alcove between them both, staring Lucille in the eyes.

Growing nervous, Lucille found the courage to answer. "Yes, I did. Did you do as I asked?" She took a step back, the smell of this rugged, once noble man lingered in the air around her.

Torick stroked his stubbled beard as he moved past Lucille. "I did, Luci. An unusual request, to be sure, but one I took pride in doing." He looked Lucille in the eyes again, a look of shame, of disappointment. "Oh Luci. How could you lose our daughter?" He shook his head.

Lucille rolled her eyes. "It was exactly how I had planned it, Torick. I told you everything." She watched as he rummaged through a stone cabinet, filled with different coloured potions and vials of thick liquids.

"You're lucky I still had a few of these left." Torick shook a vial of thick, red liquid in Lucille's face, before flicking off the cap and drinking it whole. "It tastes like you, Sunflower." He smiled, wiping his mouth.

Folding her arms, Lucille gave Torick a look of annoyance. "That's because it *is* me, it's my blood."

"Well not everybody is fortunate enough to be raised an elf, Luci. Some of us have to resort to dirty, filthy doings to tap into our affinity to magic." Lucille caught on to the sense of sarcasm in his tone. Torick tested the liquid, conjuring a small fireball in the palm of his hands, which separated into a multitude of smaller, though equally dangerous, balls of flame which illuminated the room by the different sconces mounted on the walls.

Lucille grew impatient. "So? Where is she? What is she doing?" She demanded answers.

"Relax, Sunflower. She's only killed a few people." He hesitated. "Well, by a few I mean a lot. Horrifically. I'm oddly proud of my daughter."

"Please, no more." Lucille covered her ears briefly. Her disgust turned to anger. "You turned her into this monster, Torick."

Her former lover laughed. "Me? You dumped her on me! The second my parents knew I was harbouring a Majless elf-child it was all over for me! For the two of us!" He moved closer to Lucille, as though he was reprimanding a child. "I ran with her Lucille, I escaped the mob wanting to kill us both. Yes, we wound up in a gang of outlaws, yes, they made us do things I wish we hadn't done. Perhaps, Lucille, they were the ones responsible for our daughter's downfall. Perhaps they twisted her mind and made her want to kill for sport. They were outlaws!"

Lucille knew she had failed in raising Torril. "I blamed you, I never blamed myself. I know the truth now." Lucille moved closer to Torick, falling into him and burying her head in his chest. "I wanted us to be a family. But I failed us all. You, Torril, poor Ethril. I even failed myself."

Torick embraced the weeping mage. "There is still time, Lucille. We can try again."

Lucille turned her nose at the thought. "No, Torick. I cannot fail a third time. I don't have the strength anymore."

The sympathetic human kissed Lucille's forehead. "What about this girl? Gothwen? She has no parents, she needs guidance. We can take her in. Raise her how we would have raised Torril, or Ethril. Raise her together."

Lucille sighed. "She's nineteen, Torick. She's an adult." Lucille wiped her eyes. "No, there is nothing we can do now other than ensure our daughter does not succeed in her contract and murder the poor girl."

Torick took a step back from Lucille. "Then I am afraid we must act quickly, Sunflower." He hesitated for a moment, before continuing. "I am afraid she is close to her target. Though I do not know when she plans to strike."

Torick turned to face a circular, stone table which stood in the centre of his cave. The entire surface was flat, as though it had been carved this way. He held his palm above it, until a spectral, golden image depicting all of Oreldas appeared. Three red dots pulsated like artificial heartbeats, one merely glowed with no movement. Torick point to the two dots which stood less than a millimetre apart. "Those two are us." His finger moved to the glowing dot which stood perfectly still. "That is the tree within which our daughter Ethril resides. Her blood may not flow, but it still remains within her." His final movement was towards the red dot which was the furthest South. "Torril is there, in Coryphia. She is close to Gothwen, we need to act quickly."

Lucille examined the ghostly map. She looked back at Torick. "Our daughter must be stopped, whatever the cost." The thought of her putting an end to her daughter was enough to form a tear in Lucille's eyes. She fell into Torick's arms, burying her head within his chest. He sighed, holding Lucille in silence.

"I can't believe they really did it." Gothwen looked up, at the ring of charred bark around the tier of the tree which once held her apartment. "Everything I owned was in that apartment, Filli. All the memories from my childhood, my clothes, everything." She looked back at Fillinel, who still looked the same as ever to her. "Did this potion work? Do people really not see us for who we are?"

Fillinel looked back at Gothwen, examining her face, before looking at the people walking the streets around them. "Well we aren't getting any strange looks from anybody, so I suppose so." She scanned the area around them, an elven girl was walking in their direction. Fillinel stopped her in her path. "Excuse me, Miss."

The elven girl looked at Fillinel in disgust. "What." She eyed her distraction up before doing the same to Gothwen.

She sighed to herself. "Make it quick."

Fillinel stood in shock, her nerves getting the best of her. "Well, my name is Glandris, and this is my friend Rose. We were just wondering. We're writers, you see, and we would like to know what's the best way to describe us both?"

"Are you serious?" The girl toyed with the blade at her waist. "I'd cut you down right now if I didn't find you both so damn attractive." The girl continued. "OK, so, you." She pointed to Fillinel; her blade used as a pointer. "You have beautiful blonde hair, deep, blue eyes, and puffy pink lips I could make out with all day. You." She moved her pointer blade to Gothwen. "You have black, flowing hair, chocolate brown eyes, and beautiful lips I could also make out with all day." The girl flipped her blade and sunk it back into the scabbard at her hip. "The name's Torril. Remember it, I'll be coming back for you two." She winked at Fillinel.

Gothwen's heart began to race. She knew who the girl was, she knew Torril had murdered Lucille. She needed Fillinel's attention. "Fill- uh, Glandris?" She tapped her arm.

Torril's eyes narrowed. She nodded to the burnt apartment. "You know who used to live here?" She looked up at the tree herself. "A woman by the name of Gothwen Darkarrow. I've been sent here all the way from Marrivel to find her. I'm a bounty hunter, you see." Torril moved closer to Fillinel. "A bad girl, through and through."

Fillinel gulped, looking back at the visibly panicked Gothwen. "Who sent you? Why? I heard she was just a sweet, innocent little girl." Fillinel laughed, she too seemed to be growing alarmed.

"Now." Torril caressed the panicked mage's cheek. Fillinel didn't feel anything. "If I told you that, I'd have to kill you." She looked at Gothwen. "Chocolate Eyes over there would have me all to herself. As much as I'd like that, I feel like taking you both on at once would be so much more fun." Torril stroked Fillinel's lips. "Now, Golden Hair, do you have any more questions for me?"

Fillinel shook her head, quicker than any head shake she had done before.

"Good. Then I'll be on my way." She kissed her fingers and placed them against Fillinel's lips. "When my job is done, I will come back for you two. Remember that" She moved past Fillinel, winking as she moved past Gothwen, her hand brushing against her waist.

Gothwen ran into the stone-arched foyer of the apartment tree she once called home. She was hyperventilating. Fillinel ran in after her. "Gothwen? Who was she?" She wrapped her arm around Gothwen, who used her shoulder to try and return her rate of breathing to normal.

"She was Lucille's daughter. She killed her. Now she wants to kill me too." Gothwen sunk her head deeper into her love. "I don't want her to kill me, Filli. Please don't let her!"

Fillinel held Gothwen. "That will never happen, ever. I'd sooner let myself fall to her blade than watch her cut you down." She turned her attention to one of the portals within the circular room of the lobby. Each tier of the tree was connected to a portal leading here, each one acting as a front door to every residence. They only opened to the hand print of the apartment's owner. "Gothwen. Can you still access your tier?"

Pulling herself out of Fillinel's arms, Gothwen turned to face her portal. "I suppose it's possible. I still register as the owner of this place, I think. Would it still work? With us both like this?"

Fillinel thought for a moment. "It should, only our faces and hair should have changed. Our hand prints should still be the same."

Gothwen walked cautiously to the orange, ball-like object at the side of her portal. She wrapped her hand around it, the standard activation method. The ball began to glow, and with it, a warbled, broken noise. "They tried to remove my hand print from my own door." Gothwen sighed. She was about to turn away, when she noticed the portal had begun to open. Slowly, as though it was resisting reality itself, the flaming outline of the tear in the mortal world beginning to form. It spread outwards, sometimes retreating back in parts as though the flames were at war with the air around them. It was as though Gothwen and Fillinel were looking at the spread of a thick liquid from above, watching as it filled the container around it, the twisted vine edges of the portal doorway serving as the barrier where the liquid could spread no further. Eventually, the portal was complete, and the apartment within began to appear.

Gothwen took a sigh of relief. "That took longer than usual. It was clear the portal was trying to resist me." She looked inside, most of her furniture was black, along with the walls, the floor, even the ceiling. Everything had been burned. Gothwen felt her heart turn cold.

"Are you sure this is something you wish to do, Gothwen?" Fillinel held her partner's hand, though Gothwen had already begun to enter.

"No, Filli. It isn't something I wish to do. But it's something I need to do. A need requires more direct attention than a wish." They passed through the arch-shaped portal together. It closed behind them.

Before the fire, the floor of Gothwen's circular apartment reflected the natural look of the tree it had been created in. Much like the walls, and the ceiling, the floor was made from the tree itself. The rings of the tree's interior, as Gothwen thought, was a perfect, natural addition to the apartment which, along almost every other elf who lived within the confines of a tree, was a shared opinion citywide. Now, as Gothwen and Fillinel stepped cautiously around what once was Gothwen's living room, their eyes found no rings of wood, no beautifully carved walls, nothing Gothwen remembered. Instead, her apartment was black, grey in some places, with a pungent smell of ash dominating the incense Gothwen usually burned. Everything, from the furniture to the fixtures, even the cloth doors to Gothwen's washroom and bedroom on either side of her living area were blackened or destroyed completely.

"Gothwen, I don't know what to say." Fillinel reached out her hand, holding Gothwen's in front of her. She used it to pull herself forwards, releasing her grip to wrap her arms around Gothwen's stomach. She rested her head on Gothwen's shoulder.

Unknown to Fillinel, Gothwen's attention was on the only item of colour in the apartment. A rose, in a pot of marble, placed recently on the window ledge in Gothwen's bedroom. It could be seen from where the two stood. "No, Filli. This is the motivation I need. The push I've been waiting for, to move on from here and do something with my life. This story, Filli, ends with me. The Count, that bounty hunter, Luci's death, they are all a part of my tale, but I have the power to write the final word." She placed her hands over Fillinel's, clasped firmly together at her stomach. "We both do, Filli."

Fillinel kissed Gothwen's neck, before leaning her head against her again.

"Now." Gothwen smiled again. "We have a Count to stop."

CHAPTER ELEVEN

The Plan Executed

Footsteps. Either good news or bad news. The Count could not be bothered to lend his ear either way. He was still attached to the contraption that made up his throne, the artificial blood still pumping into his body. The Count was reading, while sipping a tea brewed from a leaf grown from the vines on the side of a working man's house in Balmira from a golden teacup. The book was one written generations ago, by a human warlord who had conquered half of Oakenheim before the elves had surrendered to him and his tyrannical laws. The Count needed ideas for when his own reign began.

The footsteps stopped, and The Count looked up. It was his servant, a poor elf boy who had lost both of his parents to unfortunate matters. The Count never told him his parents were killed under his command, they were rebels considering aligning themselves with The Apostates. The boy knelt before him. "My Lord." He spoke with a scared tone, his voice quiet, almost like a whisper. "I bring good news from the mages you sent to Ald Rosimeris."

The corner of The Count's mouth twisted upwards, ever so slightly. "Do tell, boy."

The servant cleared his throat. "The wand of the fallen

High Transmuter Marill has succeeded in converting a single tree into fifty Oaken Warriors. The numbers would be significantly higher if the spell was focused, the mages believe."

The Count clasped his hands together. "That, my dear boy, is the reason for The Engines I have had constructed." He leaned forward, lecturing the boy before him. "Listen, learn the how these Engines work. They are cone-shaped devices, elevated on two stands, one either end, both wheeled on the bottom and within a circular track. One man stands on the larger end of the device, one of the shorter end. The man on the larger end places a wand within the larger ring, pointing it down the coned barrel. The finely attuned crystals, protected by the stone barrel, purify and focus the spell cast from the wand, creating a beam of energy, or a ball, or whatever the spell would initially create, only a hundred times more powerful. With Marill's wand, or in fact any of the High Transmuter's, we are able to transmute the appearance of anything, alive, dead, or inanimate, into anything we desire. With it, I will build an army to outnumber the Humans ten to one, so I can take and hold Ald Rosimeris for as long as I require."

The boy nodded solemnly. "They also wished for me to tell you that they have successfully used these fifty men to form a stable portal within the central fortress of Ald Rosimeris large enough for siege weapons to be constructed at our war camp, to be passed through, ready for battle."

The Count leaned back in his chair. "Excellent. Ensuring we have a portal within the fortress means we can make our forces look considerably smaller than they are. When the Humans see our apparent weak army and send a small force to meet it, we will crush them with our true power."

The Count stood from his chair. "Come now, boy. It would be wise to begin our invasion of the city now." He gestured to the lever, which the boy immediately pulled. He stepped down from the elevated position of his throne, detaching the tubing from his flesh, leaving them to dangle as what remained of the artificial blood soaked the floor of his throne room. "Come with me, I may need assistance in collecting the four gemstones." The boy began to follow sheepishly.

"Ready my carriage, I will pick up my new crown and a security detail. Tell the guards to allow the mercenaries another half hour of rest. I will return, the we shall depart immediately."

The boy nodded, before running off in the opposite direction of The Count.

The wooden chair shattered against the stone wall. Torril screamed a roar of defeat. She swung her arms at the table in front of her, knocking the hastily left half-eaten meal to the ground. She picked up the empty bottles by their necks and flung them at the wall behind her. Turning back, she flipped the table, sending what had not already been thrown to the ground hurtling across the room. Torril marched towards the alchemy table she spied at the far end of Fillinel's chamber. The bowl was still wet with the liquid which had been prepared beforehand.

She dipped her finger into the bowl, scraping it along the edges to pick up traces of what had been left. "Now, what were you two up to, I wonder?" She sunk her finger into her mouth, knocking the residue around with her tongue. "Milkweed, sugar water, fungus." Torril continued, a surprising look of happy disgust filled her face. "Saliva." She grabbed the potion book beside her, flicking through it until she found a potion which matched the ingredients she had tasted. "This one." She tore the page out of the book, before storming back out of the room, and out of the ruins themselves.

"Now, if I am correct, they should be disguised as anyone. This was not what I was expecting." Torril furrowed her brow, frowning at herself. "They appear to be proving themselves as worthy opponents." Torril smiled. "This just means slicing their throats will be all the more satisfying."

Torril came to the main door of the ruin. She had no time for locks, with one swift kick the door fell to the ground. "Now, I just have to narrow down the possible locations where they would be." She was almost blinded by the outside light, a contrast to the darkness of the ruin's interior. She remained on her warpath, however, a change in lighting doing little to halt her progression.

It was the early hours of the evening, the sun was balancing on the top of the trees to the West, providing one last stand before it dipped lower over the Bluehorn Sea and disappeared into the horizon. It was about this time, Torril thought, that much of the population of Coryphia would be finishing a day of work and relaxing in their local tavern. The gears began to turn in Torril's mind, this would provide her with the perfect opportunity to gather what information she could.

These thoughts had given Torril enough time to walk from the exterior of the Old City ruins to Coryphia itself. The two locations were not too far apart from each other, in fact the Old City would still be in use if it wasn't for the majority of the Coryphian people deciding to live instead within the increasingly popular apartment trees. Torril looked up at these towering organic constructions. There were twenty of them in total, though more were being developed by the more powerful users of Chlorokinesis within the city. Each tree was moulded, sculpted practically by hand in the shape of a tree, while remaining hollow and with the basic necessities for living. The smaller trees, thinner in width though some just as tall as their more voluminous counterparts, would primarily house one family per floor, averaging twenty stories high. The wider trees, however, would be able to house four families per tier, with the tallest of these trees being around thirty stories high. Some of these organic apartments would interconnect, branches forming elegant, snake-like walkways between tiers. Much like the old ways of Nirndrelluin, some of these walkways held large, bowl-like constructs primarily used for farming, some privately owned, others open to the public. The thick canopy of leaves and thinner, uninhabitable layers of tree further upwards left much of the city in shadow, the sun occasionally poking through the gaps in the leaves on a cloudy day, the further up the plots of farming land were, the more likely it was that the plants would receive their much-needed sunlight. Though when the days were brighter, clearer, and warmer, the light turned a shade of green which glistened on the surfaces it touched and shone bright on the elven people walking below. Torril did have to admit, on these days, Coryphia was a beautiful place.

The smell of cinnamon and fresh bread became pungent in the air around Torril. She inhaled deeply, though the sweetness burned her black lungs and made her twisted stomach wretch. A tavern must be nearby. She scanned her surroundings. Of course, Torril was right. On the corner of the street before her, hugging the curved walls of one of the larger apartment trees was a building unlike any other in Coryphia. It was seemingly built by humans, there was no organic, twisted vines making up most of the walls or the roof, albeit some vines creeping down from the tree itself and wrapping themselves around the wood and stone construct. The roof was made from logs, carved to perfection, with the corners of each wall evidently the same. The doorframe and windows too were the same, simple logs carved to fit, the front door seemingly being of the same wood. Torril climbed the steps to the porch, her boots connecting with the solid wooden floor, the clicking drowned out by the noise of merriment and intoxication from within. Upon closer inspection of the door, she found carvings depicting images of happiness, merriment, and joy. Elves held hands with humans, dancing in a circle while others played various musical instruments for their entertainment. Deep in the locked abyss of Torril's mind, she was imagining how the scene would play out, had it not been carved, frozen for all eternity. Above the circle of merriment was a carved hill with a tree, protruding further up to the edges of its wooden canvas, engulfing almost the entire upper half of the door with wooden leaves. Torril deduced this as Heroes Hill, a sacred hill deep in the region of Oakenheim, where the most distinguished and honoured of the elven people would be enveloped by the trees on their death, becoming one with nature for all eternity. Almost a quarter of the trees within the expansive forest of Oakenheim served as graves for the Elven people. It was their tradition that, upon death, they would once again become one with nature as an experienced mage uses their powers to open the heart of a tree and preserve the body within. It was for this reason that every tree within the region was considered sacred, never to be touched, primarily due to the fact that there was a possibility a tree being cut down could hold a corpse.

Torril ran her fingers across the carvings. She knew exactly how many corpses she had put inside a tree. That thought made her smile. She ran her fingers down to the door handle, grabbing it and pushing the door inwards. She was hit by a tidal wave of good vibes and fun that almost made her sick. She powered through the intoxicated regulars and dancing couples to a solitary table to the far end. Fortunately, it seemed one party was a person too large, so only one chair remained at the two-person table. Torril sat, examining everyone around her for sign of anyone familiar or anyone who would be a threat to her. She sunk her dagger into the wood in disappointment, there was nobody. Nobody to kill, nobody to question. She signalled one of the bar staff, a tall human male who had his bare, muscular arm around his short, freckled elven wife. He poured her a flagon and called one of his regulars to deliver it for him. Oddly enough, they obliged.

Torril began deciding her next course of action. She needed

to find someone who knew something about Gothwen or, at the very least, someone who knew where she could possibly be going. Fortunately, Torril noticed her answer swing open the door to the tavern and perch herself on a lonesome stool at the front of the main room. She rested a lute on her lap and, after a monstrous applaud from her audience, began to sing.

Every lyric that came from her beautiful red lips resonated in Torril's hollow mind. Every pluck of her lute kept Torril on the edge of her seat. She could imagine herself running her hands through the brunette locks of hair that cascaded down the back of her head. Torril could imagine wrapping her fingers around the two braids which sat elegantly on her shoulders. More importantly, Torril could imagine asking this bard, who sang of tales and events all over Oreldas, of the potential whereabouts of Gothwen.

The bard's song was over before Torril realised, she had seemed to have been mesmerised by the song coming from her mouth. The woman left her seat for a drink. The two made eye contact, Torril, out of force of habit, winking directly at her. Once she had finished her drink of clear water, the bard made her way to Torril's table. She swung a vacant seat around, to the opposite side of Torril.

"Malukii Silverstrings. I noticed you liked what I sang." She rested her lute against the table, Torril noticed she must have earned her name by the way the strings shone in the light.

"Torril." She cursed herself in her head, she panicked before imagining a fake name. "I really did enjoy it. I'm a traveller myself, how did you come by those tales so quickly?"

"Well." Malukii smiled, she knew she should not say, though she couldn't help herself. "The Bard's Guild mainly. We share stories, think up songs, then see who makes the best one." She ran her fingers along the rim of Torril's flagon. "Do you have any tales you want to share?" Torril looked into

Malukii's eyes. She noticed the same green that made up Gothwen's eyes. At least, in the images she had seen of her.

"Actually, I have a question for you." Torril leaned back in her chair. "Do you know of anything big that's going on around here? Anything world changing?"

Malukii's face dropped. "Well, I suppose there's that march The Count was planning to Ald Rosimeris, but is that all you want?" She looked at Torril in her eyes again.

As much as it hurt her, Torril was in too much of a rush for any fun. "Listen, I have a few things to take care of. Perhaps when I get back, we can make a few tales of our own." Torril stood up, she had the information she needed. She was beginning to leave when she felt a tug at her wrist. Malukii was looking up at her.

"Be safe, Torril. This world is full of evil. Never let it consume the fire in your heart." Malukii smiled, placing an outstretched palm on her breast, to which Torril hesitantly smiled back. At least now Torril knew where Gothwen would be.

A rogue root arching above the ground provided Gothwen and Fillinel with the perfect cover to begin their plan. Vorn stood before them, no cover hiding his perfect form. Before him was the Count's palace, more specifically the breach in the outer eastern wall. He turned his head to where the couple hid, winking in their direction, though neither knew who the target was, most likely them both. He cleared his throat, outstretching his hand in the direction of the breach. From his palms he conjured balls of fire, narrowly missing the guard perched nearby, facing inwards. That got his attention.

Vorn began to yell, his fist pumping the air above him, the hand holding the torch waving the flame carelessly. "The Count will not blindfold his people and lead them over a cliff!" He fired a few more fireballs, one of them hitting a guard and knocking him off the wall.

This was enough to convince the guards to give chase. One by one, they clambered down the ruined stone of the breach. Vorn began to take a step back, readying his stance to run at the perfect time. Once all the guards visible had made their way to the hole in the wall, Vorn cast one last fireball, striking another guard in the chest. Like a swarm of bees, the guards all gave chase. Vorn ran in the opposite direction to where Gothwen and Fillinel were crouched. This gave the couple the perfect opportunity to slip through the breach unseen and towards the barracks where the rest of the mercenaries lay.

The exterior of The Count's palace was not the same as Gothwen remembered on her trip with The Ark during her studies. The interior remained relatively similar, as she had found out a few days before, though the walls and spires which now rose, casting an elongated shadow down onto them, were constructed from the finest marble, with very little organic infrastructure visible. There were, however, at various points, branches piercing the gaps between the stone, though there were no leaves growing upon them. They were dead, drooping in a serpentine fashion to the ground.

The palace, however, was not Gothwen and Fillinel's target. To their left was the guest house, where The Count was allegedly keeping his small force of mercenaries. In truth, using the Engines would provide an army of countless wooden soldiers, though it seemed wise to begin with a small force of elven warriors to oversee and create them in the first place. At least a hundred soldiers slept on the floor of the guest house, there was hardly space for Gothwen and Fillinel to step as they opened the door and entered the main room. One of the men was, however, awake. He was smoking what Gothwen deduced to be Blackweed from a pipe while sitting on the ledge of a window to the back of the building.

"What happened with you two? I thought everyone was asleep." Smoke left his mouth as he spoke. He leaned towards the window, blowing the rest out.

Gothwen hastily thought up an excuse. "We heard a noise outside, we both left for some fresh air when we saw all the guards running towards that hole in the wall."

The soldier gave Gothwen a quick nod. "Fairs. I saw most of it from the window. I also saw you two sneaking your way in." He smiled at them both. "But don't worry, your secret is safe with me."

Both Gothwen and Fillinel felt their hearts skip a beat. Gothwen's face dropped. "Our secret?" She noticed Fillinel had grasped the hilt of the sword at her waist. Gothwen gave her a look of disapproval.

"Well yes. We don't know what's going to happen after today." The soldier inhaled from his pipe again. "You two met when we all joined up. You both liked what you saw so you hit it off. Of course, a room of a hundred sleeping men isn't exactly the most private of places, so you decided to sneak back out through the wall to have some fun, then creep back in while the guards were distracted." A few others had begun to wake with all the noise, though the conversation continued as normal.

Gothwen and Fillinel both sighed with relief. "That's exactly what happened." Fillinel wrapped her arm around Gothwen. "It was love at first sight." The beaming elf kissed Gothwen's cheek, proving the soldier's fake story.

He smiled at them both, before jumping back to the ground. "Congratulations. I hope we all make it back from Ald Rosimeris in one piece then, I for one would love to see how this romantic tale turns out."

A heavily armoured elven male shoved his way past Gothwen and Fillinel before either of the two could reply. In his left hand he held a large bell, which he lifted and rung ten times unintentionally into Gothwen's ear. The sleeping soldiers on the ground grumbled before standing up to face him, rubbing their eyes and their heads. They all stood looking at this skeletal man, his bleach blonde hair cascading down onto his solid, enchanted wooden breastplate. The accents crafted with sap glistened as he moved.

"Nap time is over, soldiers." The elf spoke with a deep, hoarse voice which made Gothwen shudder in fright. "Count Vlastoril has ordered the commencing of our march. We leave in half an hour through the North exit, avoiding the city. Under cover of darkness, we shall march for several hours until we reach the halfway camp. From there, after a short, hour-long rest, we shall continue for several more hours until we reach the final portal base. Half of you will remain there, constructing the siege weapons and The Count's Engines, while the other half will continue through the portal to the central fortress of Ald Rosimeris. You will be briefed further when we reach the portal camp." The elf left as swiftly as he entered, and the grumbling among the soldiers began.

Gothwen turned to Fillinel. "I suppose the plan worked." They both smiled at each other. "We're in."

CHAPTER TWELVE

The March of Mages

Gothwen adjusted the bow at her back, while Fillinel examined her sword. She looked up at her lover, who was clearly unnerved by the situation that had befallen them. "Filli." Gothwen looked at Fillinel in the eyes. "Is it a good idea we do this?"

Fillinel frowned. "Are you doubting the plan, Gothwen? It'll work, and we will reach Ald Rosimeris together." Fillinel cleaned her blade with the sleeve of her jacket. She had picked up a silken one from her wardrobe before they left. It was burgundy, with a few tears and stains. Underneath she wore a vest, suitable for the warm weather of the forests while keeping her cool enough to continue wearing the jacket. She wanted to wear something with enough pocket space, none of her robes met those standards.

Gothwen, however, was still wearing the same armour plating with the same leaf green top and skirt. She was aware The Count had already seen her wear this outfit, though until the potion wore off, she would have a completely different appearance, so this thought affected her very little. What affected her even less was the fact it was highly unlikely The Count would even notice her among his own soldiers, he struck Gothwen as the type to care very little about the wellbeing of the people he hired.

One by one, the soldiers left their temporary accommodation, gathering instead beside the fountain in the centre of the courtyard. The main building of the palace wrapped its stone right arm around an area of grass and cobblestone, where a fountain spewed crystal-clear water, and various groups of flowers dotted the ground. Of course, most of these flowers were now flattened, trampled on by careless, still tired soldiers. Gothwen and Fillinel joined their ranks, integrating themselves among the crowd. That was, however, until another bell rang.

The same elf who deafened Gothwen and Fillinel earlier, the leader as Gothwen presumed, rung his ear-piercing bell thrice again, getting the attention of everyone who stood around the misfit couple. He begun to shout something, though Gothwen and Fillinel were both too far away to hear, and too short to see past the mercenaries in front of them to see what he was gesturing. Those in front, however, did, and begun to line themselves up in rows of three, the muddled group of clueless mercenaries all beginning to follow and change their organisation. When it came to Gothwen and Fillinel, there was no third member to complete their row, so they remained as a couple.

When the marching group was assembled, the walk began. Gothwen and Fillinel kept their eyes to the front, in an attempt to see where they could be going. Though of course, this early in their journey, it was difficult to say.

The babble of a nearby stream running along the side of the pathway somehow managed to dwarf the sound of marching soldiers. Gothwen looked down as she walked, into the shimmering reflected light of the water, the reflection of the torches glimmering. The light of the day was starting to fade, obscuring the pebbled bottom of the stream from Gothwen's view despite the water itself being as clear as one of her drinking glasses. Gothwen's attention turned away from the stream, her head tilting upwards. The treetops rustled in the breeze, a light wind which brushed against her hair. She could feel it only as far as her actual hair grew, the extensions provided by the potions could not be felt by Gothwen.

Eventually, though fearful for what was going on, Fillinel spoke up. "Gothwen, what will we do when we reach the final camp?" She turned to face Gothwen, hoping for a look of reassurance, though one did not come.

"I suppose we see what The Count is planning, find him in Ald Rosimeris, and stop him before war breaks out and millions of lives are lost." Gothwen kept her head facing firmly forwards. "It seems he's leading me to my destiny."

Fillinel reached out, holding Gothwen's hand. "What happens then? When you've achieved what you were brought into this world to achieve. What will you do?"

Gothwen finally turned her head to Fillinel. "No, Filli. It's not what will *I* do, it's what will *we* do."

The thought of a life afterwards, with Gothwen, brought a glimmer of hope back to Fillinel. "Together, Gothwen. We will live together, in a house we built together, deep in the Rosimer forest. All alone, with nobody to disturb us."

Gothwen smiled back at Fillinel, who was now grinning the largest grin she had ever seen from her cute, freckled face. "If that's the life you want, then it's the life I will give you."

The couple were disrupted from their fantasy by the sound of another person joining their row. "I didn't expect to find you two here." The sound of this particular voice made Gothwen's heart stop, before almost jumping out of her chest. "Glandris. Rose. You remember me, don't you?"

Gothwen turned her head, slowly and cautiously. Her eyes met with a deathly stare from the speaker. "Torril. What are you doing here?"

Torril grinned. "I could ask you two the same question. What are a couple of writers doing in a march made up of mercenaries?"

Fillinel was quick to jump in. "We wanted a genuine war story. A tale of battle."

Gothwen continued. "A story to bring in the money, basically. What better way to find a war story then to take part in a battle? Or at least, I hope this leads to a battle."

Torril laughed. "Two writers taking on an army in battle? I'd love to see that." She placed her hand on Fillinel's shoulder. She flinched. "Don't worry though, I'll protect you. We can't have fun if you're dead. Well, we could, but it's less fun when they can't scream the safe-word."

Both Gothwen and Fillinel shivered. They didn't want to imagine Torril's idea of 'fun', though for someone as deranged as her, it was bound to be something horrific. Fillinel was imagining ropes, Gothwen had the image of a whip in her mind. Neither wanted to imagine anything further.

Torril rummaged around in her pocket. She pulled out the torn page from Fillinel's book, showing them both.

Fillinel squeaked. "Is that from... A book?" She recognised the page; it was the one on the potion they were both using.

Torril narrowed her eyes. "Have you seen this page before? Do you know where it's from?"

Fillinel tried to think up an excuse. Gothwen helped her. "We read books together usually, I remember us reading one that had a page like that. It's a shame you had to tear a page out."

Torril looked at the couple, confused. "I didn't think it was possible to care so deeply for a damn book. It's an object"

Gothwen had to stop the situation escalating. It was clear Fillinel was becoming agitated. "We're writers. We do care deeply for books, Torril. We never write on one, we never tear one up, we never burn them."

Torril shrugged. "I suppose it's each to their own." She continued. "Anyway, this potion is for a transfiguration spell. I found it where Gothwen and Fillinel were hiding. They could be anyone, and they could be anywhere." Torril looked them both in the eyes. "Have you two seen anything suspicious? A couple who seem out of place perhaps?" Torril closely examined Fillinel. "Though of course, no duo is safe from my scrutiny."

The walk continued in silence. Torril began plotting what she would do once she had found her prey. Gothwen and Fillinel both knew it was going to be a long night.

Eventually, night descended on the marching group. After a few uneventful hours of walking in almost complete darkness, in which the road ahead was illuminated only by occasional street lanterns and the handheld lantern of a horse-mounted sentry which passed by every few minutes, Gothwen, Fillinel, and their new companion arrived at the halfway camp. A clearing in the forest opened up to reveal a collection of tents, fires, and supplies. It seemed some mercenaries had even hacked down a few trees to serve as benches for the weariest of the walkers.

Gothwen and Fillinel separated themselves from the larger group, as they dispersed to get the best seats by the fires. Torril ran ahead too, barging people out of the way, even lightly slicing them with her dagger if they got too close. She was hungry, and she wanted food, nobody would dare get in her way.

Fillinel pressed her back against one of the larger trees to the edge of the clearing, she had begun to panic. "She knows, Gothwen. She knows the potion we've made. She knows who we really are, we need to get away from her as quickly as possible. We can't go through with this anymore."

Gothwen joined her against the tree, holding her agitated body steady. She looked around, seeing whether or not Torril was in earshot. "She doesn't know it's us, Filli. She'll never find out." Gothwen ran her fingers through Fillinel's hair, this evidently seemed to comfort her.

The bushes behind them seemed to rustle. For a moment

the couple thought someone had eavesdropped on their conversation, and that they were about to be caught by every mercenary in Rosimer. Gothwen and Fillinel both drew their blades, edging closer to the noise's source. Their arms were shaking, Gothwen could feel her heart pounding. They were inches from the shrubbery when the figure emerged. It was not a mercenary or a spy, or even Torril, it was something far worse. Gothwen should have realised by the smell of where they stood, but now it was too late. A half-decomposed corpse lunged towards them both, groaning through the top half of its mouth, the bottom section of the jaw seemed to have fallen off completely. Gothwen and Fillinel both dodged the being, now separated by this decomposing mess of a creature, though Filli definitely made her presence known by her screams. The creature's skin was a deep grey, fungus growing out of some parts, insects crawling over others. The head had been caved in by what looked to be a blunt weapon, the insides had been completely cleaned out and replaced with a glowing red organism. It stared at Gothwen through one milky eye, the other, like the jaw, seemed to have fallen off. It reached out at Gothwen with a skeletal hand, two of the digits were missing, two others were missing flesh. Gothwen swung her dagger, slicing off one more and temporarily dazing the attacker. They were no longer alone with the creature, a third sword joined them, and with one swift swoop completely sliced off the being's head.

Torril crouched down, examining her kill. "Dread Ghoul. I knew one was here. I could smell it." She tilted the body back and forth. "Poor sod, no idea when it got him."

The organism from inside the decapitated head began to ooze out of the cavity in the skull. It rolled along the ground for a short while. Torril stood back up, pushing Gothwen and Fillinel back as she watched it move. "We have half an hour. That thing will be going back to it's hive to lure in another puppet." She looked at Gothwen, then Fillinel, who was still in tears and shaking uncontrollably. "We need to find the Demon controlling it. Now. I hate it when things steal my kills."

Gothwen and Fillinel looked at each other, before deciding to join Torril on her hunt. She was already in an attack stance, dagger in hand just in case the Demon was nearby, as impossible as that was. Nevertheless, the trio continued, following the rolling pile of glowing red slime into the forest.

The couple walked in fear for ten minutes, following Torril hesitantly, until eventually the rolling slime brought the three to a small cave, a circular outcropping of rock which seemed to sink into the ground below them. There was a pungent smell coming from within, similar to that of the Dread Ghoul Torril had previously slain though worsened tenfold. The guiding slime cascaded down the vertical drop into the pool of black nothingness within. A faint splat could be heard a few seconds afterwards.

Torril peered over the edge. "Roughly two hundred feet. Directly down, nothing to break our falls. We'd be dead in an instant" Gothwen had the sudden urge to push her down, just to prove her point.

Gothwen outstretched her arms, before slapping her waist, sighing. "So, there's nothing we can do? Nothing at all?"

Torril crouched, twisting the bag slung over her shoulder to her front. She rummaged around in it, reaching as far in as her arms would allow, before finally pulling out a black, wrinkled object. It would have been, if not for the dents and creases, a perfect circle. "Ghoulfruit. They grow where a Ghoul's been, where the operating slime has dripped out of a crack in the possessed corpse's skull and onto the soil below, if the corpse in question is particularly, well, decomposed." Torril cupped the fruit with both hands, twisting them with enough force to crack it open, perfectly in two, impressing even Fillinel. A nauseating gas erupted from within, dissipating in the air around them. The interior of the fruit reminded Gothwen of one of the geodes she had seen on display in The Ark. It was a deep blood red, glistening in the light of the moon above them, a secret beauty born of evil and encased in a cloud of toxicity. Torril tossed the hidden treasure down the hole. Gothwen flinched as she heard the shatter of the gem-like object echo below.

"The shattering of a Ghoulfruit tells the Demon the air above is toxic. It's like a duelling glove, the gas provides the opening to which the Demon can grace our world with its presence for a few brief moments before the magics around us cleanse the air again. It can come up here and accept the combat challenge of the mortal who made it all possible." Torril turned her head to face Gothwen as she took a few steps back. Fillinel was cowering behind her, holding Gothwen's shoulders. Torril winked. "I've only ever fought a Demon twice. Don't worry."

From the darkness of the cave below them, spectral tendrils began to rise. They remained relatively close to the area where Gothwen and her companions stood, any tendril which exceeded the spiritual boundary would dissipate almost instantly into a cloud of black smoke. It became clear to Gothwen that the tendrils were not the Demon, they were instead it's means of transportation. Slowly, from the depths, a deep, red, horned humanoid appeared. The thing was being elevated out of the mouth of the cave, standing on a platform made from the intertwining vines of evil. These vines extended, creating a walkway on which the Demon could gracefully dismount its tendril elevator. It towered over Torril, at least twice her size, lifting one red, horned arm to the side. It was the arm of a body which had clearly been looked after. Black veins seemed practically ready to burst out of the blood red skin. In the clenched fist of the Demon grew more tendrils, though these twisted and contorted not into the form of a new means of transportation, but of a blade. Gothwen wondered how inky black tentacles dripping some sort of spectral goop would make an effective weapon, that was until she saw how they flattened and turned what seemed to be solid, shining like a metal, and not as though it had been writhing in the ocean for a few hours.

Torril stared into the flaming orange eyes of the Demon. The beast bore his enormous black fangs. Torril flipped her blade, holding it horizontally across her body. She continued to stare, bearing her own white fangs. They were tiny compared to those of the monster which towered over her. "So" Torril broke the haunting silence. "You accept my offer?"

Lucille lay in the skin of a deer. Torick had been using one as a bed cover for a few days now, he would change it every so often, at least until the current one started to smell. She missed the elegance of the beds she was used to, the grandeur of the halls she had become accustomed to, the sophistication of the lifestyle she had grown to love. Then she realised what her former lover had been reduced to. She realised whose fault it had been.

"You took advantage of me." Lucille stared at the stone ceiling above her. There was no chandelier, no golden swirls, no paintings of cherubs and roses. She turned her head. Torick lay beside her. "You knew the situation I was in and took advantage of me."

Torick turned to face Lucille, lying on his side. "We both needed this, Luci. That was why we both agreed to it."

Lucille sighed. She remembered how she consented. "I suppose we did. My life is full of regrets, I was sure that, when I awoke a few minutes ago, this was to be another."

Torick inched himself closer to Lucille. "I never would have done anything that you would not agree to, Sunflower." He kissed her shoulder, something he had waited far too long to do again.

A tear began to fall from Lucille's eye. "Not all of us are

given the option to decline. I consider myself lucky to have had even the slightest remnant of a family with a man such as yourself, Torick." He wiped away the tear falling from Lucille's eye. Though when she turned her head to look at him again, she saw not the eyes of the man she loved, but of the daughter she failed. "You remind me of her, Torick. She has your eyes."

"She has your heart, Sunflower. Brash, headstrong, and sometimes arrogant." He smiled, insinuating the last word of his list was a joke, though Lucille knew the truth behind it. "She is a far more extreme version of the woman you once were, Luci."

Lucille nodded in agreement. "When I was her age, I found my cause. No longer did I act in the interest of myself, but for all of Oreldas." She looked at Torick again, through the veil of his face, and into the soul of Torril. "Do you believe that if she found a purpose in life, she too could change for the better?"

Torick sighed. He rubbed his forehead as he lay on his back again. "Her mind is far gone, Lucille. I do not think she can ever return."

It was Lucille now who turned to her side, facing Torick. "Do you believe we could be a family again? Do you believe we still have the potential to raise a new child?"

Torick smiled. "Would we have spent an evening together, like this, if I did not?"

Lucille paused for a moment. "Come with me. To Rosimer. I know a clearing in the forest that is little more than a day's ride from Coryphia. We could build a house there, we could live together. Maybe grow a few vegetables, a few flowers, perhaps."

Torick's heart agreed, though his mind wandered. "I'd be run out of there too. Surely there are elves in Rosimer who are half as hostile as the humans in Marrivel."

"I would care little." Lucille felt her heart begin to beat

faster. "We would be happy, and that is all that would matter."

Torick tried to rummage around his mind for another excuse. None could present themselves. "We need to sort out this situation with Torril and Gothwen first. We cannot allow one to kill the other. Then, Sunflower, then we can live together in peace and happiness. With a new family of our own."

Lucille smiled, rolling in bliss onto her back again. "As long as we are together, Torick. To make up for lost time. To bring a new child into this world together." Lucille looked around Torick's simple cave. Her attention turned to the shelf of potions to her left, hand-crafted and nailed haphazardly above what looked to be a workbench. Specifically, her attention turned to a potion which was much older than the others. "Torick. Is that what I think it is?" Her face dropped.

Torick managed to decipher what Lucille was focused on. "That Obliterate potion? Yes. It is. I kept it, for you. So you could do the same thing the person who made it did for you."

A look of disgust washed over Lucille's face. I would never allow it. I would never allow anyone I knew to make the same mistake she did. She kept her child, I kept my child, and I would like to think the next woman after me would keep their child."

Torick attempted to calm the discomforted mage. "It is there to give someone a choice, Lucille. Not everyone has the opportunity to decide, to make the choice that you both did not, despite your circumstances."

Lucille began to seem calmer. "I suppose it is a wise choice, Torick." Her thoughts were suddenly disrupted by the ringing of bells, louder than any Lucille had ever heard.

"By the King's blade I thought we would be asleep." Torick threw himself out of the bed, clutching his ears.

"Fear not, Torick." Lucille did the same, though as she did she outstretched her arm, clenching her fist. There seemed to be some sort of spiritual resistance, though Lucille fought it with considerable strength. When her fingers finally reached her palm, and her hand snapped shut into a fist, the hourglass which was the source of the ringing shattered entirely.

"Well." Torick sighed. "There goes my last enchanted hourglass."

Lucille groaned. "What did you set it at this time for?" She yawned, it seemed the spell she had cast had drained a lot of her energy already.

Torick rubbed his head. It was taking a while for the ringing to stop for him. "At this time, the March that Torril has joined with the disguised Gothwen and Fillinel would be reaching the halfway point, while Vlastoril would be reaching his portal camp. I decided now would be a good time to prepare ourselves for what lies ahead. We need to get to Ald Rosimeris." Torick noticed Lucille was giving him a look of confusion. "This was why I planned this. I needed time to explain to you what is going on too." He paused for a moment. "Yes, it will also cover why I have been monitoring Vlastoril too."

Lucille shook the confusion out of her mind for a few minutes. "Then I will open the way to Ald Rosimeris. Though first." She fluttered her fingers before her, the loose, white shirt Torick was wearing began to change. It became a deep, blue jacket, lined with gold and made from fine silk. His trousers changed to match too. She turned her fingers to herself, causing the nightgown she was wearing to also change. It switched to a corset in a similar design to Torick's, with deep blue frills and golden laces. "Battle ready, I assume?" She thought for a second, before mentally setting the destination of a portal which swirled to life before them.

Torick grabbed the belt from the stone serving as a table beside him, sheathing the dagger which was once propped up against the bed, but now lay flat on the floor, in the holster on his waist. "Battle ready, Sunflower." Holding each other by the hand, the new couple entered what was to be, fundamentally, the largest arena in Oreldas.

Gothwen could feel her heart pounding faster than ever before. She could almost feel Fillinel's reacting similarly to the Demon towering over them. It was clear neither of them had faced such a haunting evil before. Torril, however, seemed to be in her element. She was smiling, never breaking eye contact with the beast before her, not even when a tendril lashed out at her. She simply sliced it clean off, like the head of a particularly vicious serpent.

Gothwen cautiously drew the bow from her shoulder, she too had not broken eye contact with the Demon, though clearly this was due to fear and not the thrill of the fight, as it was in Torril's case. Fillinel was still whimpering behind Gothwen, though even she knew a battle was imminent, and she would have to fight too.

"It would be my pleasure to wipe this magical scourge off the face of Oreldas." Torril began to strafe her target, walking sideways away from Gothwen and Fillinel. "You're stealing my kills. I can't allow that." Torril tilted her head. "Tell me. How many have you killed? Personally?"

A deep voice, deeper than any Gothwen had ever heard, bellowed through the air around them. "Three hundred and fifty-six." The Demon began to take a step towards Torril. The ground below it turning a dead, grey colour.

Torril stopped moving. "Impressive. It will be an honour to add your kills to my list. Once I have decapitated you and ripped out whatever is the equivalent of your heart."

The Demon seemed to begin to laugh, though it was difficult to tell, as Gothwen could not see any movement which would accompany one. Even the area of the Demon's face which constituted a mouth was nothing more than small, grey horns bending to form lips from which pointed teeth protruded. "You will make a fine addition to my collection of elven suits, girl. I will try not to cause too much damage to your beautiful little body."

With those final words, the Demon swung his tendril blade at Torril, who rolled backwards to avoid it, narrowly missing the oozing blade. Torril threw her arm in an arc in front of her, launching a multitude of tiny, poison darts from her sleeve. Two tendrils flew between her and her assailant, blocking her attack and absorbing her darts. After a few seconds, they both fell to the ground, writhing in pain before seeping into the ground below them. The Demon swung his blade again, this time in the direction of Gothwen and Fillinel. Throwing Fillinel to the ground, Gothwen managed to avoid the blade, which instead struck a tree with such force that it fell to the ground almost instantly.

Fillinel crawled on her stomach inside a hollowed-out log on Gothwen's orders, while she stood back on her feet and picked up her bow again. She drew one of the arrows from her back, placing it in the bow and aiming directly at the Demon's face, who by now was distracted by Torril again. Her athleticism was antagonising the beast, she seemed to dodge and roll away from every attack it was making. Gothwen fired the arrow, lodging it exactly where the Demon's cheekbones should have been. This did little to stop the attack of the Demon, who simply pulled the arrow from its face with its free skeletal hand. It turned to face Gothwen again, launching the arrow back at her, twice as fast as any shot Gothwen would have made herself. The aim of the Demon was perfect, if Gothwen had not have ducked at the last second, the arrow would have pierced her forehead and would have possibly continued out the back of her head. Gothwen did not see where the arrow hit the ground, though judging by Fillinel's scream which came after Gothwen ducked, it must have struck the log she was hiding in. The Demon began to float on a bed of black mist to Gothwen's location, much to the annoyance of Torril.

"Dammit Rose! I had it!" Gothwen was confused for a

second, before she realised, she was still under the influence of the potion and she was, in fact, Rose.

Gothwen flung herself over the log Fillinel was hiding in, hoping it would at least slow the Demon down. Unfortunately, it did not. Two more tendrils flew at the log, twisting around either side and lifting it high over Gothwen's head. As the Demon tilted it, Fillinel seemed to lose balance, falling while still screaming, out of the lower end and rolling back onto the ground and into the open. The Demon, who seemed to miss Fillinel roll out of the log, tossed it towards Gothwen, who spun herself behind a tree to take cover. The log landed diagonally, lodging itself between the tree Gothwen was hiding behind and the tree beside it. The Demon moved past the two trees, closer still to Gothwen who could do little but back herself up even further. Torril had mentally assessed these new surroundings and had already planned her next move.

The Demon swung its blade at Gothwen, who took a few more quick steps back. Unfortunately, these steps were not enough, as the tip of the blade sliced a thin cut along her stomach. It was not deep, though the demonic source of the blade stung worse than anything Gothwen had felt. She fell on her back, clutching her stomach, watching as the Demon lifted its blade above its head, preparing one final blow to Gothwen which would slice her clean in half. Gothwen closed her eyes, though the fall of the blade never came.

Torril ran up the log which the Demon had thrown between the two trees, launching herself off the edge and sinking her dagger into the Demon's spine. She pulled with everything she had, bending the Demon on its back, until she could feel the grass against the back of her neck. Though with Gothwen injured, Torril's plan was missing one crucial thing. Someone to sink their blade into the Demon's heart and kill it. Torril could feel the Demon resisting, releasing one of her blades to hold it in a headlock in an attempt to strangle it to death. This did not seem to work. Torril was certain this was to be her end.

What she did not anticipate, however, was the scream of an emboldened Fillinel, running with her sword in the air to where the Demon lay. She ran up the Demon's legs, closing her eyes and sinking her blade into the chest of the dying beast. The deep screams of the Demon could be heard for miles, as Fillinel continued to stab at the beast's heart. Black smoke rose from every cavity, until eventually, no sound, no movement came from the Demon. All of the tendrils, even the blade, turned to nothing more than black smoke. All that remained of the Demon was a wrinkled, charred husk, with Fillinel's blade piercing triumphantly from the chest. Fillinel fell onto her back, exhausted and in shock. She was joined shortly by Torril, who fell backwards onto a pile of fallen leaves. Gothwen did not move from where she lay already.

The three of them remained on the ground, breathless from their battle for what felt like an eternity. However, as Torril knew, it was time for them all to return to camp, before the final journey to the portal camp. Torril stood first, offering her hand to Fillinel, who reluctantly took it. With one swift pull Fillinel was on her feet. Torril moved to Gothwen, who simply looked at her as she towered over her injured body.

"You getting up? Or are we going to have to put you out of your misery?" Torril toyed with her blade. In her head she knew the option she wanted to take.

Gothwen sighed. "I suppose I should stand. Though that blade stung pretty bad. It was only a flesh wound, but it felt as though it sliced me in half."

Torril laughed. "That's a Demon blade for you. Looks like crap but hurts like a bitch." Torril outstretched her arm to Gothwen. "Come on, Rosy Rose, up you get." Gothwen hesitantly took Torril's hand. It was inhumanly cold. Fillinel grabbed Gothwen's other hand. She smiled at the warmth of Fillinel's skin.

Gothwen dusted herself off, Fillinel helped in places Gothwen could not reach. "How long do we have until the mercenaries leave?"

Torril looked up at the stars. "Roughly five minutes. If we take a shortcut, we can re-join the group just as they march off, latch ourselves on to the back end again."

Fillinel held Gothwen close, the fight had startled her to the point she was shaking uncontrollably. She sunk her face into Gothwen's shoulder. Torril had already begun walking ahead. This gave Gothwen the perfect opportunity to speak to Fillinel directly. She whispered into Fillinel's ear. "We survived, Filli. Nothing bad will ever happen to you, I promise."

Fillinel looked up at Gothwen, their eyes met properly for the first time all night. While Torril's back was turned, the couple shared a kiss. For the entirety of the journey back to the army of mercenaries, even as far as the portal camp itself, Fillinel never let go of Gothwen.

CHAPTER THIRTEEN

Battle Preparations

Lucille and Torick stood in an elegant hall larger than any Torick had set foot in for many years. The grandeur of the room was enough to make him speechless, even though some of the walls had begun to crumble, and vines from the exterior had begun to meander their way around the banisters, tumbling down the stairs which clung to the sides of the room like rapids of green. Torick did not recognise the hall, though he felt at home within the walls. He looked up, the chandelier which had once hung from the ceiling had fallen, taking a chunk of the stone with it as it fell. Various items of furniture which looked to have been part of a bedroom lay on top of what remained of the crystal lighting piece, dusty and broken beyond repair.

"Where did you bring us, Sunflower?" Torick ran his hand along the bottom of one of the banisters, taking a chunk of vines with his hand and letting them fall with grace to the cracked, stone floor.

"You can have one guess." Lucille was also taking in the view. She knew exactly where she had brought the two of them, though she decided to withhold this information. "It is somewhere in Ald Rosimeris. Far enough so that we would not be caught upon our arrival, though close enough to

Central Tower as not to have me travel too far." Lucille stopped, realising that perhaps this had given away their location.

Torick began to climb the stairs, admiring the paintings which remained. Some had fallen, others had been torn up. All of the paintings which could still be looked at were of elven women, this was clear by the pointed ears and flowing, golden hair, some of which had been tied in braids, others in pompous, elaborate hairstyles. Torick's attention turned to one painting, which, unlike all of the others still hanging upon the wall, was in pristine condition. It looked as though it had been cleaned regularly, the golden frame outlining the woman within had clearly been looked after, it shone in the dilapidated ruin of the home. Torick stroked his stubbled beard, there was a hint of familiarity with the woman in the painting.

"She has your eyes, Lucille." The same sky-blue eyes that Torick now stood beside were reflected in the painting before him. "Your hair too. She is a beautiful young lady." Torick smiled, he had begun to realise where they were.

"She was, Torick. She *was* a beautiful young lady." Lucille sighed. "You do realise where we are now, do you not?" Torick had little time to respond. "This was my home. This was what would have been *our* home. This." She stroked the face of the girl in the painting. "This was Ethril. You had never seen her in the years leading to her death. I thought perhaps you wanted to."

Torick turned to look at Lucille. Her eyes had begun to fill with tears. "You are wrong, Sunflower." He wiped away Lucille's tears. "I did see her, recently." Lucille held Torick's hand as he stroked her face. "I was at her embalming ceremony. I saw her from a distance, as you carried her body into the tree. I do admit, I myself shed a few tears as you sealed it shut behind her. I wept at the roots of her tree once you had all left. I shall never forget where it is."

Lucille's eyes began to light up. "You were there? I understand the need for discretion, though you should have told me you would be attending. We would have wept together."

Torick pulled Lucille close. "You chose a beautiful spot. The view of Heroes Hill, the sound of the stream running beside her, the light dancing on the bark of the tree she will spend all of eternity within. She would be at peace, Luci. If her spirit roams those grounds, like most are said to, she would truly be happy with the place you chose for her."

Lucille looked at the painting. "She is in so much pain. I need to help her, I need to join her again."

Torick seemed confused. "Luci? She is gone, she is in no pain, there is no need to join her." It became clear that perhaps Ethril's death had shook Lucille's mind as well as her spirit.

"Maybe it was all just a dream. I do miss her very much." Lucille held Torick tighter. "I know not if Torril deserves redemption. She is my daughter, *our* daughter, though to take her own sister away from us all is something I can never forgive her for."

"When the time comes, Sunflower, you will know how to handle her. You will know exactly the punishment she deserves for her actions of late. The deaths cannot go without consequence, if she learns that, then perhaps the fire that boils her very soul would fade ever so slightly, but enough to see reason. Enough to see that every living thing in this world does not deserve to die by her hand." Torick ran his hand through Lucille's hair again. He loved how soft it always felt, he imagined Ethril's would have felt the same. He kissed the top of her head. The distant sound of a horn could be heard through the broken walls of the Magelight Estate. We should make our way to Central Tower, I suspect Vlastoril will be there gathering his forces against King Malthus, he too will be here, or at the very least on his way. The Humans have a very long way to walk.

Lucille took one last look at the painting of Ethril. "There is still much to be done, my sweet. You will not go unavenged."

"There." Torril pointed ahead, a light in the distance signalling the end of a journey which had diminished more of the party's strength then had been planned. The final camp now lay before them, an organised mess of various siege weapon parts, separated by tents within which a handful of sleeping mercenaries lay, while others performed various workout routines. These were not, however, what grabbed the attention of the trio. At the farthest end of the camp, guarded by an almost countless number of mercenaries, stood the largest portal ever witnessed by any of the group. It was active, though sealed, a glossy shine signalling impassibility. The sun had begun to rise, the ball of flames balancing precariously on the top of the portal frame. Beyond, Gothwen recognised the ruined citadel of Ald Rosimeris, specifically the area immediately before the main gates of Central Tower. The leaves she had fallen into when the Tower had denied her entry were gone, trampled by the army which now marched around the portal itself. Gothwen now realised how the camp worked, the closer she moved to the portal, the clearer the system had become. The closest siege weapons to the towering gate would be constructed first, in fact some already were reaching the end of their assembly. Four trebuchets already stood, two either side of the portal, almost ready to be transported the few hundred miles in a matter of seconds. Gothwen, Torril, and Fillinel sat together in a tent close to the portal, one which appeared to be empty, most likely used by a group who had already passed to Ald Rosimeris.

"So, we're here. What next?" Unfortunately, being in close proximity to the camp meant Fillinel had been forced to release her grip on Gothwen, though as she spoke, she inconspicuously moved her hand on top of Gothwen's.

"I guess we wait until the next group passes through and

join them." Torril had torn a piece of fabric from the bedroll on the ground. She was using it to clean her blade, which was still dirty from their fight. "No idea how long it'll take, so get some rest. I'll wake you."

As much as Gothwen hated agreeing with a being as evil as Torril, it was a good idea. Besides, if Gothwen and Fillinel were well-rested, they would have the upper hand against an exhausted Torril, should a battle between them come soon. "I agree. Glandris? Your thoughts?"

Fillinel was still not used to being called by this name, though she eventually realised. "If you think so, then perhaps we should. I *am* exhausted, after all." Fillinel stretched, exposing a slender stomach which made Gothwen's heart skip a beat. She fell back onto one of the bedrolls, barely having time to relax before Gothwen joined her. They both turned onto their sides to face each other, smiling as they made eye contact.

"We're almost there, Sweetleaf." Realising Torril was not watching them, Gothwen began to stroke Fillinel's face. This seemed to comfort her, she bit her lip as she let out a shy smile. A movement from Torril caused an abrupt end to the couple's happiness.

"I'm going to go and find more information on this place. What these people plan on doing. Perhaps Gothwen and Fillinel are already here, they could already be beyond that portal for all I know." Torril stood herself up, examining the area around them with eyes which darted back and forth almost impossibly quick.

This, at the very least, gave Gothwen and Fillinel time to rest, together, for once. They both closed their eyes, though neither knew they would actually fall asleep.

Torril, however, began to wander. She remained cautious, though she explored with a sense of confidence, as not to arouse suspicion, of course. She was faced with countless living souls, none of which, in her perception, would provide a worthy enough opponent. They would each fall by her blade, if she would be given the opportunity. Torril toyed with her blade in her hand, pacing the length of one of the trebuchet support beams, belonging to one that had not yet been put together.

"Nobody here looks suspicious. None look as though they are not who they say they are." Torril scanned everyone who passed her in great detail, while remaining invisible to the people she was investigating. Eventually, one elven man caught her eye. He was the same man who had organised the march Torril had found herself on, she recognised him by his sap plated armour. She immediately put on a new persona.

"General. How goes the efforts? How long until the next squad is permitted through the portal?" Torril stood straight, for the first time in a long time.

"Every thirty minutes, as is standard." The General narrowed his eyes. "Though of course, you should have known that."

Torril sighed, perhaps this one needed a blade at his neck to keep him quiet. "Apologies, the march here disoriented a few of my men, they required rest, as do I." Torril was quick to respond to most situations. She thought again, she still needed information. "Any news on Darkarrow? I heard rumours she would be at Ald Rosimeris when the conflict begins."

The General raised an eyebrow. "I do hope this rumour is reliable. Your neck will be on the line if it turns out to be false. Rest assured extra security measures have been taken to ensure that the meddlesome Darkarrow and her Apostate accomplice will never reach The Count and prevent his plan from coming to fruition." The General looked towards the portal. The frame of the construct seemed to be made out of humanoid objects, intertwining and connecting to form a gargantuan arch. Some of them were glowing, it seemed to be a pattern from the bottom-left side, moving up and around the arch until the glowing hit the bottom-right side. By now, it was almost to the bottom-right, one more humanoid had begun to glow.

"That is the signal, rally more men to pass through. Take some who are well rested, then get some sleep yourself." The General left, barging his way past Torril.

Running back to where Gothwen and Fillinel lay, Torril still examined everyone exceptionally closely. They all seemed to be ordinary people, which led to Torril fearing for the worst. Pieces were beginning to form together in her head, the jigsaw which was her predicament coming together in the black depths of her mind. Her worst fears became a reality, when she returned to the tent where the so-called Glandris and Rose should have been lying. There was nobody there. Torril had been made a fool of, she would never let this go.

Gothwen and Fillinel had managed to make their way near to the front of the next group to pass into Ald Rosimeris. They needed to get as far away from Torril as possible. Once everybody was apparently in position, The General ordered the march to begin again. In rows of two, the elven mercenaries marched through the portal, which had lost its glossy shine and was now, temporarily, just an ordinary portal again. As both Gothwen and Fillinel passed through, they felt the chill of the ruined city freeze their bones once again. Gothwen had forgotten how high up they both were. The green of the forest was now replaced by the ruined browns and greys of the broken walls around them, the only essence of green coming from the moss and vines which hung from the battlements. Gothwen and Fillinel looked at each other, neither wanted to be back, though both knew why they had to be.

"As soon as the march disperses, we vanish." Gothwen looked into the fiery eyes of her partner again. "We'll be okay, Fillinel, we might not even have to use more of our potion."

Fillinel had almost forgot about their potion plan. "I suppose we have no need for it anymore. Or any potion for that matter." She smiled at Gothwen, who briefly held a look of confusion on her face.

"The Liquid Laughter." Gothwen's eyes opened wider. "I haven't drunk any for a few days!" Gothwen held Fillinel's hand. "I believe it was you, Fillinel. You're my Liquid Laughter now. The most beautiful little potion around."

Fillinel smiled at her happy lover. "You never needed it in the first place. The people around you alone should provide you with enough happiness to last a lifetime. Always remember that, Gothy." Fillinel brought Gothwen's hand to her lips, kissing it, before letting it fall again.

Gothwen sighed. "I suppose I just needed someone to soak up all my love and give some back to me." This time Gothwen lifted Fillinel's hand, kissed it, and let it fall.

By now, the marching group had begun to disperse, which Gothwen took as an opportunity to tug Fillinel away from the multitude of people around them. There was a partially hidden door in one of the corners of the fortress, ivy had obscured much of the wood. Gothwen pulled Fillinel into it.

"Alone, finally. No Torril, no mercenaries, no Count." Fillinel did not seem interested in talking. She grabbed Gothwen by the collar of her shirt, pulling her close and giving her the most passionate kiss the two had shared in a long time. It was a moment they both wanted to last forever, and for a moment, it felt like it would. That was when they both realised that neither of them were able to move, they were locked in an eternal kiss.

"I do apologise for my intrusion. I had no idea emotions such as love existed within Vlastoril's ranks. Gothwen could not turn her head to face her assailant, though judging by Fillinel's heavy breathing and increasing heartbeat, something Gothwen could feel as her hand had been frozen in possibly the worst location on Fillinel's body, the person responsible was someone Fillinel despised.

"Give me one good reason why I should not turn you both into worms and step on you while you wriggled." Gothwen found the voice familiar, though she knew it was impossible.

Fillinel let out a muffled yell, it resonated against Gothwen's lips. She tried to imitate, to get the attention of the woman who had joined them.

"Very well. I shall let you explain yourselves. Then we are going to tie you up and leave you here until somebody finds you." Gothwen felt the spell release. Her lips were no longer frozen on Fillinel's, and her hand was no longer cupping Fillinel's breast.

"Gothwen! We are Gothwen and Fillinel!" Fillinel was quick to reply, a lot quicker than Gothwen was. "I know who you are, Conjurer Magelight." Gothwen's jaw began to drop as she turned her head. "You will not force us to comply to your rules any more, the mages of Ald Rosimeris are gone, none shall restrict us!"

"Intriguing. You have the voice of the Apostate, that I can see. Though your physical appearances are not of that I would have expected. Besides, I have spent time with Miss Darkarrow myself, I know how she looks. This." She gestured an elegant finger at Gothwen. "This person is not her."

Gothwen decided now was a good enough time to speak up. "No, Lucille. It really is us. We used Perceptiplasm to infiltrate The Count's mercenaries and get here without being caught by..." Gothwen hesitated. "...Your daughter."

Lucille scoffed. "Torril is nearby? That girl failed in ending my life, I can very well guarantee that she will fail in ending yours too. There is no need for you to worry, Gothwen." Lucille waved her hand in front of Gothwen and Fillinel, the Perceptiplasm immediately began to wear off, working from the top of their heads down to their feet. "Ah, now that is better." Lucille looked at Gothwen. "How long has it been, Gothwen? A week? A little longer perhaps?" She smiled, nodding her head, before turning to Fillinel. Her smile was replaced by a solemn look of disrespect, the same one Gothwen received when the two first met. "It is about time I made your acquaintance, Apostate. As much as you may despise me, I do believe we should set aside our differences and work to eliminate this threat together."

Fillinel reluctantly agreed, though she still kept within shoulder-touching distance of Gothwen. Perhaps, as Gothwen thought, a method of showing who had the most influence over herself. In all fairness to Lucille, it was Fillinel, simply because of the connection between the two of them, which had developed over their time together.

A human male appeared from around the of the room, presumably the same corner Lucille had entered from. "Torick, Lucille's partner and father to her children, it is an honour, Miss Darkarrow."

Gothwen nodded. "So, you're the one who co-created Torril?" Gothwen smiled jokingly. "Nice work on that one."

Torick shook Gothwen's hand. "What has happened is a tragedy. These events, I hope, will pave the road for her redemption."

The two couples stood together, huddled in a circle. Lucille began to speak. "The plan is, Gothwen and Fillinel, you will travel to the Well of Abundant Magics. I will open the way for you. I am unsure how current events will lead to what I saw in my vision all those years ago, so I do believe that if you have one of your own, things will hopefully become a little clearer." Lucille looked at Fillinel. "Apostate, I will allow you to look inside the Well, though if it deems you unworthy for a vision, that is not my concern." Fillinel understood, though deep inside she knew she just wanted to see the Well of Abundant Magic for herself.

Gothwen and Fillinel looked at each other, they nodded in agreement with Lucille's plan.

"It is settled then." Lucille took a few steps back. "Torick, you shall ensure the Engines can do no harm, I shall handle Vlastoril, and you two will…" Lucille stopped moving, she froze, just like Gothwen and Fillinel had before.

"Mother dearest is not supposed to be alive." Torril stepped to the side, revealing herself from behind Lucille. Her dagger was pressed against Lucille's spine. "Mother dearest should be lying in the dirt." Torril stared directly at Gothwen. "Mother dearest shall watch as I gut her precious apprentice."

Torick stepped forward. "Torril put the dagger down."

The girl's head snapped in Torick's direction. "Stay back, old man. I don't know who you are, but I'll cut you in half if you come any closer."

Torick shook his head. "It is a sad day when your daughter no longer recognises your face."

Torril lowered her dagger slightly. "Father? You're alive?" Lucille began to feel the dagger fall further down her back.

"I am, Little One. Now please, let your mother go." Torick offered his arm to Torril, who stared longingly at the digits of her father. There was no desire for death in her eyes any more, she just wanted to be with the man who had raised her.

Unfortunately, Lucille could not see the brief sparkle which shone in Torril's eye, a glimmer of hope in a corrupted, tormented soul. As Torril reached out to touch the hand of her father, Lucille jolted her elbow back, striking Torril in the stomach. Lucille swung herself around and, while Torril clutched herself in shock, Lucille struck her down with an uppercut which sent her daughter to the ground. She turned once more to face Gothwen and Fillinel, conjuring a portal which seemed to swirl to life in a far more complex manner than any other Gothwen had ever travelled through. It seemed to show signs of electrical charge, sparks flying out of the edges as it grew.

"Quickly, you must travel to the Well, do as I have asked! Your destiny must be fulfilled!"

Lucille was, without warning, thrown to the ground.

"Pathetic. How dare you strike me down." Blood trickled down Torril's chin. Gothwen turned to Fillinel, grabbing her and pulling her through the portal. The room within was dark, they were stepping blindly into the unknown.

CHAPTER FOURTEEN
Abundant Magics

Lucille had little time to stand up before Torril was upon her. Pinning her to the ground by her throat, Torril attempted to finish the job she had started by choking her mother where she lay. Lucille stared into the whites of her eyes, bloodshot and filled with a rage Lucille had never seen before, not even in the most feared of Demons. Fortunately for Lucille, she was not alone this time. Torick came to her aid, pouncing on Torril and pulling her off his panicking lover. Torril clawed at her father, scraping his skin and leaving bleeding red marks across his arm. Luckily for him, Torril's small frame made picking her up and throwing her to the side much easier, though like a feline Torril landed perfectly on all fours, springing back to her feet and drawing her dagger.

"Leave me alone, Father. I do not wish to harm you any further than I already have."

Torick flicked his arm, Torril's claws had sunk in deep in some parts. "I will not harm you either, Little One." He looked at Lucille, who was still gathering her breath on the floor, rubbing her throat. "Leave your mother alone. Leave us." Next, he looked at the whirring portal in the corner of the room. "Leave Gothwen and Fillinel. Make a new life for yourself. An honest one. No killing, no stealing."

Torril's eyes darted to the portal. She thought for a moment. "Very well, Father. I shall." She sheathed her blade, standing upright in front of Torick. She kept her hand at the hilt of her blade, toying with the pommel. Torick seemed confused, wondering why such a ball would be of interest to her. Then, he remembered the old outlaw trick. Before he could turn and call out to Lucille, Torril had dislocated the pommel of her blade and slammed it against the ground. The entire room erupted in a cloud of smoke, obscuring Torick's vision the second he grabbed hold of Lucille's outstretched hand. He felt a shape move between his legs, rolling through before jumping to their feet and running into the grey cloud in front of him.

"Luci, close the portal!" Torick had realised Torril's plan, now Lucille had too.

Lucille outstretched her hand in the direction she believed the portal to be in. Fortunately, it was the correct direction, as was clear by the sound of the mystical gateway sealing. Before she could gather her strength, she was grabbed by her collar and dragged out of the room.

The smoke dissipated as it spread to the outside world on the opposite side of the door. This was the way Lucille and Torick had initially entered, through a door on the opposite side of Gothwen and Fillinel's entry point. Lucille looked up, into the eyes of Torick, who examined the injured woman thoroughly and with great care.

"Where is Torril?" Torick looked around, even as the smoke cleared there was no sign of his daughter. He helped Lucille to her feet, who simply brushed herself off as she stood up straight.

"She matters not. Attacking me for a second time proves her soul is beyond saving." Lucille looked into Torick's eyes. As much as he could not bear to agree, he knew Lucille spoke the truth.

"Then Gothwen cannot be saved." He paused for a

moment. "Though the destiny that you spoke of, the one you foresaw, perhaps it relies on Torril. Perhaps her black heart is the key to allowing Gothwen to fulfil her role in this battle."

Lucille's eyes lit up, as did her heart. "That thought had never crossed my mind. The person who hired Torril, they too must know of her role in Gothwen's story." Lucille placed her finger on her lips. "Though who would have such a power in Oreldas. Who would know of Gothwen's destiny?"

Torick held Lucille by her shoulders. "Sunflower, this is something we cannot control. We must let Gothwen's story come to an end."

"You may be right." Lucille picked up the hand on her shoulder, pulling Torick back towards the smoky room. "All we can do is stall Vlastoril as long as possible, and I know where he will be."

A third door, invisible to Torick though remembered by Lucille, provided the couple with easy access into the Central Tower. The purpose of this room became clear. It looked to have once been a storage room, for maintenance staff. Clearly, however, there had not been any maintenance for a long time, and the room was now bare, with holes in the walls and ceiling. Torick wondered what the city had been like before it was abandoned. Lucille knew all too well.

Lucille turned, her back facing the door, stopping Torick from entering. "If the Central Fortress is ever compromised, four portals can be opened within the Main Hall, the only portals which will allow access to the four gemstones. Their containment cells are filled with Obscurials." Lucille pinched together her thumb and index finger. "Tiny, invisible, but immensely magical objects lighter than air which reject all attempts at opening a portal at a location where even one is present. The only way in or out is through the portals which can only be opened in a specific place." Lucille smiled. "They were my discovery. I thought about why opening a portal inside a living being was not possible." She shrugged.

"Morbid I know, but my research paid off. It is all in our bloodstreams." Lucille winked at a confused Torick. It became clear that now she was simply gloating.

"Congratulations?" Torick squinted his eyes. "Should we continue or are there any other discoveries you wish to fill me in about?" He smiled, Lucille reluctantly smiled back. Her face began to turn a shade of red.

Lucille turned again, slowly and carefully opening the door slightly to provide her with a view inside. "I see him. He has already opened the four portals." She gasped, muttering what Torick presumed to be ancient insults. "He has already retrieved one of the gems." The glitter of the Ruby shone in his skeletal grasp. The portal he had left, one which shone with a deep red border, sealed itself shut with a high-pitched hissing sound. Vlastoril's deep laugh of triumph resonated through the ruined hall. It pierced Lucille's soul, a solitary tear fell from her eye.

"Torick. Head to the battlements. I noticed Vlastoril has set up his Destruction Engines there. Their power could obliterate any who get too close to the Fortress. They block our exit as well as Human advancements." Torick nodded, slipping away up the stairs leading to the Fortress Battlements. As the tear fell from Lucille's cheek, she burst open the door, presenting herself and Torick to an astonished opponent.

"Lady Magelight. I see you figured out my intentions." He shook the Ruby in his hand, taunting an already enraged Lucille. "One down, Conjurer. Can you protect the rest?"

Lucille outstretched her arm. Like her duel with Torril, the same, silver blade extended, trailed by golden dust. She flourished the blade in her hand. "I cannot let you destroy what our people have built. The natural balance in our world must not be destroyed."

Vlastoril smiled. His yellowed teeth made Lucille nauseous. "You do not see the power at our disposal, Magelight. The armies of Humans at our doorstep, those savage Akteen in the East, they can both be suppressed. We owned Nirndrelluin." Vlastoril stretched his arms to the side. "Is it so wrong to want us to return to our prior state of social bliss?"

Lucille thought for a moment. She thought about Fillinel and Gothwen. One a promising mage of incredible potential, the other a woman who despised everything Lucille stood for. All because of the limitations the mages of Ald Rosimeris, a city now nothing more than a ruin, a monument of a bygone era, had forced on lower mages. It was for their own safety, or so Lucille had thought. Vlastoril, like Lucille, had extended his own blade, a summoned sword of pure gold. This helped her snap out of her deep thought. It seemed the two were ready to fight. Lucille lunged at Vlastoril. Her emotions fired up by his plan, as well as the sight of the room around them, the ruins of the city she once loved. She swung her blade, Vlastoril moved to defend. As their blades crossed, sparks of white-hot fire flew into the air. Lucille felt the burning heat. It would not stop her.

Gothwen and Fillinel had fallen on top of each other as they entered the portal. There was no light anywhere, apart from around the edges of the portal they had come through. Fillinel patted Gothwen's arm until she found her hand, before wrapping her fingers between Gothwen's and holding it tight. Fillinel's hand felt cold, Gothwen could feel her fear.

"Is this where The Well is, Gothwen?" Fillinel spoke in a hushed whisper. She grabbed onto Gothwen's arm with her hand which wasn't already holding her tight.

"Lucille opened the portal, so I suppose it is." Gothwen took one step forward, the second her boot heel hit the ground, the entire room came to life. Braziers of blue flames lit up like a tidal wave down the corridor ahead of them, which was built so high even this new light couldn't reach the top. At the end of the hall was a circular room, where the last braziers met and burst into life. Something was glowing now, too. Something in the ground at the centre of the circular room. "It must be that, over there."

Fillinel never let go of Gothwen as they made their way down the corridor. There was no sound, apart from the flicker of the flames and the sound of their boots on the stone floor. "I don't like this, my love. Please, be careful." Fillinel's whispers tickled Gothwen's neck, her breaths as sensual as ever. It seemed that, even faced with the unknown, Gothwen was still deeply in love with this little elf, and nothing would ever distract her from her emotions.

Gothwen smirked. "You're hot when you're scared, Fillinel." Unfortunately, Fillinel did not share Gothwen's humour.

They eventually came to the circular room. Just like the corridor, it soared upwards, so far that the light could not find the end. They stood on a ledge, overlooking one of the most beautiful sights Gothwen had ever seen. It was The Well of Abundant Magics. Gothwen could see where the name came from. The well had the impression that it held a liquid. Blue streaks of light danced among what looked like glowing flames. Every so often, the Well would attempt to reach out at the pair with glowing, blue tendrils, dissipating when they moved so far they severed from the body of the Well. On the far side of the Well was a cage, attached to a chained pulley system. Gothwen came to the conclusion that was what the mages used to allow new members of The Council to have their visions. The thought of Lucille being strapped inside it almost made her sick.

Gothwen was shocked, Fillinel shared her feelings. She shared them to the extent she felt confident enough to release Gothwen from her loving grip. "This is it, my love. This is The Well. It's the most beautiful thing I have ever seen." She turned to Gothwen. "Other than you of course."

Gothwen barely had the ability to mutter out a "likewise" to counter Fillinel. She was hypnotised by what the Well was doing to her mind. It was then she began to have a vision of her own. "Filli. The Well is trying to show me something." Gothwen knelt down, the vision became clearer.

Fillinel joined her lover. "What is it? What do you see?"

"I see... Myself. Living in a house. I'm holding you in my arms. We have two children. A human daughter and an elven son. We're... Happy." A tear fell from Gothwen's eye, into the Well. Somehow, the dancing flames rippled, changing colours where they had come into contact with the salty liquid. "We grow old together, we die together, we are embalmed in the same tree, high on the top of Heroes Hill in Oakenheim."

Fillinel swung her arm around Gothwen, who leaned against her. "The only life I would ever want." Fillinel watched the Well, though no visions came to her. "Gothwen, why can't I see a vision? Do I have to do something? Is it because our future is the same, together?"

Gothwen frowned. "It should just come to you." She could see the hopefulness in Fillinel's eyes fade as it became clear no visions were coming.

"What if I have no future, Gothwen?" Fillinel grew fearful.

"If you had no future then you wouldn't be in my vision either." Gothwen reassured her sniffling companion.

A new voice echoed through the empty halls. "Neither of you will have a future now that I have cornered you."

Gothwen and Fillinel turned around to face the source of the voice. Torril stood, dagger in hand, eyeing up Gothwen as though she was a slab of succulent meat. "Finally, after so long, I have the perfect opportunity to end you *and* the mages once and for all."

"Torril. How did Lucille let you past her?" She signalled for Fillinel to stand behind her.

"Mother became a little... Preoccupied." Torril smiled, bearing her fangs. She began to edge closer to Gothwen and the trembling Fillinel standing behind her.

"Keep your distance, murderer. Tell me who sent you, so I can send them my regards." Gothwen wanted to protect Fillinel, making herself look tougher to make her swoon.

Torril shrugged. "Can't. She told me I'd be paid half if I did, and believe me, she's paying me a *lot* to silence you. It's worth every coin." Torril began to use her dagger as a pointer. "She told me who you are. You're supposed to be a Majless. A girl born completely incapable of using magic. You're supposed to be an outcast, like I was."

Gothwen took a step forward. "You're nothing, Torril. You never were, and you never will be. Lucille was right to abandon you. I'm so much better than you, in every way possible. We were right under your pathetic little nose and you never realised."

Her words threw Torril into a rage. "You were Glandris and Rose. Yes, you tricked me. It was only when I returned to the tent I left you in at the portal camp did it all begin to make sense. Two companions, making out and touching each other up behind my back." Torril frowned, a deathly rage filled her eyes. "How dare you toy with me, Worms!" She screamed a hoarse battle roar, tossing her dagger directly at Gothwen's chest. Gothwen closed her eyes, knowing this was her destiny. For a brief moment, she knew it would all end here. It wasn't until she heard Fillinel's screams and felt her hands push her to the side did Gothwen open them again. She lost her balance, falling onto the stone beside her. Fillinel, however, took the full force of Torril's dagger, thrown in the perfect position to land with the blade lodged in the middle of her chest. The stricken elf stumbled; her legs weakened. She reached out to Gothwen, who, in the brief moment she had, reached out too, to touch her hand one more time. The entire world felt as though it was moving in slow motion, until the moment the tip of Fillinel's finger brushed Gothwen's, and their eyes met for one last time. The beautiful, flaming amber eyes Gothwen had stared into all this time now looked tired, dying, apologising without the use of words. Then, the world returned to normal speed, and she fell back into the Well behind her. Gothwen crawled as fast as she could to the edge of the ledge, observing in horror as the woman she loved fell into the blue flames below, her body completely disintegrating as it made contact with the dancing fires. Gothwen, who was still leaning over the ledge, collapsed. Her head hit the stone floor, and she began to weep. She called Fillinel's name into the flames, reaching with her hand down, deep into the Well. It was unbearably hot, but she still thought her love could return. She knew the pain of the heat was a small price to pay to have her lover back by her side, though Fillinel never came back.

Torril sighed. "Piffle. How am I going to get that dagger back now?"

This complete disregard for her actions made Gothwen's blood boil. She stood herself up, turning to face her lover's murderer. She felt a surge of energy build up inside her, the electrical pulses from her forehead growing stronger and more powerful. She held out her hand, her fingers beginning to outstretch and grow longer, turning green as they spread. Her hands were becoming indestructible vines, a force of nature none would dare toy with. She pointed her vine fingers at Torril, wrapping them around her, holding her tight. As her hands grew, the sense of fear in Gothwen's face turned to rage, she began to realise she had the power to crush anyone who stood in her way. Her first target was Torril. She raised her hand, lifting Torril into the dark of the room, before throwing her through one of the pillars. In a cloud of dust and stone, the hired assassin had been incapacitated. Gothwen released her grip, allowing Torril to fall to the ground, seemingly asleep. Gothwen finally had time to mourn alone.

Standing at the edge of the Well again, Gothwen looked back into the deep blue flames. "I needed you, Filli. More than anything in this world." Another tear fell, this time ripples of black formed. Another vision began to appear. This one was as though Gothwen was looking into a mirror, it was exactly what was happening. Eventually, however, Gothwen jumped, and fell into the Well. That was where the vision ended.

Wiping a tear away with her sleeve, Gothwen took a deep breath. "Then that's what I'll do. My future was with Fillinel, without her it seems I don't have one." She closed her eyes, leaning forwards, not stopping until she had completely lost her balance and fell into the Well. The flames engulfed her entirely, her final sensation was the scouring heat of the fires. This too must have been Fillinel's last feeling. Gothwen realised how afraid she would have been. The entire world around her fell silent, until she could not even feel her own heartbeat.

Vlastoril narrowly missed Lucille. His blade instead striking the stone pillar beside them. Lucille moved to a defensive stance, moving backwards on an invisible line, one foot behind the other. She was not fighting her rage-filled daughter, this battle was one she needed to win. She blocked every attack with a horizontal twist of her blade. There was little time for her to tie up her hair, this made her fight increasingly difficult.

Eventually, a flaw in Vlastoril's stance led to an opening. One Lucille took the second she realised it. Keeping to her stance, gripping her blade in her right hand, she moved to attack. She swung her blade at Vlastoril, spinning on her heels after various strikes. Vlastoril managed to block every attack. It seemed neither of them were getting anywhere.

"Combat is futile, Magelight. You cannot succeed. With one gem, I have already won." Vlastoril stared at Lucille through dead eyes.

"You will never succeed, for as long as I shall live these

gems will be protected." The two crossed blades again, sparks flying as they attempted to push their blades towards each other.

Torick had been watching the fight from various gaps in the battlements. The Engines, while Vlastoril's forces had been gathering, were mostly unmanned, making it far easier to remove the wands. Now, he believed, it was time for him to re-join Lucille. He ran as quick as he could back down the stairs and into the hall where Lucille and Vlastoril fought. He reached into his pocket, taking out another vial of Lucille's blood. He hastily drank it, feeling the life essence of his lover burning through him. He held out his arm, a blade, much like Lucille's, appeared from his hand. He ran at Vlastoril, keeping the sound of his footsteps to a minimum.

Vlastoril only heard Torick at the last second, though it was long enough to swing his blade behind him and block Torick's attack. He now found himself outnumbered. "Two against one? This will still prove to be easy." He pushed Torick back with his blade, striking at Lucille again before switching, knocking back Lucille and striking Torick. This continued for a while, Vlastoril seemingly getting nowhere with his collection of the gems. Neither Lucille nor Torick, however had seen Vlastoril's servant enter the chamber of the Diamond.

"Count Vlastoril! I have…" The servant's sentence was cut off. Vlastoril turned.

"You fool! Throw me the Diamond, quickly!" He threw back Lucille again, striking Torick with a backhanded slap which sent him to the ground. He held out his arm.

"Count. What's happening?" The servant's movements had been slowed.

"Toss me the gem, boy!" The Count had become more forceful.

The servant threw the gem, which was caught by Vlastoril. "The chamber is trapped, foolish boy. Those who entered the chamber of The Diamond of The Bracing Winds would find their bodies turning into one thing which would forever remain unaffected by the winds. They would turn to stone."

This was, evidently true. The servant's body had begun to turn a greyish colour, originating from the ground up, most likely the source of the trap.

Vlastoril turned away, waving his hand. The portal sealed shut behind the begging boy as the trap consumed his body.

The Diamond attached itself to the crown on Vlastoril's forehead, alongside the ruby.

Lucille stood herself up again, trying not to think of what she had just witnessed. "Two down, Magelight. Two remain." A breeze blew through the holes in the wall. "I suppose I should test this gemstone." The breeze turned into a gust powerful enough to knock Lucille back to the ground. "Perfect." Vlastoril's laugh seemed to echo through the breeze.

The Count's attention now turned to the chamber containing the Sapphire of The Unbridled Maelstrom. The winds made Lucille and Torick unable to stand. "The trap here is simple to avoid. The second the gem is removed; the entire room fills with an untameable wave swallowing everything. The trick..." He flicked his wrist towards the portal. A gust of wind knocked the Sapphire to Vlastoril's feet. "The trick is to seal it just as the gemstone is moved." As he predicted, the entire chamber filled with water. As Vlastoril sealed the portal, a tidal wave managed to burst through, soaking the floor of the hall.

Vlastoril turned to Lucille and Torick. He tossed the Sapphire in his hand. "Three collected." Both Torick and Lucille threw themselves towards The Count. The battle now depended on them.

CHAPTER FIFTEEN
Darkarrow's Destiny

Gothwen's eyes opened. She took a deep breath in, coughing and choking from the lack of air beforehand. She lay on the ground, writhing like a fish out of water until she finally regained her ability to breathe normally. She rolled over, onto her stomach, before pushing herself onto her hands and knees. The edges of her sleeves were torn and blackened, burned at the edges and smelling of smoke. Tears were falling down her face, causing her eyeliner to run, tracing black marks which followed the beads of salty water. She tilted her head upwards, looking at what was directly in front of her. She was no longer in Ald Rosimeris, before her was a castle, the largest she had ever seen before. The white stone almost burned her eyes as each brick shone in the sunlight, the red, pointed spires rose higher than some of the tallest trees in Coryphia, and, as Gothwen's gaze met ground level, she began to make out what seemed to be one of the largest beds of roses in all of Oreldas. The specks of red were dotted all around the base of the castle. In the areas of grass which sloped downwards into what Gothwen expected to be a moat, a stagnant river of flowers flowed. The moat itself was devoid of water, it too was also filled with roses, not a blade of grass could be seen. This, as Gothwen thought, must be Rose

Castle, the seat of power for the Elven people, built upon elven soil located on the outskirts of Marrivel, the city of Humans. It was a sight she had only ever seen within the pages of a book.

Gothwen managed to stand herself up. There were a few aches and pains in various parts of her body, causing her to think that maybe she had fallen from a few feet in the air before waking up. She clutched her stomach with one arm, she had begun to feel a stinging pain. She lifted her shirt, only to find no fresh wound other than the slash of the Demon's blade the night before, sullying her toned torso. She began to walk forwards, every step unlocking a brief but severe pain in her legs. She looked around. For a castle which served as the primary residence for the Elven Queen, there was a significant lack of guardsmen. It felt as though the entire castle had been deserted.

The clicking of her boots against the ground was the only noise being made by a living being. The sway of the trees surrounding the castle and the sound of the breeze in Gothwen's ears provided the soundtrack to her mysterious walk. Eventually, she reached the main door. There was still no sign of any guards. She reached out, placing the palm of her hand against the arching wooden door. Initially, the door felt as though it would burn her hand, though peculiarly, it cooled, to the standard temperature expected of a common door. There was a quiet click, and the door seemed to unlock, allowing Gothwen to push it open. For a door of this considerable size, it was remarkably easy to push aside.

The first room Gothwen came across was, as to be expected, the entry hall. There were paintings hung at equidistant intervals along the side walls, a grand staircase layered in red carpet, a crystal chandelier which hung from the ceiling, frozen in place. Gothwen called out. There was no response. She looked at the paintings, they were of men and women not that different from herself. Their emerald eyes all seemed to follow her as she stepped towards the staircase, the piercing looks of privilege and status seemingly belittling the poor elf.

Gothwen gripped the shining marble banister with one dirt covered, slightly bloodied hand. It felt wrong for her to dirty such an elegantly designed object, though in her current state it seemed wise to use whatever possible for balance. Gothwen had climbed halfway up the staircase when she heard the door at the top open, slowly, creaking as though it was trying to get her attention. This, she thought, must be where she was supposed to go.

The door at the top of the stairs was made of the same, deep brown wood of the first door she had opened. This one, however, was engraved with various images and patterns. In the centre, split in two, towered an oak tree, some of the leaves curling and flowing in a stagnant breeze. Gothwen squeezed through the small opening, she did not want to open it any further, especially considering how hot the main door initially was, she did not want to take the chance that this one would actually burn her, leaving a fiery red imprint of half a tree on her back.

The opposite side of the door held a similar basic design to the main hall. The same gleaming white walls holding paintings of elves whose emerald gazes still followed Gothwen wherever she walked. The crimson carpet which had trailed up the staircase from the main door continued into this new room, a room that Gothwen had come to realise was some form of throne room. The room was mostly empty, rising at least two levels, as was evident by the two levels of balconies on either side of the walls.

Gothwen's gaze, however, was on the throne at the farthest end of the hall. There was a woman sitting within it. Her hair cascaded down her head and, as Gothwen guessed, fell as far down as the bottom of her back. Two braids hung down her front, like golden ropes holding her in place, made clearer by the shining white dress she wore. The woman stood, elegantly sauntering down the steps upon which her throne sat. Gothwen could see two slits in her dress, one either side of her legs, exposing her skin as far up as her waist. Her eyes shone in Gothwen's direction, the same emerald green gaze Gothwen returned.

Before Gothwen knew it, the woman was directly in front of her, she had become entranced by the seductive nature of her walk. The woman spoke, a tone hushed and smooth, a voice so soft it made Gothwen smile. "It has been so long." The woman reached out to Gothwen, cupping her cheeks with both her hands. "I suppose you do not remember me, nor do you remember who you are?"

Gothwen stared into the woman's eyes. Her hands felt so soft, though there was a hint of familiarity within her. "I know who you are, Queen Aastere, but I'm sure I'd remember a place like this, and a woman like you if I had been here before."

The woman smiled. Releasing her grip on Gothwen's face. "Ah yes, that is understandable. You were very young, after all."

Gothwen's eyes narrowed. The room had suddenly gotten much colder. "Very young? What do you mean?"

Smiling, the woman continued. "My dear Aastarinwe, you are my daughter." A shining layer of tears began to form in Aastere's eyes. "I guess this was something you kept from her." Gothwen realised Aastere was no longer looking at her, but beyond her. She turned around, to where Elaina stood.

"I did what I had to, ma'am. For her own safety, and your own. If less reputable forces found the truth, they would have hunted her down. I had grown too attached to her."

Gothwen knew Elaina had survived the attempt on her life, the rose in her room was a mark of her safety. It was Elaina's idea. If something was to ever happen to either of them, they would place a rose inside the other's bedroom, as a symbol that they were, in fact, alive, no matter the odds against them. Gothwen now knew why this rose was important.

Aastere sighed. "So, what name does my daughter go by now, then?"

Gothwen had little time to answer for herself before Elaina had replied. "The caravan you had her delivered on was attacked. I could not reach it in time to save the owners, but I was able to save your child. I named her after the young couple. I named her Gothwen."

Aastere looked at her daughter. "Gothwen." She smiled. "It suits you better than Princess Aastarinwe."

Gothwen shivered. "If you don't mind, I'd like to keep the name Gothwen. I don't suit the role of Princess."

Elaina took a step forward. "I am afraid public life has altered her personality, my Queen. I know not if she would ever make a successful monarch."

Aastere sighed. "You still have the Emerald, I see. I suppose every cloud has a silver lining."

The mention of the gemstone in her circlet was enough to cause another electrical pulse which pierced her forehead. "Is it supposed to create so much static? It keeps zapping me." She rubbed her head underneath her circlet.

Aastere's face dropped. "By the gemstones, no. It's bonding to you." She clearly began to become increasingly panicked. "I knew giving you one of the gems was dangerous. I never should have done that. Deep down I knew this would happen." She leaned forwards, holding Gothwen tight. "I am so sorry, my child."

Gothwen began to realise what the gemstone in her circlet was. "Are you telling me that all this time I've been walking around with the Emerald of Natural Balance on my forehead?"

She could feel Aastere nodding against her neck. "I did not know it would do this to you, Aastarinwe."

"I suppose it explains why vines grew out of my hands

earlier." This seemed to cause Aastere to pull herself away from her daughter.

"Vines? Were they dangerous?" Her eyes had opened wider than usual.

Gothwen nodded. "I knocked out an assassin that had come to kill me."

"Ah." Aastere laughed an embarrassed laugh. "Torril. You met her?"

Gothwen stared at her mother. "I did. She killed the woman I loved."

Aastere's smile left her face. "I had no idea she would do that. I sent her to find you. I have been tracking her movements. I did not expect her to actually try to kill you. I told her there was an elf out there like her, an outcast. I wanted you found and brought to me, nothing more."

Gothwen could barely look at Aastere. "You picked the right assassin for a Search and Retrieve job."

"I deeply apologise, my dear." Aastere held a sincere tone. It seemed she meant it.

Gothwen shook her head. "Don't worry, I don't blame you. Well, not entirely. I understand the underworld of assassins and mercenaries can be confusing to a woman of your... Status."

Aastere looked to the ground. "Her mother. Lucille. You blame her, do you not?" She shook her head. "I never wanted her to live a life of regret. When I was with child, carrying you around inside me, I brewed myself a potion. An Obliterate Potion. If I drank it, the life inside me would cease to be. It was something many of the female mages of Ald Rosimeris did, their careers often came before their families. I know many lives which should have been, reduced to little more than breath on the wind. However, I did not drink it. Instead, I left it for Lucille, to give her the same choice I gave myself."

Gothwen folded her arms. "You were going to Obliterate

me?"

"You do not know the whole truth, Aastarinwe." Aastere attempted to console her daughter, though Gothwen merely swatted away the hand which moved towards her shoulder. "The means for your conception were not exactly... Consensual." Aastere hesitated. Gothwen grew less hostile towards her mother.

Gothwen moved heavy footed towards an open bottle of wine on a side table. She picked it up, leaning against the wall, emptying most of the contents into her mouth.

"I did not know what to do. I was unsure if I was ready for a child. Though I remained on the same course and followed it through to the end."

Gothwen wiped her mouth with her sleeve. "I only have one question, Aastere. Who was my father?"

The entire mountain shook with enough force to throw Lucille to the ground. Above her, the stone spires which made up most of the Capital building began to crumble, falling onto the arena around her. The bells in the central tower rung louder than ever before, before even they succumbed to the collapse themselves. They signalled the start of the battle, a battle which was raging throughout all of Ald Rosimeris. Lucille still stood, with Torick at her back, watching with a dagger-like stare at The Count in front of her. He stood, undisrupted by the collapsing building around them, wielding his golden blade pointed at Lucille. One portal remained open. The portal to The Emerald of Natural Balance.

"One remains, Magelight. It is only fitting that I cut you down before I steal the gem you swore to defend with your life." The portal began to move, gliding with elegance along the ground between them, towards the villainous leader.

Lucille yelled back. "You will never succeed, Vlastoril. One man cannot hold the power of all four gems. It will tear you apart."

Vlastoril's voice echoed through the hall. "Only a weak-bodied fool would be torn apart by the power these gems hold. Elves made them, another elf can handle them."

With little option remaining, Lucille threw herself at The Count, her silver blade leaving a spectral trail in its path. Realising her plan, The Count simply waved his fingers in Lucille's direction, causing her to be thrown several feet into the air and directly into one of the fallen chunks of spire. Torick ran to his fallen ally, luckily, she was still alive, scratched and bruised but barely harmed. "You forget, Magelight. I control every aspect of this world apart from its greenery. The skies, the winds, the seas, they all answer to me!" With the mage no longer a threat, he began his collection of the final gemstone, The Emerald.

Torick helped his wounded love to her feet, though the couple could do nothing but watch. The Count had already stepped through the portal, sealing it shut behind him, turning the portal into a glossy, window-like apparition. The power of three gemstones had severely altered his motor functions. The power coursing through him rendering his ability to simply reach out and grab the final stone a challenge. Eventually, however, he did manage to wrap his skeletal fingers around it.

Lucille screamed in horror as the final gem was placed in the Count's Crown. Though she did not anticipate the explosion which followed. The Count was thrown back, shattering his own sealed portal and landing on his back at Lucille and Torick's feet, the Emerald seemingly vanishing from its position on his forehead, leaving little more than a charred mark. She released herself from Torick's grasp, sprinting towards the now open portal. She peered inwards, scanning the broken shards on the ground. She reached in, picked one up, and inspected it closely.

She turned to Torick, who had not moved from his position, now watching over The Count. "It is glass. The Emerald was a fake, seemingly designed to self-destruct on contact."

Torick looked in confusion at Lucille. "Then what happened to the real Emerald?"

Lucille's faced dropped. Like a jigsaw puzzle, all the pieces were coming together in her mind. "Aastere."

"The Queen? What does she have to do with this?" Torick stared at the incapacitated Count. Before he could look back at Lucille, he found himself falling through the floor. Vlastoril, who had simply been pretending to lie incapacitated, had opened a portal directly below himself, allowing him to fall through and land on his feet on the opposite side. Torick, however, completely lost his balance.

"Aastere has the final gemstone then? I suppose it is time to pay her a visit." Vlastoril brushed himself off with his bony hands, picking up his golden blade once more.

"That is not necessary, Vlastoril." Aastere had swung open the doors to the main hall, a beaten-up Gothwen and battle-ready Elaina behind her.

The Count held out his arms to his Queen. "At last, we meet. I have heard promising things about you. Things involving the whereabouts of the Emerald?"

Gothwen felt another electrical sting at her forehead. Aastere looked around the room. "I do so believe it is right here, Vlastoril. Though it can only be seen by those worthy of its presence."

The Count's face dropped. "Of course, I am worthy. Gaze upon my forehead, there lies the remaining three gems. Am I not worthy enough to hold three? Why should one more elude me?"

Gothwen stepped forward. "You are not worthy to hold any gemstone, father." Gothwen felt the eyes of the entire room fall upon her. Aastere sighed.

Vlastoril burned a gaze of shock into Gothwen's own eyes. "Impossible. I would remember if I fathered a child."

Aastere moved in front of Gothwen. "What about one born of evil? One born from a night of unlawfulness?"

Vlastoril swallowed. He had become agitated. "That never happened. There is no evidence of this. We had never even met!"

Aastere grabbed Gothwen's arm, dragging her between the two of them. "Here. Here is your evidence. Your daughter. Our daughter."

Gothwen now realised her hatred of this man was even more justified. Not only was he a man twisted by evil intention, but an accidental father who had used her mother.

Lucille began to show signs of discomfort. She clutched her throat, falling to her knees at Torick's side. Vlastoril's gaze pierced Aastere. She realised what was happening. "Release her, Vlastoril. She is an innocent in this." Vlastoril persevered, continuing to block Lucille's ability to breathe through the alteration of the air around her. He was using the Diamond to create a vacuum within which only Lucille's head resided.

"She is no more an innocent than I am. Leave this place, take your 'accident' with you." Vlastoril glared at Gothwen. "Give me the Emerald, and the Mage will live."

The pulses in Gothwen's forehead worsened. Her breathing became heavier. She could take no more. She was not an accident. She refused to accept it. Gothwen screamed. The entire room shook with the power of her voice. Every standing being was thrown to the ground, unconscious. The windows shattered, pillars fell, and every door was thrown from its hinges. Gothwen stood for a moment, examining the damage she had made. She too then fell to the ground, unconscious with the rest of the group.

Gothwen awoke, as though from a deep sleep. Aastere towered over her, her eyes staring into Gothwen's. She had no idea how long Aastere had been watching over her. Gothwen looked around. The dust had barely settled, and the room seemed to be a lot more damaged than before. Aastere placed her hands upon her waist.

"So, the Emerald really has bonded to you then. You need to learn how to control it." She outstretched her arm. Gothwen, weakened by the blast that came from her own head, reluctantly took it. "Though I suppose there are more important tasks at hand. Another time, perhaps."

"I don't know what happened, Aastere. I just couldn't take any more. Before I knew it, I was lying on the floor, unable to move. My eyes were closed, they wouldn't open." Gothwen was clearly shaken by her experience.

Aastere looked back at Lucille and Torick, then to Vlastoril, who all lay unconscious around the hall. "This whole thing needs to end, now." A long stick of wood extended from her sleeve, she caught it perfectly by the handle. She offered the stick to Gothwen, who examined it closely. She recognised the design. The black leather handle, tied by silver string and lined at either end by grey fur, the glass pommel holding an emerald, suspended in glass, the curvature of the wand itself. It was Lucille's wand.

"This was given to me by one of my agents. They oversaw the fight between Lucille and her daughter, and they retrieved this for me afterwards. I know what Lucille saw in The Well, I saw it too. I know this is when and where it happens." Aastere wrapped her slender hand around Gothwen's, as her daughter gripped the wand's handle. "It is time, Aastarinwe of House Sibbil, for you to fulfil your destiny."

Gothwen looked at her mother. "Darkarrow. Gothwen. Darkarrow. I do not accept any pompous titles or elegant estates. I'm a nobody. I always have been, I always will be. What I do, I do for the good of our People, not for pride or honour among a family I never knew."

Aastere looked to the ground. She solemnly nodded. "So be it, Gothwen. I accept the path you take. Please, nevertheless, just end the battle raging on the other side of those walls, bring peace to our island before it erupts in war."

Aastere released her grip on Gothwen's hand. The courageous young elf turned, facing the main door which seemed to have withstood the full force of Gothwen's blast. She took a few steps towards it. Before she could reach it, however, the door swung open. For the first time in as long as she could remember, an enchanted door accepted Gothwen. This was the first step, she thought, in her path to social acceptance.

The sound of the door caused Lucille to stir. It was a familiar sound. It filled her mind with dread and caused her heart to race. She turned her head to face the door. Gothwen stood, exactly as the vision predicted, bloodied and broken, her clothes torn, grasping Lucille's wand, staring out into the flaming ruins of Ald Rosimeris. Gothwen turned, examining the ruins and bodies around her. The battlefield. Where all of Lucille's allies had fallen. Outside the door, beyond the walls of the fortress, Gothwen could hear the sound of blades clashing and screaming soldiers. She could see the smoke rising from burning buildings, the stray fireballs escaping from the hands of mages and disappearing into the clouds above. The smell of smoke mixed with blood and burning flesh stung her nostrils and made her eyes water. She needed to end this.

Gothwen aimed Lucille's wand at the fortress gate, a towering metal gate sealed shut by Vlastoril. In truth, she had no idea how to operate the wand, or if it would even work for her and not the golden-haired mage. She had no idea what spell she was casting, but she felt a tremor underneath the ground where she stood. Before her, a gargantuan vine burst from the ground, penetrating the gate and tearing the metal door completely from its hinges, before disappearing in a cloud of brown, red, and golden leaves. Gothwen's forehead stung once again.

The main street greeted Gothwen with open but broken

arms. The battle had raged here recently, most of the building which had stood before, when Gothwen and Fillinel had explored the city together, were little more than piles of rubble. Corpses were strewn across the road, some crushed by large chunks of rubble or entire buildings, which looked to have been brought down by the skill of mages, or expertly placed explosive arrows at a building's weak point. Gothwen could see flames in the distance, the source of what she assumed to be the smell of burning flesh.

A squadron of human soldiers charged at Gothwen. They were hiding behind what was left of the armoury. They were scared, that much was clear, the looks on their faces gave it all away. This was to be expected, most humans feared the magical capabilities of Elves. Gothwen closed her eyes and outstretched the wand again. The same vines sprung from the ground, knocking the soldiers off-balance. Before they could hit the ground, the vines grabbed them each, all five of them, by a leg, or an arm, forcing them into the air and causing them to hang precariously from a newly-formed vine arch. They were unharmed, in shock if anything. One of them had passed out by the time Gothwen opened her eyes again. She yelled an apology, before continuing down the road.

The main battle seemed to be raging in the Gardens to the West, where most of the High Mage Estates stood, and where the largest open space could provide the largest open battle. It took Gothwen a few minutes of sneaking and climbing to reach the gardens, she had no desire to lift any more soldiers off the ground and onto magical vines. Gothwen climbed one of the buildings on the edge of the gardens. It looked to be a huge forest, surrounded by grassy plains and a river running diagonally through it. At least, this was what seemed to be there, before the battle had destroyed most of the trees, turned the grass a deep brown, and left the water running in the river no more. To the right of the gardens were the Emerald and Diamond estates, these included the Magelight Estate, from which the Human flag of Marrivel hung, the outstretched eagle adorning a shield of gold and red watching over the battlefield with ever open eyes. It slapped the walls of Lucille's home as it flapped in the breeze.

Gothwen hopped down from the roof of one of the Estates, down a convenient pile of rubble which provided her with a haphazard staircase to ground level. The sound of clashing blades and ferocious spells became clearer. Gothwen needed to act quickly, the more clashes she heard, the more lives would be lost. Gothwen took a deep breath, charging headfirst into the clouds of smoke ahead of her. She was not alone anymore, soldiers battled, and mages threw fireballs all around her, though without Fillinel she had never felt more isolated. None of them seemed to mind Gothwen, it was as though she was invisible to the battle around her. Those who did see her saw she was unarmed, unprotected. Any blade which did end up being swung in her direction was swatted away by a serpentine vine which would spring from the ground and vanish in another cloud of leaves.

Gothwen continued to run until she found herself in what she deemed to be the closest to the centre of the Gardens as was possible. She had been here before with Fillinel, after Lucille had told her of the vision which Gothwen now knew to be this moment. A decorative pile of boulders stood before her, they were climbable, which helped greatly. This, she believed, would be where the battle ended.

Gothwen tried to remember what had caused the earlier blast which incapacitated everyone nearby, including herself. She believed this was what she needed to do to stop the battle, to allow those fighting to see the truth and come together again. She closed her eyes, attempting to tap into the passion in her heart which would create a shock-wave a hundred times stronger. Countless thoughts tumbled through her mind, but one remained prominent among them all; her memory of Fillinel.

Gothwen lifted the wand above her head, opening her teary eyes and screaming louder than she had ever screamed in her life. Her throat began to sting, though somehow, despite taking no breaths, she continued. The ground began to shake, all of the soldiers on the ground stopped to look up at the emotional girl. A forest of vines sprung up from the ground, penetrating The Count's organic wooden soldiers. The orange sap which burned within them turned a leaf-green, before they all seemed to fall asleep. The human and elven fighters too all seemed to fall to the ground, unconscious as though Gothwen's scream had broken their minds.

Completely out of breath, Gothwen's weak body fell. She hit the boulder below the one she was stood atop, then the boulder after that, before finally landing on the dying grass.

CHAPTER SIXTEEN

Dealing with The Darkness

Lucille stared at the unconscious body of her daughter. Torick shook his head in disbelief. Aastere muttered under her breath how this was all her fault. Elaina simply folded her arms. Torril's eyes opened, she sighed, knowing this was where her journey would end.

"You've got me, Mother. I can't move, there's chunks of mountain on my legs." Torril looked down, one of the pillars Gothwen had thrown her though had, in fact, trapped her legs. "What are you going to do now? Have me put down? Replace me with your little green-eyed puppy that does nothing but hump your leg all day?"

Lucille placed her hands on her hips. "I have half a mind to leave you here to rot you murderous worm."

"Mother! Language! There are children present!" Torril held a look of shock, one which was not shared by the remaining four standing around her. Torril's glare met Aastere. "I did the job, lady. One elf dead. So what if it wasn't the right one. Pay up."

Aastere glared at Torril, a stare to match hers. "I wanted you to *find* Gothwen, not kill her. I never wanted anybody to die."

Torril began to count on her hands. "Then that's…. Twenty

unnecessary deaths, fifteen severely wounded, and ten men who can't piss. I'd say that's a job well done. Pay. Me. Now."

Shaking her head, Aastere denied Torril's demand.

Lucille kicked Torril in her ribs. "I gave you too many chances, all I asked was that you backed down. You murdered, you slaughtered, and you manipulated your way here, and what do you have to show for it? Defeat."

Torril scowled. "I have not lost. I've simply been slowed down."

"No more." Lucille silenced Torril. "You will remain here under the watchful gaze of the Queen's Agent while we deal with Vlastoril. You will be brought to justice for your crimes, Torril." With this, Aastere, Torick, and Lucille all left through the portal re-opened by Lucille. Elaina sat on a chunk of fallen pillar, her arms still folded. The portal closed behind them, giving Torril time to think. The gears in her head began to turn, plotting her success.

Elaina was the first of the two to speak. "I knew Fillinel. Poor girl. Gothwen fell in love with her a while back, she always told me how cute she was." Elaina toyed with her fingernails. "Gothwen had always thrown around subtle hints that she was bisexual. She never said it, she just knew. I remember getting her ready for her dates with boys, seeing the discontent in her eyes. She knew where here heart lay; it was always Fillinel."

Torril scoffed. "Selfish bitch. Only she would demand the attention of anyone. I prefer a woman's touch so much more than a man's." Torril smiled, remembering her last time. She glared at Elaina. "Are you trying to guilt trip me? It won't work. I don't regret what I did. In fact, the only regret I do have is the fact that I can't get my dagger back."

"You killed an innocent girl. A girl who was loved, a girl who had a future. Does that not make you feel anything?" Elaina held a look of confusion.

Torril stared blankly into the darkness behind Elaina. Her

eyes opened, and her jaw dropped. "Fillinel. You're alive?"

Elaina's eyes opened. She turned her head, staring into nothing but darkness. By the time she had realised her mistake, it was too late. Torril had already thrown a chunk of debris at her head, knocking her backwards off the broken pillar serving as her bench. Elaina stood herself up, just in time to receive a swift punch in the stomach and an uppercut which sent her to the ground. She remained there, in a daze, unable to move.

Torril towered over her, her foot placed against the side of her head. "Be grateful I don't have my dagger. I swear your throat would be slit and I would be feeding you your fingers one by one through the gushing crevice." Torril stomped her foot, Elaina's eyes closed.

Torril fumbled in the darkness behind one of the pillars. Before revealing herself to Gothwen and Fillinel, she had stashed a vial of liquid, to be used as a secondary plan if something went wrong, which it did. "I'm glad that was over quick, I don't know how much longer I could have held that chunk of rubble for. Any longer and it would have really crushed me." She found the vial. "If I can't complete one contract, then I shall fulfil another. Torril wandered back to the Well, standing where Gothwen and Fillinel had stood. Fillinel's blood had already begun to dry on the stone floor of the ledge. Torril unscrewed the lid of the vial, outstretching her arm and pouring it into the living liquid below. It appeared to scream, lashing out with magical tendrils at Torril, before sinking in a haze of white smoke, deeper and deeper into the mountain.

Torril looked down at her handiwork, smiling. "Bye bye, Magic."

Vlastoril pointed his blade at the three allies inching towards him. He had awoken shortly before they returned from The Well's chamber, he had enough time to locate the crown he had placed the gemstones in, though not enough to plan his escape. He was still confused at what had happened, the brash, dark persona he had carried with him at all times now replaced by fear and uncertainty.

"You cannot best me. I will win. The Emerald will be mine!" He turned the tip of his blade from Aastere, to Lucille, then to Torick.

A sharp pain overtook all sensation in his brain. The same could be said for Lucille and Aastere, who both clutched their heads in pain. Lucille fell to her knees, Torick was seemingly oblivious to what was going on around him. Lucille looked up, tears of blood dripping from her eyes.

"My body is on fire, Torick!" Lucille screamed, Aastere and Vlastoril were both experiencing the same. "My blood is boiling; my head feels as though it may explode!"

With Torick tending to Lucille and Aastere, Vlastoril took this as his opportunity to fight his pain and escape. His golden blade melted in his hand, giving himself a free palm to outstretch, in an attempt to open a portal. With great reluctance, one opened. It crackled to life, groaning as it tore the veil of reality before him. Unlike every other portal, however, this one did not have a clear destination. The opposite end was a pool of deep, purple liquid, something Vlastoril did not anticipate as he ran, distracted by the pain coursing through his body. Before he could realise his mistake, he had come into contact with the hazardous portal. Dropping the crown on the floor behind him, he entered, his body becoming one with the liquid, vanishing into the unknown. The portal sealed shut behind him, smoke rising where the centre had been.

Lucille and Aastere managed to come to their senses, the burning pain resonating through their bodies had subsided. Lucille wiped the blood from her nose, every opening on her face had appeared to serve as an exit point for the red liquid inside her. Aastere had evidently been the same.

"Aastere, Torick, return the gemstones. Something bigger is at play here, and I do not like it." Lucille's eyes burned with a rage fiercer than any both Torick and Aastere had ever seen in her. Nevertheless, they agreed, each taking a gemstone, attempting to re-open the portals Vlastoril had used. The room filled with a deathly silence. No portals opened; the hall remained as it should be. Lucille attempted to cast a fireball. A single spark flickered from her palm, nothing more.

A voice the three of them recognised sent a chill down Lucille's spine. Her theories were proven right. "What's wrong, Mother? No spells? Something must have gone horribly wrong with The Well." Torril sauntered into the hall. "Of course, that is but a guess."

"Torril. What have you done?" Lucille's voice boomed throughout the stone hall.

"You don't honestly think this was the *only* job I took, do you?" Torril examined her fingernails. "I searched all over Coryphia for Darkarrow. I ended up in the Apostate hideout. Pretty little thing by the name of Malina told me their leader had gone soft. Fallen for the girl Gothwen. Hired me to do another job. A secondary one. One Fillinel was supposed to do. Paid up front, I really like that woman." Torril leaned against one of the pillars. "Sexy mage gave me a vial. Sexy mage told me to pour it into the Well. Sexy mage and I will have a hell of a good time later, Mother." Torril smiled, her fangs glistening in the sunset. "I killed Fillinel on purpose. I knew she'd protect that stupid girl. She was supposed to have done it, but I did it instead. I mean, I had the money, I could have just left it. When she told me what it did though, I couldn't refuse."

Lucille clenched her fists. "What was it, Torril?"

Her daughter laughed. "A much stronger Obliterate potion. One that was modified to remove all traces of Magic, as well as life. It completely destroyed the Well. I suppose it took your precious Magic with it. That moronic Well sucked me and Elaina's little body straight out of the chamber."

"Our Magic is not completely gone." Aastere interrupted Torril's victory speech. "You merely weakened it. The Well cannot be destroyed, only weakened temporarily. One potion does not have the volume to eliminate an entity that large."

Torril's face dropped. "So, the Magic in the world is not completely gone?"

Lucille shook her head. "It never will be, Torril."

In a panic, Lucille's daughter attempted to make a run for the exit. She was swiftly apprehended by Lucille, who lifted her off her feet before throwing her back to the ground. "You cannot escape this time, Torril. You will pay for your crimes."

Torril lowered her head, punching the ground. This time there really was no escape.

A few of the fighters who had been battling in the Gardens had begun to wake up. Most of the magically fabricated flames had died out, all that was left was a thin layer of smoke which settled above the scorched grass. Sitting with her back against a fallen tree was a mage, nursing a bruised knee and taking a sip out of the flask on her hip. She was met by a Human, clad in armour and brandishing a steel blade. He sheathed it, offering his hand instead. The mage reluctantly took it, being dragged to her feet by the Human before her.

"You saw it too?" The mage brushed herself down, she was covered in dust from the buildings, and loose dirt from the gardens around them.

"So much raw emotion in one being. I wonder who she was." The Human began to walk, signalling the mage to follow.

The mage spoke up. "Do you think those things were real? That they were true?" She began to retell what she had seen. They felt as though they were memories, from the perspective of another being. Vlastoril, Fillinel, Torril, they were Gothwen's memories, though neither of them knew this.

"Whatever they were, they got us all to stop fighting. I mean, what were we fighting for? This old city? It's nothing but ruins." The human gestured towards the outlying estates.

"Count yourself lucky." The mage laughed. "Our leader wanted to enslave all Humans and lead the entire world with the power of all the gemstones." She looked to the ground. "I don't know how none of us realised."

The Human looked at his newfound friend. Blood seemed to decorate her collar as well as the ends of her sleeves. It was clear that, in some areas of her face, she had wiped some of her blood away, red streaks covered her cheeks. "Are you injured? You're covered in blood."

The Mage looked at her hand, some of it had gotten in her fingernails, her skin was tainted a light red. "It appears so. Odd, I don't remember taking a hit. Perhaps something happened while we lay unconscious."

The couple came across the boulder formation at the centre of The Gardens. Through the thinning smoke they could make out silhouettes of wandering figures, disillusioned with their leader's orders and forced to wander the silent battlefield. Both pairs of eyes settled on one specific feature of the battlefield image before them, a pair of feet, protruding from one of the boulders on the ground before them.

The Mage furrowed her brow. "Why is this one not awake? Everybody else seems to be perfectly fine. A little disoriented perhaps, but up and walking at least." They walked slowly around the stone before them. The feet extended into legs, the legs extended into a torso, the torso sprouted arms which outstretched to either side. Finally, the boulders revealed the head. The head of a young woman who seemed oddly familiar to the two, yet neither of them could recall where from.

The unconscious woman was clearly elven, the couple could tell by the points of her ears and the smouldering remains of a wand grasped firmly in her right hand. Her hair was white, shoulder length, though it looked as though it had been electrocuted, standing on end in various parts. Her limbs were spread out, they had gone limp during her fall, a fall which also looked to have created a few more cuts and bruises upon her skin. The clothes she wore were now torn, especially across her stomach, with the end of the sleeve on her right arm scorched and burned past her wrist. This was the hand within which the wand was gripped. The curved, wooden shaft was now nothing more than a charred stick, still smoking. Her hand had been badly burned, almost fusing to the handle of the wand itself. It was the sleeping body of Gothwen, a name neither of the two knew, but a face they had seen before from the images which had previously flooded their minds.

"I know her. Yet I cannot place where from." The human scratched his chin, the mage rubbed her temple.

"Me too, I feel as though I've known her all my life." The mage placed her hands on her hips. "I do remember something about Central Tower, though. Perhaps we should take her there."

The Human looked around. "We have a medical tent not too far from here. We can find her a stretcher or a cart, carry her to that tower. You know the way, don't you?"

Nodding, the mage bit her lip. "She won't be too heavy, will she?"

"I suppose we'll find out." The Human laughed, kneeling down and wrapping one of Gothwen's arms around his shoulder. The mage knelt beside her opposite arm, doing the same. On three, they lifted Gothwen, dragging her towards the Human tent.

CHAPTER SEVENTEEN

The Trial of Torril Magelight

"Two boulders, a Demon's blade, an explosion, a lot of wine, and an incredibly addictive antidepressant." Lucille sighed. "Is there anything your little body cannot handle?" She held a stone tablet, on it was a sheet of paper. She looked over it again. "Ah yes, the bonding of an Elemental Gemstone to your brain. How could I have missed that one?"

Gothwen heard Lucille's voice in her head. She had regained consciousness while she spoke, yet the world around her remained in eternal darkness. Mustering up enough strength, Gothwen opened her weary eyes. She found herself lying in a bed, bandaged in places where she was in the most pain, as well as places where she had no idea needed it, she felt dizzy, like she had spent the night before drinking heavily and sobbing into her bedsheets. That was something she did often. "Speaking of wine, do you have any more? My head is killing me." Gothwen felt her forehead. The gemstone was not there. "Where's my circlet?"

Lucille gave Gothwen a look of discontent. "You mean that woven leather band?" Lucille shook her head. "All these years of watching over you and even I never saw through it."

Gothwen narrowed her eyes. "Woven what? Where is it, Lucille?"

"It's not here. Aastere took it for a while. Just in case it got stolen again." Lucille looked at Gothwen. "She was pretty clever. All these years I saw that band around your forehead as plain leather." She smiled. "It had a perception filter. A Chameleon Enchantment. They're rare but by the green of the forest are they good."

Gothwen was still confused. She did not know if Lucille was talking nonsense or this was just the result of hitting her head too hard. "So, what? What are you saying?"

Lucille thought for a moment. She had forgotten Gothwen was not as academically adept as herself. "Aastere enchanted your circlet. To those who considered themselves higher than you, the likes of me, Vlastoril, the tutors at The Ark, those unworthy of witnessing it for what it really is, they saw it as a plain leather band, nothing more. A harmless accessory. Anybody who would not be a threat, however, the people of this world who passed you by as their equal, or someone who you were above in our society, such as the students who, might I say, rightfully called you 'Princess', or the common people of Oreldas, they would see it in all of its beauty."

Gothwen spoke up, she had thought of a question. "What about Fillinel? She saw it for what it was, yet she led the Apostates, the very people who wanted an end to the restrictions of the mages. She could have been a threat to the Emerald."

Sighing, Lucille answered. "Fillinel was a caring young woman. She treated the Apostates as though they were family, she was equal among them, despite being their leader. I suppose the enchantment saw that as a good enough reason to consider her worthy."

Gothwen wiped a tear from her eye. "She was worthy. Worthier than anyone I ever knew." Gothwen paused for a moment, before looking around, examining the elegance of the room she had found herself in. "Where are we, anyway? This isn't Ald Rosimeris."

"This was to be your bedroom, Miss Darkarrow." Aastere stood in the doorway, one hand on her hip. She entered the room, her hips swaying as she moved, like the most beautiful of flowers in the breeze. "It appeared our Magic had been temporarily disabled. We moved your slumbering body to Marrivel. You have been sleeping for almost a month." Aastere gestured around herself. "This is one of the prettiest rooms in Rose Castle. I had it kept spotless for your return."

Gothwen sighed. She allowed her head to fall forward. "How many times, Aastere? I don't want this. I want to be me."

"I know." Aastere looked away from her daughter. She gestured to one of the walls. It was empty, apart from the golden, floral design found upon every wall of the room, as well as the ceiling, which flowed to form a border around the empty space. "You could have had the greatest book collection in Marrivel here. Every book you ever wanted, every ancient tome, every fairy tale, a book on every language upon this world."

Gothwen rolled her eyes. "You can tempt me as much as you like, your silver tongue won't convince me."

"Perhaps I should move your room to one of the storage rooms within my basement. You can have the one next to the wine cellar. Would that convince you?" Aastere was growing visibly agitated, annoyed at the way her own daughter was dismissing a place within her home.

Gothwen merely smiled. She sat herself up, turning to the side of her bed. Using up most of her strength, she stood up, her head spinning and most of the bones in her little body aching. She walked, bare-footed and cautious, to where her mother stood. Gothwen wrapped her bandaged arms around her mother's waist, resting her head against her chest.

"Just because I don't want to live here doesn't mean I don't love you, mum." She sunk her head deeper, she could feel a tear forming in her eyes. Aastere too wrapped her arms around her daughter, kissing the top of her head. It still smelled of smoke. She had waited far too long to be called 'mum'.

"It's not because of you I don't want to live here. In fact, if I'm ever in Marrivel, I would gladly stay here every so often and visit for a few days. I just don't want all of this extravagance. I want to live a simple life, not one of royalty. No matter how it seems, I love you. I always will. Now that I know you're here."

A solitary tear fell from Aastere, falling on Gothwen's head. "Okay. I understand. Aast-" Aastere hesitated. "Gothwen. I love you too, my daughter." For a few minutes, the mother and daughter shared a loving embrace, not leaving from the other's grasp. Lucille looked on, this was something she missed.

Lucille cleared her throat. "I believe we have matters to attend to, Aastere." Lucille smiled, observing the two in each other's arms.

"I suppose we should let Gothwen rest." Aastere unwrapped herself from around her daughter. She led the weakened elf back to her bed, where Gothwen threw herself back down in agonising pain, wincing as she positioned herself back in a comfortable enough position to lie back.

"What's so important that you both have to leave me?" Gothwen's eyes darted between Aastere and Lucille.

"A trial, Gothwen." Lucille spoke up. "The trial of Torril Magelight." She fell silent again.

After a few moments, Aastere continued. "Normally, an elven woman would be tried in either Coryphia under the eyes of the ruling Count, or Ald Rosimeris under the judgment of the High Mages. However, with Vlastoril disappearing and the Council of High Mages being nothing more than Lucille, it is up to her to decide her daughter's fate."

Gothwen turned her attention to Lucille, who still sat in silence "You're okay with that, Lucille?"

Lucille shook her head. "Of course I am not, she is my daughter."

"It's tough." Gothwen placed her hand on Lucille's. "Whatever you choose, I know you'll choose right. Fillinel will have justice." Gothwen smiled, as Lucille and Aastere stood up to leave. "The countless lives she's ruined will have justice too."

Lucille closed her eyes as she left Gothwen's room, there was a pain in her heart Gothwen could not see, though Aastere could see it perfectly clear. Aastere turned to Gothwen. "If you have the strength, you should watch over the proceedings. There is a carriage outside which can take you there." Aastere smiled. "I do not want my daughter to be in too much pain, though I do want her to see her lover's killer come to justice."

Aastere left, leaving Gothwen alone in her room. She was right, it was something Gothwen wanted to see. She leaned back in her bed; the pillows were the most comfortable she had ever rested her head on. One short nap would not hurt.

Lucille held the main door of the castle for Aastere. Before them waited a carriage, a white carriage which, much like most of the castle, was lined with gold. Two white stallions stood patiently at the front, while the coach driver smoked a pipe while reading the latest Detective Brambles instalment. It was a popular story, one which was added every week to the end of the Marrivel Weekly magazine under an anonymous name. It was much loved, even by Lucille and Aastere. The carriage was to Lucille's taste, though as she walked towards it, she was signalled by Aastere to continue walking a path she herself had chosen instead.

"The carriage shall be left for Gothwen, Lucille. We go by foot, it will give us enough time to prepare, and to have a little chat." Aastere had picked up a cloak before leaving her castle, she had crossed her arms, gripping it below her shoulders. It was not until they reached the bridge to Marrivel did Lucille realise why she had done this. The winds had picked up significantly, Lucille's free-flowing hair constantly got caught up in her mouth and around her eyes, she found herself swiping it out of the way frequently.

"Why do you believe Gothwen is who she is?" Aastere had thought of a question Lucille struggled to think up an answer to.

"I suppose it was what happened. You left her with Elaina." Lucille continued to think. "Believe me, leaving your child with somebody else, somebody who is the world apart, is a bad idea."

Aastere smiled. "It seems we both failed our children, Lucille." Aastere looked over the bridge at Marrivel, the city bathing in the light of the midday sun, smoke rising from the taverns and houses where lunch would be being served. "Have you ever wondered what life would have been like without our children?"

Lucille laughed shyly. "A lot easier, Aastere. A lot easier."

Aastere smiled at Lucille. "I do so believe our sexual desires got the better of us, Luci."

Lucille stopped smiling. "Gothwen's means of conception were not consensual, that was not what you desired."

Aastere looked to the ground, watching one foot step before the other. "With her, I suppose not. Though Gothwen has a brother, Corym. It is something I shall tell her at a later date, just not yet."

"A brother?" Lucille kept her gaze on Aastere.

"An older brother, I gave birth to him a few years before you came to me. I sent him away too, to be raised by another of my agents in Anchor. I figured a small coastal town would be ideal to raise a child. I took a gamble with Coryphia and look how that turned out."

Lucille nodded. "I took a gamble too, Aastere. It was one of the biggest regrets of my life. All I wanted was a family to call my own. A couple of children I could treat to a day out. A picnic, a day in the forest, something nice. I wanted Torril and Ethril to get along, to play together while I lay watching them in Torick's arms. Of course, nothing ever goes that way, does it."

Aastere agreed. "Corym and Gothwen are two very different people. I fear the day they meet. When Corym reached sixteen I had him trained as a military strategist. He's twenty-one now, with a wife and young child far to the East, past the core."

Lucille narrowed her eyes. A map of the world appeared in her vision. "Far to the East? Do you mean with the Cave Elves?"

Aastere nodded, admiring the view as they walked. "He married a sweet young Cave Elf by the name of Alesi, yes. He remains there to strengthen our ties to their civilisation. Though I know one day he shall return here. Do I believe Gothwen is ready to meet him? I most certainly do not."

By now the pair had finished crossing the bridge, entering the city of Marrivel. The Courthouse could be seen in the distance, rising atop an angry mob of Humans. Aastere and Lucille both looked at each other, they knew the severity of the situation.

"It appears your daughter has done well to anger every Human in Marrivel." Aastere slowly turned her head forward again.

"I believe the protestors are split." Lucille attempted to listen in on the shouting as they walked closer. "One group wants to see Torril put to the sword for her crimes." Her walking pace quickened. "I believe another is protesting the use of Elven Law on Human soil." Lucille tilted her head. "I believe a third group just wants to see Gothwen. Soldiers, I presume. The ones she saved from death at Ald Rosimeris." Lucille smiled. "I impress myself with my hearing abilities."

Aastere shoved Lucille down one of the side streets. "We shall take the rear entrance." She raised the hood of her cloak, leading Lucille around the winding back streets of Marrivel.

Torick paced the width of the holding cell. Within it sat her daughter, alone yet concealing a look of contempt on her face. He caressed the greying brown beard on his chin. Every few moments he would glance in Torril's direction, though she would not move. She kept the same position she held in her previous cell; sitting cross-legged, her palms placed firmly on her knees, her head bowed as though in a deep meditation. Her tongue slid out of her mouth like a pink serpent, wrapping its body around the piercing in her bottom lip.

"Your mother will not have you executed, Torril." Torick continued his pacing, this time refraining from making eye contact with his daughter. "She cannot stand to lose another of her children." Finally, he turned, shrugging his shoulders. "I suppose you can find some form of relief in that."

Torril lifted her head, slowly. Her pale eyes stared into Torick's soul. "I know she will not have me killed. Mother is weak." Torril tilted her head to the right. "What punishment do you think she has for me instead then, Father?"

Torick ran his hand down one of the bars. "She knows there is good in you, Torril. Please, help her find it. Give your poor mother a break for once in her life."

Torril laughed, her hyena-like shrieks echoing throughout the cell, resonating against the metal bars. "A break? Mother will never take a break. The weight set upon her shoulders will cripple her. Though, if that does not end her life, the cold steel I run across her throat the first chance I get will." She closed her eyes as though experiencing a sensation of immense bliss. She threw her head back. "The eternal break which comes with death. Ah, it is but a fantasy." She ran her own hands down her face, still shrieking with laughter. "I did what had to be done. Now, all those people who said 'hello' to my blade are taking the longest break of their pathetic little lives."

Torick took a step back, the sight of his daughter groping her own flesh made him uneasy. "What has become of you, Torril? My child?"

Torril rolled her head back towards her father, piercing him with her deathly glare once again. "I am who I am, and I wish to be nobody else." She smiled a smile which sent shivers down Torick's spine. Torril tilted her head again, continuing to laugh.

"You. You are insane." Torick shook his head in disbelief at what his own flesh and blood had become. "You deserve to rot in a cell. A cell locked with an unbreakable lock, with the key thrown into the deepest, darkest abyss in Oreldas."

Torril frowned. "A little harsh, Father."

"No, Torril." Torick snapped back. "The lives you took must be avenged, and you must be brought to justice."

His daughter stopped laughing, bowing her head. "Very well, Father."

The Usher of Torril's trial, a man dressed in long, black robes which flowed as he walked, entered the room where Torick stood, staring blankly at his daughter.

"The courtroom is ready for her now, Torick." He scribbled a few notes on the clipboard he held close to his chest.

"I will see her brought in now." Torick nodded, giving the Usher a brief but awkward smile.

Torril looked up, she knew there was no escape now.

Lucille entered the Courtroom. Everybody, from the prosecutors providing evidence to worsen Torril's case, to the civilians observing the trial itself, even Aastere, were all standing, staring at Lucille. She knew the trial would take every ounce of strength she had left. The nervous judge took her seat, behind a freshly varnished oaken desk. Every person in the room did the same, taking their seats in silence.

"Please, bring in my dau-" Lucille closed her eyes. "Torril Magelight."

The door to the left of the courtroom opened, two human soldiers entered first, taking up a defensive position at either side of it. Torril entered next, clad entirely in chains, her neck unmovable within a rusted iron clamp. Torril entered the cage which had been specially prepared for her beside the door she had entered from. She stood, staring blankly at the heightened desk on which her mother sat, alone despite the fact the desk was built for at least nine.

Lucille took a deep breath. "Torril Magelight. You have been found guilty of first-degree murder on twenty counts, with twenty-five counts of grievous bodily harm. The Court today will provide the material necessary to aid my decision in what your punishment shall be."

Torril attempted to bow her head, though this was made difficult by the iron around her neck.

One cloaked man stood up. "Torril Magelight should be sent to her death for the crimes she has committed. The countless lives she has affected must see justice. Observe, the extent of which Torril would go to see her dastardly deeds carried out." The man pointed upwards, to the ceiling which appeared to ripple, like a lake confined within a container and thrown around by a child. Human magic was artificial, concocted by potions and liquids elves would never have the desire nor necessity to create. It was because of this reason Human Magic had been, on the whole, unaffected by Torril's actions. The magical floods subsided, revealing a blurred projection of Torril, sinking her blade into innocents. After every murder, the image would change, showing another, then another.

Gothwen opened the door to the rear of the courtroom. She did not want to draw attention to herself, her brief nap had extended too far, making her late. Fortunately, the entire courtroom was distracted by the images swirling and reforming above them. Gothwen took her seat quietly, ushered by a human guard who must have led her through the back door, avoiding the large crowd outside. As Gothwen moved, she masked her pain as best as possible. She looked up too, realising she had arrived in time to witness Torril's final murder, the murder of Fillinel. She watched the scene play out again, looking on helplessly as Fillinel sacrificed herself to save her lover. Gothwen wanted to reach up and push Fillinel away, saving her yet allowing the dagger to strike her own chest. A tear formed in her eye; she was not ready to see this again.

Lucille and Aastere looked at each other, they both saw Gothwen enter the courtroom, they both knew how much it hurt her.

"That is enough." Lucille held out her hand. She watched Gothwen wipe away the tears with her sleeve. "Torril Magelight, my daughter. I do not wish to see you put to the blade, though I know the black heart within you can be destroyed, and the light in your soul redeemed." The members of the audience began to murmur. "I deem it fitting for a half-elven woman with no magical affinity to be placed within the most secure prison cell of Ald Rosimeris; the Dread Demon's Pit." The audience erupted in disagreement. "A doorless cell, built from the impenetrable enchanted stone of the mountain itself, where you will be monitored by the mages through solid, enchanted glass, unbreakable by any means." Lucille had begun to see how restless the courtroom had become. She raised her voice. "However." She seemed to have gotten the attention of the court again. "If you fail to prove to me, when I call upon you to do good, that your soul can be saved from the eternal darkness, then you will be put to the blade and executed." This appeared to have worked, it was the best the people of Oreldas were going to get.

Lucille signalled to the guards to move Torril. "Bring her before the court, I shall personally confine her to her cell. With this, Lucille stood up, taking the stairs down to meet Torril in the middle of the courtroom. Lucille waved her hands, the chains and clamps binding her fell to the ground.

Torril stared at her mother with her pale eyes. "You have bested me, Mother, for now." She smiled, licking her lips. "You knew my weakness. Magic. You knew this would hurt me worse than any blade."

Lucille opened the portal behind her daughter. "Today, Torril, you learn." She grabbed Torril by the throat. "You learn that your actions have consequences, and that you must atone for the foul deeds you have committed." Lucille threw her backwards. Torril tripped on the bottom of the portal itself, landing upon her back against the stone floor on the other side. She looked up at her mother, giving her a look she had given none other, a look of respect.

"A worthy opponent is she who made me. For I am half the woman she will ever be." Torril stared at her mother through a deathly, pale stare.

Lucille stared back at her daughter, until the portal sealed shut. It was then she found herself staring into nothing more than the blank, empty space before her. The audience had left, as had the members of the court. All that remained was Lucille, who had been joined by Gothwen and Aastere.

"So, it's all done?" Gothwen's voice snapped Lucille out of her trance. "We can go back to live our normal lives?"

Lucille agreed. She had begun to walk towards the exit. Aastere and Gothwen followed. "I suppose we do." She sighed. "I shall have the Mages rebuild Ald Rosimeris, calling upon the remaining former High Mages to return and take up their positions. I believe it is time for me to lead them properly."

Aastere nodded. "My position within Marrivel needs to be solidified. The unity between Elves and Humans is fragile. I must return to Rose Castle and make sure the voices of the Elven people within the Human provinces are heard, while keeping the peace within our territories."

Gothwen walked a little further ahead. "Perhaps I'll build a little house in the forest, live there for a while in peace and quiet." She swung open the front doors of the courts, she could not allow two of the most powerful elves to do that themselves.

A roar of applause erupted from the opposite side. Gothwen found herself staring into a crowd of both Elves and Humans, waving flags bearing her face, some bearing The Apostate logo. There were crude mannequins of herself bobbing up and down above the crowd of applauding people, leaves were being tossed from the roof of the courthouse. Aastere and Lucille had taken their positions either side of Gothwen, two towering mages sandwiching the small woman. They too were applauding her. Gothwen smiled at them both, her heart was racing.

Aastere looked down at her daughter. "Do you really think it will be so peaceful?"

Gothwen's smile fell from her face. She turned back towards the crowd, letting out a long sigh. "I'm going to need a hell of a lot more wine."

CHAPTER EIGHTEEN

Epilogue

"Is this what The Hero of Ald Rosimeris is reduced to these days?" Lucille slapped the pipe of Blackweed out of Gothwen's mouth. "There are people who need saving, buildings to be opened, ceremonies to attend, and what do I find you doing? Smoking some illegal leaf in the middle of nowhere."

Gothwen sighed as she picked up her pipe from the ground. "That was two years ago, *Lady* Magelight. Can I not have some peace and quiet now?" She slumped back in the chair on her porch. Gothwen had built herself a small hut in the middle of the Rosimer forest. She had never desired a life in the city, whether it be Coryphia or Ald Rosimeris, or even some place as far as Balmira.

Lucille shook her head. "You turned down the position of Countess of Coryphia, no, Princess of the *entire* elven people, for this?" Lucille gestured to the handmade house. There were clearly some aspects of it where Gothwen had used Chlorokinesis spells to bend a couple of trees, but it seemed partway through she had given up, fashioning a hut out of carved logs and stone instead. It looked homey enough, though Lucille knew Gothwen had easy access to a life of extravagance and excess that she seemingly turned her nose at.

"Sometimes, Gothwen. Sometimes you confuse me." Lucille shook her head.

Gothwen looked blankly at the canopy of the forest. Leaves fell around her, swirling in the breeze. "I never wanted to be Aastarinwe, Princess of the Elves, Luci. I wanted *this* life. Living in the forest, in a house built by myself, with a good history book, a bottle of wine, and some Blackweed."

"You imagined it would be with Fillinel, though, did you not?" Lucille folded her arms; the mention of her name was met by a deathly stare from Gothwen.

"If I remember correctly, it was your flesh and blood that murdered her. If you hadn't have gotten yourself knocked up nineteen years ago, she'd still be here with me now." Gothwen stood up, poking Lucille in the chest. "You disobeyed Ald Rosimeris laws. You, of all people. A special High Conjurer of shitty little portals, because that's all I've ever seen you summon. Oh, but little did you know seventeen years after you gave birth, I'd be the one to pay the price."

Lucille sighed, moving closer to Gothwen. "I've been here before. I look into the windows to see how you are doing, I have done for quite some time, after I knew where you were, that is. I know you play those memories countless times, Gothwen. I know the reason why you came to me to learn the Liquid Memory charm was so you could see Fillinel again. I had no idea, in that short journey you took, that short amount of time you spent together, the two of you had become so close." Lucille poked Gothwen back. "Besides, I was not the one who twisted my daughter into a deranged psychopath."

Gothwen sighed. "I'd loved her for years, Lucille. We studied together, we spent days, weeks, years laughing with each other. I could never find the courage to tell her how I felt. While you were playing dead two years ago, that was when I told her. I said it for the first time, how it made me feel to be around her. It was less than a week later she took a knife to the chest for me. Two years on, and I still can't pry that dagger from my own heart. When I look at you, I see your daughter. When I see my mother, I'm reminded of the family I can never have with her." Gothwen wiped a tear from her eye with her sleeve. "Why are you here, Luci?" She reached underneath her chair, pulling out an unopened bottle of wine. She pulled out the cork with her teeth and spat it on the ground, taking one big gulp out of it.

Lucille, who had clearly taken Gothwen's speech to heart, explained herself. "As you may or may not be aware, my fortieth birthday is next month. All those who are of a high status; the new Count of Coryphia, the human Queen of Marrivel, even your Mother is attending. I wanted you to be there, Gothwen. Not as a student of mine, or as a Hero, but as my friend. Like we once were, briefly." Lucille looked at Gothwen's tired eyes. "I want to put this whole thing behind us, once and for all. Forget this whole Torril thing and just spend a night with me, drinking and having fun. We never got around to doing that." She handed Gothwen a piece of silver paper, emblazoned with gold writing and patterns around the edges. "Please, take your time to read it thoroughly. It will be worth your time, I guarantee it."

Gothwen scoffed. "You want me to go to some fancy ball where every person knows my name and has seen my face, where everyone calls me their hero and kisses me like Filli did?" Gothwen stopped, tears began to form in her eyes. "I will never, ever, move on from her, Lucille. It doesn't matter how much time passes, I will always miss her fiery hair, her beautiful orange eyes, and that skin. That amazing skin! I could have spent years caressing it. We promised each other we would. When it was all over, we'd be together, never leaving each other's side. Now look. She's dead and I'm alone. Fate is a cruel mistress, Lucille Magelight. I'm fully aware you know that too."

Lucille began to walk away. She could no longer hold back

the pain in her own heart. "Read the letter, Gothwen. I am telling you this now. It is of the upmost importance that you read it." She stormed away from Gothwen's house, her right arm making a circular motion. A flaming portal opened before her, though it did not hinder her current pace.

Looking down at the ground, Gothwen shook her head. "I'm sorry Luci. It was never your fault. I know that." She looked at where the portal flickered. Lucille had stopped. "What in Oreldas did we do to deserve so much pain."

Lucille turned her head to the side; she could not look at Gothwen while she had her back to her. Though of course, she also did not want Gothwen to see the tears on her cheek. "Losing a loved one is never easy. Especially if you were close. The pain you are feeling, it never goes away. It cannot go away, not while the memory of that person lives on." Lucille smiled. "You're a strong woman, Gothwen Darkarrow. I know you can get through anything." Lucille stepped through the portal, and in an instant, she was gone, leaving Gothwen alone once again.

Gothwen looked at the invitation Lucille had handed to her. Something was off about it. Protruding from one of the edges was a separate, torn note, different to the gilded paper the invitation was written on. She opened the note, and, just as she had thought, there *was* an alien note inside. Lucille had clearly written on it in one of her fancy silver pens. Gothwen read it aloud. "Found by farmer half hour from Balmira. Investigation required, inform G.D." Gothwen's brow furrowed, she opened this second note. She read this one aloud too, though she immediately recognised the handwriting. "To my dearest and most beautiful Gothy." Gothwen's eyes began to fill again, the letter became harder to read. "It seems that blasted Well sent me through some sort of portal. If you are reading this, and you survived whatever madness followed my apparent death, you must know that I am alive, and that I never stopped thinking about you, my love. I awoke on the coast of Akten, the Bracket Isle, and have been nursed back to health by the native Akteen. An odd species, might I add, like elongated lizard-fish. Unfortunately, a knife wound so deep did take a while to heal fully, and longer still did it take to regain my ability to cast spells and use my hands for writing. It seemed passing through the Well severely altered my ability to use magic." Gothwen wiped her eyes. "The portal I opened to send this letter was weak, you must know I did not have the strength to allow living matter through, or even keep it open for longer than five seconds. I do hope it reached you, I miss you dearly, my love. I look forward to our many nights together again. I do miss that morning in my quarters after we made that potion. The way you used that wine bottle to-" Gothwen's eyes opened wider, and she blushed. She cleared her throat, skipping that section of the letter and hoping Lucille had not read it. "You are forever in my heart, Gothwen. You always will be. With all the love in Oreldas and beyond, your beautiful Fireheart, Fillinel."

Gothwen was speechless for a few minutes, pacing up and down her front garden. Eventually, she realised what she had to do. She ran inside, picking up her bow, putting on her bandolier, and attaching her quiver. She picked up her daggers and added them to her belt. She swung open her front door again, walking out into the shining light of the outside world. Somewhere, Fillinel was waiting for her. She looked up, taking a deep breath of the forest air. "I suppose one more adventure isn't going to kill me."

Printed in Great Britain
by Amazon